FINDING YOU

CHIKALU FALLS
BOOK 1

LENA HENDRIX

Edited by Nancy Smay, Evident Ink

Proofreads by Sara Burgess, Telltail Editing

Cover by Kim Bailey, Bailey Cover Boutique

ABOUT THIS BOOK

I never thought I'd find her.

After eight years in the Marines, I'm still looking for the mysterious woman I've obsessed over since her first letter. When she shows up in my small town, I'm thrilled.

But when she turns out to be my brother's best friend—and the girl he's always loved—I'm caught between the two people who matter to me the most.

I'm a Marine, which means honor and duty run deep. Joanna is off-limits. That would be a whole lot easier if she hadn't already agreed to help run my brother's fishing guide business for the summer, forcing me to work side by side with the woman I've fantasized about for years.

I try to keep her at a distance, push her away, man up. But she draws me in without even trying, and I can't get enough of how she makes me feel. I'm stealing moments with her, and I know it's wrong. She may not be my brother's girl-friend, but I know a landmine when I see one.

How can a good man choose his heart over his honor?

ONE

LINCOLN

THE JOLT from the blast rattled through the truck, blowing out the front window. All of the doors flew open. Unlatched, I was ejected from the vehicle—thrown onto the open road. I slid before coming to a grunting halt against a nearby building.

I remember every second of it. There's no way to describe how it feels when you think you're going to die. No white light, no moment of clarity. The one thing that crossed my mind was that I wanted to kill the motherfuckers who did this.

With so much adrenaline pumping through my veins, I couldn't feel a thing. The blast from the IED into the truck as we were leaving a neighboring village also meant that I couldn't hear shit. I knew from his anguished face Duke was screaming, writhing on the ground, but as I stared at him, I heard nothing but a low ringing between my ears.

Smoke swirled around me as I fought to get my bearings. My eyes felt like they were lined with sandpaper, and my lungs couldn't seem to drag in enough air.

Get up. You're a sitting duck. Get. The fuck. UP.

Dragging myself to my knees, I patted down my most tender places, and except for my right arm, which hurt like a bitch, I was fine. I looked back at Duke, whose face had gone still. Although I already knew, I checked his vitals, but it was pointless. Fanned out around us were eight or nine other casualties—some Americans, some villagers. One set of little feet in sandals I just couldn't look at.

Ducking behind another car, I drew my gun and swept the crowd. *Come on, motherfucker, show yourself.* Civilians were getting up, walking past like nothing had happened. Those affected by the blast were screaming, begging. It was a total clusterfuck. My eyes darted around the area, but I couldn't find the trigger man. He'd melted into the crowd.

I ran back toward the mangled, smoking remains of our Humvee. Fuck. It was a twisted mess of metal and blood. Crouching around the base of the truck, I moved to find the guys. Lying in the dirt, knocked halfway out of the doorframe, was Keith, hanging on by the cables of the radio, his left leg torn at a sickening angle. He was dazed, staring at the pooling blood staining the dirt around him and growing at an alarming rate. Without my med kit, I had to improvise. I ripped his belt from his waist and using that and a piece of metal, successfully made the world's worst tourniquet around his upper thigh.

Over the constant, shrill ringing in my ears, I yelled at him, "I got you! FOCUS. Look at me . . . We got this!"

His nod was weak, and his color pallid. He probably only had minutes, and that was not going to fucking happen. I grabbed the radio mic. The crackle of the speaker let me know we weren't totally fucked. Calling in a bird was the only way we were getting out of this shithole.

"This is Corpsman Lincoln Scott. Medevac needed. Multiple down."

"10-4. This is Chop-4. Extent of injuries."

"We've got a couple hit here. Ah, fuck, Wade took two in the chest. At least four down."

"Roger that. Let's get you men onboard."

Leaning back on the truck, weapon across my legs, I felt warmth spread across my neck and chest. The adrenaline was wearing off, and I became aware of the pain in my neck, shooting down my ribs and arm, vibrating through my skull. Reaching up with my left arm, I traced my fingertips along my neckline and felt my shirt stick to my skin. Moving back, I found a hot, hard lump of metal protruding from my shoulder and neck. It had buddies too—shrapnel littering my upper torso, arm, and neck. My fingers grazed the pocket of my uniform, and I held my hand there. I could feel the outline of the letter I kept in my pocket. Its presence vibrated through me. Touching my right forearm, I thought about my tattoo beneath the uniform. Looking down, all I could see were shreds of my uniform and thick, red blood.

Hold steady. Breathe.

My fingers explored. My vest was the only thing that kept the worst of the blast from reaching my vital organs. This neck wound though . . . damn. This wasn't great.

The cold prick of panic crept up my legs and into my chest.

Calm the fuck down. Stop dumping blood because you can't keep your shit together. Breathe.

I focused on Keith's shallow, staccato breathing next to me. I tried to turn my head, but that wasn't fucking happening. "You good, man?"

"Shit, doc. Never better."

"Hah. Atta boy."

We sat in labored-breathing silence. Listened for the

medevac helicopters. As the scene around us came into focus, I realized how easily the lifeless bodies of the Marines around me could have been mine. I counted six members of my platoon killed or badly wounded. Our machine gun team, Mendez and Tex, had been among the dead. Mendez was only twenty.

Already struggling to breathe, I felt the wind knock out of me. Just last week, in a quiet moment outside our tent, Mendez told me he was afraid. He missed his mom and little sister and just wanted to go home to Chicago. Becoming a Marine was a mistake, he'd said.

"Doc, I don't wanna die out here, man."

In that quiet moment, he'd revealed what we all felt, but never spoke aloud. Instead of offering him some comfort, I'd stared out into the blackness of the desert by his side until he turned, stubbed out his cigarette, and walked back inside.

Leaning my head back, I let my own thoughts wander to Finn and Mom. His easy smile, her lilting laugh. I wondered what they were doing back home while I was slowly dying, an imposter in the desert.

When I walked off the plane, the airport had an eerie feeling of calm. I could smell the familiar summer Montana air over the lingering stale bagels and sweat of the airport. I hoisted my rucksack over my shoulder and began to walk toward the exit when a small voice floated over my right shoulder. "Thank you for your service."

My whole body shifted, I still couldn't turn my head quite right, and I peered down at a little boy—probably six or seven at most. "Hey, little man. You're welcome."

Then he clipped his heels together and saluted, and I

thought I'd die right there. He was so fucking cute. I saluted back to him and dropped to my knee.

"You know, they give these to us because we're strong and brave and love our country." I peeled the American flag patch off my shoulder, felt its soft Velcro backing run through my fingers. "I think you should have it."

The little boy's eyes went wide, and his mother put her hand over her heart, teared up, and mouthed, "Thank you." I tipped my head to her as I stood.

"Linc! LINCOLN!" I heard Finn yell above the crowd and turned to see my younger brother running through baggage claim. His body slammed into me, and we held onto each other for a moment. I ignored the electric pain sizzling down my arm. Over his shoulder, I could see Mom, tears in her eyes, running with a sign.

"Damn, kid. We missed you!" Finn laughed, his sprawling hand connecting with my shoulder. I braced myself, refusing to wince at his touch. But Finn was huge, a solid two inches taller than my six-foot-one-inches. He'd definitely grown up, reminding me that he wasn't the same gap-toothed fifteen-year-old kid I'd left behind when I enlisted.

"Kid? Don't forget I'm older and can still beat the shit out of you. Hey, Mom." I engulfed my mother in a hug. Her tiny frame reminded me why everyone called her Birdie.

"Eight years. Almost a decade and now I get to keep you forever!" We hugged again, her thin arms holding onto me tighter, nails digging into my uniform. Mom was a crier. If we didn't get this under control now, we'd be here all afternoon with her trying to fuss all over me like I was eleven and just wrecked my dirt bike. But the truth was, while I'd been home for the occasional holiday leave, Chikalu Falls, Montana hadn't been my home for over a decade.

She finally released the hug, holding me at arm's length. "I'm so happy to have you home," she sighed.

"I'm happy too, Mom." It was only a small lie, but I had to give it to her. I was happy to see her and Finn, and to put the death and dirt and sand behind me. But I'd planned on at least another tour in the Marines. I was almost through my second enlistment when the IED explosion tore through my body. The punctured lung, torn flesh, and scars were the easy part. It was the nerve damage to my right arm and neck that was the real problem.

Unreliable trigger finger wasn't something the United States Marine Corps wanted in their ranks. In the end, after the doctors couldn't get my neck to turn or the pain radiating down my right arm to settle, I'd been honorably discharged.

I glanced down at the poster board that Finn scooped off the ground. "Oh, Great. You Somehow Survived" was written in bubble letters with a haphazard smattering of sequins and glitter. Laughing, I adjusted my pack and looked at Finn. "You're such a dick." I had to mumble it under my breath to make sure Mom didn't hear me, but from the corner of my eye, I could see her smirk.

"Let's go, boys."

It was a four-hour trip from Spokane, Washington to Chikalu Falls, Montana—but only out-of-towners used its full, given name. Saying Chikalu was one way to tell the locals from the tourists.

The drive was filled with Mom's updates on day-to-day life in our small hometown. Finn eagerly filled me in on his fishing guide business, how he wanted to expand, and how I could help him run it. I listened, occasionally grunting or nodding in agreement as I stared out the window at the passing pines. Ranches and farmland dotted the landscape as we weaved through the national forest.

I was going home.

"You know, Mr. Bailey's been asking about you. He heard you were coming home and wants to make sure that you stop in...when you're settled," Mom said.

"Of course. I always liked Mr. Bailey. I'm glad to hear he's still kicking."

Finn laughed. "Still kicking? That old man's never gonna die. He's still sitting out in his creepy old farmhouse, complaining about all the college kids and how they're ruining all the fishing. I saw him walk into town with a rifle on his shoulder last week like that's not completely against the law. People straight up scatter when he walks through town. It's amazing."

Changing the subject, Mom glanced at me over her shoulder and chimed in with, "The ladies at the Chikalu Women's Club are all in a flutter, what with you coming home this week. You make five of our seven boys who've come home now." A heavy silence blanketed the car as her words floated into the air. No one acknowledged that three of the five who'd returned came home in caskets.

Clearing her throat gently, she added, "And you got everyone's letters?"

I nodded. The Chikalu Women's Club was known around my platoon for their care packages and letters. Without fail, every birthday, holiday, and sometimes "just because," I would get a small package. Sometimes because we'd moved around or simply because the mail carrier system was total shit, the packages would be weeks or months late, but inside were drawings from school kids, treats, toiletries, and letters. I'd share the candies and toiletries with the guys. We'd barter over the Girl Scout cookies. A single box of Samoas was worth its weight in gold. For me, the letters became the most important part. Mostly they were from Mom and Finn, young kids or other mothers, college students working on a project, that kind of thing.

But in one package in November, I got the letter that saved my life.

I idly touched the letter in my shirt pocket. Six years. For six years, I'd carried that letter with me. After the bombing, it was torn and stained with my blood, and you could hardly read it now, but it was with me.

"The packages were great. They really helped to boost morale around camp. I tried writing back to the kids who wrote when I could. Some of them didn't leave a return address," I said.

Mom continued filling the space with anecdotes about life around Chikalu. My thoughts drifted to the first time I'd opened the package and saw the letter that saved me.

In that package, there had been plenty of treats—trail mix, gum, cookies, beef jerky, cheese and cracker sandwiches. When you're in hell, you forget how much you miss something as simple as a cheese and cracker sandwich. Under the treats was a neat stack of envelopes. Most were addressed to "Marine" or "Soldier" or "Our Hero" and a few were addressed directly to me. I always got one from Mom and Finn. When I got the packages, I shared some of the letters with the guys in camp. The ones marked "Soldier" were always given to the grunt we were giving shit to that week. Soldiers were in the Army, but we were Marines.

On the bottom of this particular box was a thick, doodled envelope—colored swirls and shapes covering the entire outside. It was addressed directly to me in swirly feminine handwriting. Turning it over in my hands, I felt unsettled. An uncomfortable twinge in my chest had me rattled. I didn't like not feeling in control, so rather than opening it right away, I stored it in my footlocker.

I couldn't shake the feeling that the letter was calling to me. I spent three days obsessing over the doodles on the envelope—was it an art student from the college? The mystery of it was intoxicating. Why was it addressed to me if I had no idea who had written it? When I finally opened it, I was spellbound. The letter wasn't written like a traditional letter where someone was anonymously writing notes of encouragement or thanks. This letter was haphazard. Different inks, some cursive, some print, quotes on the margins.

It became clear that the letter had been written over the course of several days. The author had heard about the town letter collection and decided to write to me on a whim. It included musings about life in a small mountain town, tidbits of information learned in a college class, facts about the American West, even a knock-knock joke about desert and dessert. I read that letter every day until a new one came. Similarly decorated envelope, same nonlinear ramblings inside. A voice—her voice—came through in those letters.

There were moments in the dark I could imagine her laughter or imagine feeling her breath on my ear as she whisper-sang the lyrics she'd written. Her letters brought me comfort in those dark moments when I doubted I'd ever have my mom's buttermilk pie again or hear Finn laugh at a really good joke.

Over the years, she included small pieces of information about who she was. Not anyone I'd known pre-enlistment, but a transplant from Bozeman. She'd gone to college in Chikalu. "The mountains and the river are my home," she wrote. Her letters were funny, charming, comforting.

The one I carried with me was special. News reports of conflict in the Middle East were everywhere, and she'd assumed correctly that I was right in the thick of it. She told me the story of the Valkyrie she'd learned about in one of her courses.

In Norse mythology, Valkyrie were female goddesses who spread their wings and flew over the battlefield, choosing who lived and who died in battle. Warriors chosen by the Valkyrie died with honor and were then taken to the hall of Valhalla in the afterlife. Their souls could finally rest.

Reading her words, I felt comfort knowing that if I held my head high and fought with honor, she would come for me. I carried her words in my head. Through routine sweeps or high-intensity missions, her words would wash over me, motivate me, and steady me. She connected with something inside of my soul—deep and unfamiliar. At my next leave, I'd gotten a tattoo of the Valkyrie wings spread across my right forearm so I could have a visual reminder of her. I could always keep her with me.

Glancing down now, I slid my sleeve up, revealing the bottom edge of the tattoo. It was marred with fresh, angry scars but it was there. My goddess had been with me in battle, and I'd survived.

Pulling into town, I knew I had to find her—the woman who left every letter signed simply: *Joanna*.

TWO
JOANNA
TODAY

"Please tell me you're wearing the slutty one."

My younger sister, Honey, glanced at me from over her phone as I chewed my lip, looking back and forth between the two dresses hanging and the one I was trying on.

I looked at myself in the mirror from each angle. "I don't know. This one seems a little more me, ya know?"

"You mean boring."

I rolled my eyes at her. "No, just . . . less likely my boobs are going to have a mind of their own and pop out when I reach for the salad. Besides, it's comfortable."

Now Honey rolled her eyes at me. "Really? Comfortable? C'mon. You were the one who said that you wanted to look hot. Change it up a little! Isn't this some big party for Travis's work? Let him show you off a little."

"Yeah . . . it's their annual end-of-tax-season party or something. He says it's a big deal." I turned again, frowning at the long, loose dress on my body. It was sort of shapeless now that I was looking at it . . . and brown. Not great. I wanted to be comfortable, to look like me, but Honey was right. I also wanted to look good for Travis and his work friends. Was it the color? Maybe the hem?

Honey crossed her legs, clicked her phone off, and stared right at me. "Look, if you want to get Travis to sit up and beg, you gotta throw him a bone." She pointed at the green dress. "That one. Trust me." She went right back to her phone.

I touched the silk green fabric of the dress hanging on the back of the dressing room wall. It *was* gorgeous—an emerald-green silk wrap dress that had flowy cap sleeves and small flutter hem that landed mid-calf. It wasn't too revealing but definitely hugged my curves, and between the plunge of the wrap and the slit up the side, it was so far out of my norm that I had to admit, it was pretty perfect.

"Besides the fact that you look smokin' hot in that, you can't show up in boots and field pants."

"I wasn't going to wear boots . . ." I grumbled. But she wasn't wrong. My preference leaned toward comfortable hiking boots, field guide pants, and T-shirts. I liked to think it was because they were practical. I was a fishing guide, and that line of work wouldn't really jive with Honey's preferred dresses and pencil skirts. Her marketing and public relations job meant she was kicking ass and taking names, all in her Louboutins.

While she was back on her phone texting, I eyed my younger sister. Even though she was only two years younger than me, she definitely always had a leg up when it came to looks and fashion. She had always been polished.

In fact, sometimes I thought she didn't even realize how different we were. My mind still lingering on all the ways I wasn't like my sister, I asked her, "Do you remember Michael Drake? From high school?"

"Uhh . . . I guess. Baseball team, right? I'm pretty sure we went to a dance together."

"You did. *My* prom. When he came up to me after chem class, I thought he was going to ask me. Did I ever tell you that?"

"Stop it! You did not!" I had her attention now.

"I did—we'd been chem partners and I'd helped him with his labs a few times. We got along, and when he came up to me after class looking all nervous, I thought he might ask me to be his date to prom."

Honey just looked at me, her eyebrows moving up, making her look a little uncomfortable. "Anyway," I continued, "I was wrong. He *was* really nervous, but it was just because he was afraid to ask me for your number so he could take *you* to the dance."

I looked away, not sure why I'd just told her that story. I wasn't jealous of Honey. Not all the time, at least. But there were times when softness and femininity came so easily to her—it was just who she was.

Everything, including her name, exuded sexiness—blond hair, long thin limbs, bright blue eyes . . . She was always put together, but that was just Honey. I, on the other hand, had always felt out of place with my not-really-blond but not-really-brown hair, muddled green-gray eyes, and a body that was strong from years of hiking. I was fit but didn't have any of Honey's softness. The only thing we seemed to have in common was the inheritance of grandma Nana's boobs. They were literally the only thing that felt feminine about me, and they were mostly in the way.

"Well, now I feel like an asshole," Honey said as she wrapped her arms around my shoulders and leaned her head against mine.

"You're not an asshole. Besides, who cares about

Michael Drake? He kind of smelled like baby powder anyway."

That got her. She burst out laughing. "Oh my god, you're right! I'd totally forgotten about that. Maybe he had sweaty balls . . ."

Scrunching my face, I said, "Ew! Now I can never think about Michael Drake without thinking about his nasty, sweaty balls." I shook my head. "So gross . . ."

I looked at Honey through the mirror and squeezed her arms again. She could be my polar opposite, but she was my sister and it never mattered to her how different we were. She never asked me to change, or when I was going to finally settle into a routine, move off the couch in her apartment into my own place, have a family, a life. Thinking about all that made me frown.

With a breath, I decided it was too nice of a day to think about the things I wanted but didn't have, so I brought my attention back to the Big Dress Decision.

"Jesus, do you want Travis to stop treating you like one of the guys or not? Weren't you saying he wasn't very adventurous? With that dress," she pointed at the green dress again, "you'll be lucky if he doesn't haul you off into a closet and fuck you right in the middle of dinner." Honey looked at me, and all I could do was grin. The green dress, definitely.

I whipped the brown bag dress off my body. "You're totally right. A sexy party dress is perfect. I feel really good in it and want him to be excited to have me with him. I think this can do it . . . and I definitely wouldn't mind a little closet sex."

"WOO! Get it, girl!" We both dissolved into a fit of giggles.

I put back on my jeans and sweater (and fine, boots), so we could finish our girls' day together.

"All right, next up, midday margaritas!" Laughing and tossing my newly purchased man-grabbing dress (and the sky-high black stiletto heels Honey insisted I buy to go along with it) over my shoulder, I looped my arm through Honey's, and we set off for an afternoon of tacos and tequila.

～

WHAT THE HELL am I thinking?

In the last week since shopping with Honey, I'd tried on the party dress every day, and every day I became more and more unsure of my choice. Looking at myself with the curve-hugging green dress and heels felt good, really good, but . . . I was uneasy. Like an imposter. The nerves building in my stomach fluttered, and I put a hand to my belly to calm them.

This soft, feminine side of me wasn't something I was used to letting peek through for people to see. As the only female fishing guide in the county, I was known for my no-nonsense, shoot-it-straight approach with people. Only a handful that I let in saw the other sides of me. This tits-out, showstopper, while definitely a more fun part of me, was a part I'd had to shove down and hide, keeping it only to myself in order to have even a small chance of being respected out in the field.

"What do you think, Bud? Can I pull this off?" My red heeler, Bud, cocked his head and looked at me, and his tongue lolled out of his head into a goofy grin.

"You're right, it's great, we're fine." I smiled, rubbing his fur between the ears.

Glancing at the clock, I realized Travis was already nine minutes late . . . No text either. A cold prickle ran up my arms and I rubbed them, chasing away the thought, *This isn't like him.*

A sharp rap at the door to the apartment had Bud jumping to attention and snapped me out of my nerves. I crossed the living room and opened the door.

Travis stood, looking down as I moved aside, inviting him in. He stepped in without even looking at me. "Hey!" I said, arms open, ready for our typical greeting hug.

Travis leaned forward, gave me a quick peck on the cheek and a side hug. Bud stood alert at my side and eyed him with a low, throaty growl.

What the fuck?

"Bud, enough." My dog looked at me and sighed as he curled back up in his bed by the couch.

Travis ran a hand through his neatly styled blond hair and breathed out. He was dressed in a simple but excellently tailored black suit, light blue shirt, black tie. The thought that he looked exactly like the accountant he *was* flipped through my mind. Simple, safe.

"Um, everything all good?" I asked, trying not to feel hurt that he still hadn't noticed my outfit.

"Yeah . . ." He looked up, surprise taking over the stressed expression on his face. "Wow."

Giddy over the small approval, I gave a little twirl to show off the dress, but it was short-lived. His shoulders hung and his head was down, but his eyes shot over to me as he simply said, "Nice."

I could feel my good mood slowly deflating. "What's up? You seem . . .off. Are you sure everything's ok?"

Rubbing the back of his neck he finally looked at me. "Yeah . . . Jo, I think we need to talk. Can we sit down?" As he sighed, I smelled a hint of booze. Probably vodka—he wasn't usually a big drinker, and vodka martinis or cranberry vodkas were the only hard liquor I'd ever seen him drink.

Panic crept up my spine. *Talk? We need to talk?* Was there a worse phrase in the history of the world? Nothing good ever came from "we need to talk," especially if the someone you had to talk to had also been drinking.

I stared at Travis blankly. He stood in front of me, his lean arms at his sides.

In the six months we'd been dating, I was surprised that things hadn't really gotten any more serious. Sure, our relationship wasn't exactly exciting, but he was kind, sort of funny, and we'd gotten along just fine.

Just fine. That was the problem. Honey would have *died* if I told her that's how I was describing my current relationship.

She felt like any relationship, especially someone who was seeing you naked, shouldn't be anything less than live-wire electric. Sure, a fun and spontaneous relationship was something I would love in my life, but that hadn't been my experience. I wasn't the girl a guy thought of when he wanted to spend an afternoon with his face between someone's legs. Certainly not Travis. He'd never even tried to go down on me.

Our relationship included rounds of planned Thursday or Saturday night sex, if I happened to be in town. Even then, that meant some small kisses, him on top for a few minutes, finishing, and rolling off before he gave a second thought to whether or not I was close to enjoying it too. I liked sex, I really did, and I hated to admit that even though I was dating Travis, my vibrator was getting just as much use as before we met. With him, it never was the mind-blowing, multiple-orgasm sex that Honey claimed was every woman's god-given right.

"All right, then let's talk," I said, crossing my arms and lifting my chin. I could feel my walls going up, and I needed to cover myself in this ridiculous dress. I felt my right eyebrow tip up, my unintentional Resting Bitch Face on full display.

"I just think that maybe we're better off as friends."

"Friends? We are friends. I don't think I understand," I offered.

"JoJo, we are. But I think that's maybe *all* we are, you know?" He offered a sheepish smile, looking down at me like I was his little sister and he hadn't seen my tits the night before last.

It slowly occurred to me that he was more uncomfortable than normal standing in my living room. I didn't think I'd ever seen him entirely self-assured, but the nervous energy rolling off him was filling my apartment. He was hiding something. I should have been sympathetic, but all I could feel was anger.

"Are you kidding me right now? I wouldn't say we're *just* friends . . . We had sex twice this week! This is just occurring to you now? What about the party tonight?" The words tumbled out of me as I word-vomited all over him.

"Well, yeah. I have to get to the event, but I think it's best if I go alone tonight. You understand." He wasn't asking, just a simple statement of fact. Well, fuck that.

"Help me out here, Travis. What changed? This seems really out of the blue for me."

He looked around and started rattling his car keys between two fingers. Instead of rambling more, I pinned him with my gaze, unwilling to let him leave me hanging.

"Fine. I met someone . . ." He breathed out a breath I

didn't realize he'd been holding. A weight seemed to lift from his hunched shoulders as he straightened. "Her name is Heather. We met at the coffee shop on Park and Main, and we're in love."

No words. A thousand questions ran through my head, but no words came out. I opened my mouth to speak, but he cut me off. "Besides, you don't really have time for me. You're always gone looking for new places to take people hunting or fishing. I don't understand your need to be gone all of the time. You spend all of your free time dreaming of a business that's never going to happen."

That was it. Gloves off. I was *done*. Uncontrolled annoyance radiated through me, and I ground my teeth together. This asshole was breaking up with me, telling me he'd been seeing "Heather" long enough to fall in love, and then had the balls to act like me wanting a fulfilling life was the reason we couldn't be together? Well, fuck that.

"You mean my career? Yes, I'm busy, but you knew that when we met. I have to work twice as hard as any man in this business to get *half* the respect. Do you know how hard it is to get someone to sign up and pay for a woman to guide them? Plus, I invite you to come with me *all* the time. I'm sorry that you didn't want to go with me, but—"

He held up his hand, cutting me off, making my eyes flare with fury.

Bud immediately tensed at our loud voices. His hackles raised as he stalked forward, putting himself between Travis and me. I put my hand down to calm him.

That's right, pal. Fuck this guy.

"Look, you're a nice girl, beautiful and driven, and I thought we had enough in common to make this work, but the truth is, we're twenty-six already and I just need someone more . . . girly. You know what I mean," he said, gesturing toward me.

Out of steam, I sighed, rubbed my eyes. "Yeah, sure."

I choked back tears because I knew *exactly* what he meant. Travis had always been looking for me to be more soft, feminine, polished. A woman who lunches with other women, who he could bring to all of his corporate events and show off on his arm. A woman who didn't prefer to sleep in a tent rather than her sister's apartment. My ears burned with embarrassment, but I'd heard it all before.

JoJo, you're such a tomboy. Jo, you're one of the guys. It's so cool—you're like a dude with great tits!

Clearing my throat, I just looked at him. I refused to cry in front of him. If he didn't think I was feminine enough, I damn sure wasn't going to prove him wrong by crying all over him.

He reached out, placed his hand softly on my shoulder. "I'm sorry, JoJo. I mean it—we can be friends. But we're almost thirty, I need a woman I can see myself marrying." And with that he turned, as I stared at his shiny black shoes, and left my apartment with a soft click of the door's latch.

I stood like an idiot in the middle of my own living room for longer than I'm proud of. Bud sat at my feet, looking up at me with those sweet, brown eyes of his. I tried to get a handle on what the fuck just happened. Travis dumped me. Travis, who Honey said was "blander than a banana," dumped *me*.

I didn't love Travis, not even close, but it still cut deeply to feel rejected. I wasn't woman enough for him. He had found someone else who could be. I wasn't someone you brought home to meet your mom. I wasn't marriage material. I was just one of the guys. Again.

Gathering my resolve, I slipped off my black heels and

threw them across the living room with a raw yell. They smacked the back wall, rattling a frame from the shelf, sending it crashing to the floor. I let the tears fall in the quiet safety of the apartment as I tore at my green dress. It felt like every hidden part of myself that I was trying to share but couldn't. The moment I opened myself up and let someone in, my femininity was thrown back in my face. The soft silk against my skin was more than I could stand. Balling the remains of the torn dress, I tossed it away.

Is Travis right about me?

Grabbing my phone, I considered texting Honey and catching her up on the drama that was my life, but just didn't have the energy. Besides, she was probably working late at her PR firm. We could be angry together over her amazing pancakes in the morning.

I fiddled with the phone. I didn't want to sulk alone, but calling my mother also seemed like a bad idea. Against my better judgment, I tapped her name, and my fingernail toyed with the skin on my thumb.

"Hello?"

"Hey, Mom."

"Hi, who is this?" *Seriously?*

"Mom, it's Jo. Do you have a minute?" I sniffed, and she didn't seem to notice.

"I suppose, dear. Daddy and I are about to leave for book club." It wasn't surprising that Friday night book club took precedence over a phone call from me.

I cleared my throat, trying to clear the lump that had formed there. "I'm just having a bad day. Travis broke up with me."

The phone was quiet for a moment and then she started with a *hmm.* "That's a shame, JoJo. He was a catch. Did you do something to upset him?"

"He met someone else." The words burned in my throat as I fought back tears of embarrassment.

"Well, hun, to be honest, I'm not sure you two were a great match. Travis was looking to settle down, and you're always bopping around from place to place. You spend all of your time with other men in the middle of the woods. I'm actually surprised he didn't have an issue with it earlier."

I was stunned into silence. The only sound that escaped me was a small croak. I knew what she meant—and that made the burn in my chest so much worse. I was in the back half of my twenties and spent a lot of time traveling the state, sometimes even farther west, taking groups hiking and fishing on public lands most weeks in the year.

"Wow," I said, anger and disbelief bubbling up to the surface. But why should I make the effort to change when it seemed like everyone had already made up their minds about me? "I am not spending time with other men. You know that guiding is my *job,* Mother."

The work it took to build trust with the farmers, landowners, and other outfitters was hard. I just couldn't imagine giving up my dream of finding a great piece of property and transforming it into a full-service resort that helped people connect with nature. I'd take them to the best spots, feed them amazing food, teach them about the land and the animals—help them see the beauty in all of it. But that dream left very little time for things like romance, weddings, and babies.

"I'm sorry, dear, I guess I just don't understand why you feel the need to traipse around the state—"

"You know that in order to get on Forest Service land, I would have to buy out another outfitter or be given the land!" Yelling at my mother was rare, but I was steaming. "I have been saving *every* penny. You know this is my dream, and if that means that I have to scour public lands for spots that aren't already overrun or overfished, then so be it!"

"Joanna!" My mother's voice was laced with indignation. "Young lady, you will not raise your voice at me. You chose this life for yourself. Daddy and I wanted you to go to MSU, but you wasted your time at a community college in Chikalu Falls."

In my anger, I burned a path across my living room floor. As I paced, my eye landed on the fallen frame. An ache formed behind my eyes, and I pinched my nose to keep from crying. Losing steam, I slid down to sit against the wall. I sighed as Bud nestled his head on my lap.

"I know, Mother. But me being a teacher was your dream, not mine."

In the cracked frame, Pop's thick arm was around a nine-year-old me as I held up a fishing pole and my first "big bass." I couldn't help but laugh through my tears as I touched Pop's proud grin.

"I miss Pop." My voice thickened in my throat.

Pop had been gone since my freshman year of college, and his absence stung every single day. He was my rock. Visits to Pop and Gram in Chikalu Falls were the happiest moments of my childhood.

"I know you do, sweetheart. You two were bonded. He understood you in ways I never will."

It was a sad truth that stung to hear aloud. I suddenly wanted nothing more than to get off the phone with her. I was looking for comfort that she couldn't give.

"I'll let you go, Mom. I'm sorry I called and upset you. I'll be fine."

"Ok, dear. Let's talk soon."

The phone disconnected, and I sat in silence.

Pop was the only person who never treated me like I

was just a girl—like I couldn't do everything the boys in town could. He taught me to fish, hike, trap, hunt. I'd shot my first rifle with him when I was eight. It took me six shots before I even hit the old pumpkin, but he wouldn't let me give up.

When Honey and I would visit, she would peel off with Gram, learning to sew and bake and garden, and my lessons were shockingly similar. Pop showed me how to patch a tent, different ways to cook the fish we'd caught along the river, and which plants were safe to eat. He never once made me feel like I was lesser, just because I was a girl.

I traced a fingertip over the fading photo and felt the void his absence created.

In high school, I'd spend entire summers with him and Gram in their rural home near the base of the Kootenai National Forest. Their land stretched across ninety acres with access to streams for fishing, mountains for hiking, and valleys for glassing animals from across the ridge. I grew comfortable in my own skin in the silence that stretched between us—he'd encouraged me to sit and just listen. I could lay my head against his shoulder and breathe in the mountain air. I never had to be anyone other than myself in those moments.

After deciding on the community college, I took my car to visit Pop, and when he'd heard the news, he patted my leg and simply said, "Good girl. You can do this. You can do anything you set that mind to. Don't ever let anyone tell you, even your parents, that your dreams aren't good enough. You're special, little one."

Thinking back on the man who shaped so much of my life, I gently placed the cracked frame back on the shelf. I was not a wallower. I needed to stop feeling sorry for myself.

With a deep breath, I gathered my messy emotions and stuffed them back down a little. I might not be someone's arm candy tonight, but I sure as hell wasn't going to sit alone in my apartment in my underwear and cry about it.

I resigned myself to Netflix, grabbed a bottle of the expensive Syrah that Honey always bought, and curled up on the couch. I tossed a dirty look to the rumpled heap of green silk. With a pat from me, Bud hopped up, plopping his stocky body right next to mine with a deep, hearty sigh.

"I hear ya," I said to him, smoothing his fur back behind his ears. More disappointed than sad, I tried not to think about whether any man would ever see me as more than just one of the guys.

THREE

JOANNA

"So LET me get this straight, you broke up with the bland banana? That's fantastic news!" Honey's excitement radiated through her as she flipped a pancake. It smelled sweet, with a hint of vanilla, and my mouth watered. As she stirred the fresh blueberry topping, I dipped my finger in for a taste.

"First of all, Travis broke up with me . . ." I licked the tart blueberries off my finger.

"Irrelevant. You were never going to end up with him anyway," she breathed. She brushed the thought away with the flick of her hand.

For Honey, it was just that easy—turn the page, relationship over, you're dead to me. She poured another circle of batter onto the griddle. Honey worked at a successful PR firm in Butte, and we shared an apartment downtown. It started off as her apartment and in between guide jobs, I would crash at her place. Most times I slept on the couch. But after nearly a year of that, she said she couldn't stand the thought of a "homeless sister" and claimed the apartment as ours.

I paid rent and we split the bills, but the truth was that I didn't spend most nights there, but rather camping along rivers and in small-town hotels, scouting new locations. One of the biggest perks of living with Honey, however, was that she was an amazing baker.

Whenever I was home and she wasn't rushing off to work, she'd make the most amazing baked treats—scones, cinnamon buns, pancakes, crullers—all from scratch. When I'd asked her once why she never followed her dream to open a shop, she'd dismissed it with, "I gotta make bread, not just bread, ya know?"

I laughed because she was sort of right. If she was going to support her expensive lifestyle, the fancy job at the PR firm definitely made more money than a baker probably would.

"Well, you can always cook for me. These are amazing," I said.

"I know" She winked. I swear, that girl never ran out of confidence. "So tell me," she continued, "did you give that dipshit a piece of your mind? God, I'm so pissed I didn't get to see that!"

I snuck another lick of blueberries and replied, "Well, I didn't let him walk away without an explanation. But I don't know, it is what it is . . . Maybe he's got a point."

Honey looked at me with a stare only a sister could do. Part of me hated that she knew everything about me, so she knew this was total bullshit.

"Do you think he's right, though?" I asked, unable to look at her. "Is it time for me to change and give up the guide stuff? Find something different?"

"Don't even." She pointed her spatula at me. "I've had to hear about your dream resort since we were kids. You're not giving that shit up. If he can't get with the program, then fuck him. He's a cheating asshole. I swear, if I ever see him downtown, I'll tear his balls off." The sparkling gleam in her eye was slightly terrifying. Honey always seemed ready to raise hell in the name of loyalty.

She smiled sweetly, and her intensity flipped off instantly. "Pancakes?" And we both grinned.

Later that day, Honey invited me shopping with some of her friends, but I was still tending to my sour mood. Instead, I drove to the edge of the county to check out a piece of public land that offered access to a bend in the river.

I couldn't shake my crabbiness, and seeing the crowd didn't help matters. Right now, all I wanted was a little quiet. I hiked deeper into the trail, trying to find some space from the six or so anglers I'd passed on my way in. Most of them knew me, and we offered a nod in greeting, but some were newer faces. Not a girl among them, and at that, I smiled a little to myself. I may be different, but Honey was right. I was never one to back down, and a little thing like a breakup wasn't going to be enough to shake me.

My mood lifted as I got into the easy rhythm of casting, walking, and feeling the early summer sunshine on my face. Hours passed and it wasn't until I heard the familiar *ding* of my phone that I looked around to see the sun starting to dip below the tree line. I glanced down, surprised I still had service.

A wide smile took over my face when I saw that one of my favorite people, Finn Scott, had texted me.

Finn: Joanna Banana!! How was the hot date??

Me: Change of plans. You can be my hot date.

Finn: Sorry gorgeous, you're not my type.

Me: Dick.

Finn: I kid, I kid! Lincoln and I are at The Pidge if you want us to save you a seat—the band's supposed to be good tonight.

A sharp pang splintered my chest at the mention of Finn's brother, Lincoln—desire mixed with a hint of sadness.

Me: I'm ass deep in the Wise River right now. Fish are biting. Raincheck?
Finn: For you, always. And hey—save some fish for the rest of the poor sacks of shit out there.
Me: Never.
Finn: Atta girl. Also, call me tomorrow. Linc and I need your help filling in for a guide this week. I'll shoot you the details. Pretty please?
Me: Kinda busy this season but send me the details and I'll let you know.

Frowning at my phone, I felt the tug of guilt at my lie. I loved Finn from the moment we met in college—he was hilarious, a great guy, and one of my best friends. I hated lying to him that I was busy, but until I knew the details of what he was asking, I couldn't just say yes.

For the past three years, I'd successfully avoided his brother, Lincoln.

FOUR
LINCOLN

Looking around The Dirty Pigeon, I was still surprised to see that our friend Colin McCoy had turned a rundown townie bar into a legitimate dance hall in the three years he'd owned it. It still had the small-town, local-bar feel, but he'd expanded it out the back to include a stage and dance floor. Based on the crowd, it was still pretty popular in town.

After coming home, I'd learned that Wednesday night was Ladies' Night where people could come early and learn how to line dance and two-step, which also meant all the college guys were out in droves, hoping to get laid. Almost everyone that night was the dancing crowd. I'd decided Wednesday nights at The Pidge were not my thing. If it were up to me, I'd be sitting in my cabin, nursing a scotch, alone.

For a Friday night, there was a healthy mix of college students and locals—all of whom seemed to get along and enjoy the local bands. I couldn't help but scan the exits. Old habits die hard, and I felt better knowing I had at least five options for getting out if I needed to. The thrum of the guitars and laughter of a few drunks at the bar suddenly made my skin feel tight. My ears pricked, and the roof of my mouth felt like sandpaper. Someone dropped a beer bottle with a low "BOOOOO!" from the crowd. I watched in slow motion as it rolled back, the scrape of the glass against the floor intensified in my ears until it hit my stool.

"Dude, you all right?"

Finn's hand on my shoulder and his look of concern made me realize I'd jumped out of my seat, wild-eyed and ready to fight. My heart was pumping, ears ringing, and I felt like everyone was looking at me. Finn squeezed my shoulder, and I listened to my ragged breathing vibrate through my ears.

"Hey," he said. "Relax, man. Someone just dropped a bottle."

"Yeah . . ." I exhaled, but the tension stayed lodged in my chest and back. This was why I preferred to stay at home, I couldn't last five minutes without acting like a psycho.

Hearing the bottle and seeing me leap to my feet, Colin left the band he was talking with to head over to us. "Finn. Linc. Any trouble?"

Colin and I were the same age, friends from high school, and we'd always been close. His no-bullshit attitude was one of my favorite things about him. On and off the football field, he was always ready to throw down at the first sign of trouble. He was a solid dude with a lopsided grin he'd had since he was sixteen.

"'Course not, man. We are all goooood." Finn drawled it out and downed a shot of whiskey lined up on the small high-top table.

Colin turned to me and grinned. "Glad you made it out. Tonight's a great band, some pretty girls in here . . ."

At that, Finn draped his arm around my neck and winked at Colin. "Oooooohhhhweeee, boys. Maybe Lincoln will get a pretty little thing to dance with tonight."

I shrugged his arm off my back. "Not tonight."

I took a drag of my beer and looked around. I may have kept to myself, but coming into town when I needed a quick fuck was the simplest part of my week. In this town, there was no shortage of women who didn't need to know the details, just that you were a Marine, and they were ready to jump in the back of your truck. I preferred it that way. No strings, no bullshit. Fuck, sometimes they didn't even ask me what my name was.

Could she be here? Would I even know it if I saw her?

My hand dropped to my pocket. I still couldn't get out of the habit of carrying her letter with me on the hard days. I was fully aware that made me creepy as fuck, but I didn't care.

When I moved back to Chikalu after the service, I'd looked for her. I asked around if anyone knew a Joanna. There were a couple of Jos, a Josephine, a JoBeth, but no Joanna. A last name would be helpful. But for all my asking around the college, library searches, and late-night Google searches, nothing.

She was a ghost.

Colin added, "Well, it's Friday night so I'm sure you two'll have your pick. We're really tight with IDs so everyone's over twenty-one." He winked.

I noticed his eyes squinted fractionally at Finn who'd suddenly looked away uncomfortably. Finn was looking over at the main bar, at no one in particular, completely ignoring Colin's comment.

When I turned my shoulders to face Finn, he shifted back to the conversation and smiled. The kid's dimples made him a charmer with the ladies, I was sure of it, and the gleam in his eyes was either mischief or a little too much booze. Probably both.

"Well, I gotta get back to it. If you're around later, let's have another. Deck should be coming by after his shift."

In addition to Finn and Colin, Cole Decker was my closest friend. As much as I tried to avoid other people, our monthly poker games helped to keep me from drowning in my thoughts or living too long in my darkest places.

Colin drained his beer and landed a loud smack on the table. "Good to see you out, Linc. Drinks are on me tonight." He pointed at us as he walked back behind the bar.

A song later, a pretty blond waitress dropped off another two beers and looked at Finn and me. She held my gaze just long enough to let me know she liked what she saw.

"Hey there. I'm Marissa. I'm taking over for Kris, so I'll be serving you the rest of tonight."

She licked her shiny pink lips and smiled back and forth between the two of us. I'd been on leave in enough places to know the international signals for "I'm down to fuck," and she was putting off some major DTF vibes. Finn's face was in his phone so he was completely fucking oblivious to what was happening right now.

"Colin said drinks are on the house and to take care of you boys, so if there's anything," she paused, leaning her elbows on the table, tits on full display, "anything at all you need, just holler."

I looked at what she was offering, not caring that I was staring. She giggled, turned, and did that strange girl finger-wave over her shoulder. She must've thought it was cute, and it probably worked for her most nights, but I couldn't get myself interested tonight. When you spend eight years in the Marines, you learn pretty quickly that sex, let alone a good fuck, is few and far between. Some of the guys on leave took whatever they could get, but that was never my style. Unless you're up for the worst STD test on the planet —a bore punch, which, trust me, you are not—you were better off keeping your dick in your pants. There wasn't an itch I had to scratch tonight so I was going to have to disappoint this one.

Still in his phone, Finn clearly wasn't helping me out here, so I just called to her, "Thanks, we'll let you know," and turned my attention back to the band, which was midway through a song about a Voodoo lady down in Louisiana. I scanned the crowd again, letting my thoughts drift back to Joanna.

What does she look like?

What if she's married?

Fuck, what if she's really Nana's age?

I'd had to imagine all sorts of details about Joanna's life. While her letters included some things, a lot of it was a mystery, and I'd had to fill in the gaps with my own imagination. I knew she worked hard in college when she'd gone. She'd taken all sorts of classes from medieval lit to agriculture.

She liked poetry and music. I knew she loved being outdoors. She'd mentioned it in some way in every letter. She talked about her family, but never by name, and I got the feeling they weren't really close. She was closest with her grandpa, but he'd died a year into her letters. That was a strange one, feeling deep sadness for someone you'd never actually met.

I kept every letter in my footlocker and read most of them until the edges were crinkled and torn. At night I would lie awake, staring at the green ceiling of our tents and think about meeting her. I wanted her to know that her letters kept me sane. Connected me to the outside world and helped keep me from losing myself when I was faced with what needed to be done.

Nights were also when I could imagine what life could be like after we met. I'd fantasize about her lips on my skin, dragging her tongue lower down my body as she grabbed my cock. I could never clearly see her, but in the lonely nights, I tried to feel her against my skin. A few times on leave, random hookups became poor substitutes for Joanna, but they left me feeling shittier than I had before, so I'd given up trying. Thinking about the fact that I could finally meet her in my very hometown had my blood pumping hard through my veins. I could feel my cock twitch and had to shift uncomfortably so I didn't end up with a raging boner in the middle of the bar.

The worst of it was that I'd never written her back. I'd wanted to—I'd even written a few drafts to send to the Women's Club in hopes she'd get them, but I never sent a single one. I didn't want her to freak out and stop writing. Didn't want her to know how fucked up I was or that I didn't deserve her kindness. When the letters kept coming despite my lack of reply, I'd let it go and told myself that if I ever made it home, I'd find her and tell her how much her letters had meant to me.

I gave the side-eye to Finn as he smiled into his phone. "Your latest conquest?" I teased.

"Uh, not exactly." He smirked. "Jo may be able to help us with the guide next week."

I hadn't met Jo, but I knew she was a pretty big part of Finn's life. I'd asked him about her once, given her name, but he said she was from Butte. Not my Joanna. They had worked together and spent a lot of time outside of the guide service with each other. Based on how much he went on about her, I was pretty sure the poor guy had been holding a torch for this chick.

It was surprising he wasn't able to close the deal with this girl. Finn was a good-looking guy, tall and fit. Plus, he was always making someone laugh. The thought that he didn't have his pick of women in this small college town was mind-blowing to me. Maybe this girl was batshit crazy.

"So what's the deal with you two?" I asked, curious to know why he wasn't going for her.

"What do you mean?"

"I mean, are you just friends or what?"

Finn eyed me suspiciously but went on. "Jo's amazing. No asshole in this town will ever be good enough for her. She's tough as nails too."

Yeah, he definitely had it bad.

"And you fish with her? She working with another outfitter or something?" I asked.

"No, Linc. Jo's a solo guide." His voice was full of reverence. "In fact, she's the only female fishing guide in the whole fucking county. How do you not know this? This girl knows her shit—when the fish are biting, what bait to use, where they'll be based on the weather. You'd think that she'd have every asshole in town lining up to camp with her because she's also hot as fuck."

He shook his head in disbelief and downed another gulp of beer.

"Ok . . .so what's the deal?" I couldn't see what the problem was here.

"This county is old-school, you know that. None of the good ol' boys want to admit that they've got a woman showing them the ropes, let alone one who'll outfish them."

"Mmm," I grunted. That sounded about right for around here. While we'd grown up with plenty of strong women who could handle their own, including Mom, it wasn't really typical for them to go hunt and fish alone. Our small town had certainly never been progressive. But when it came to our business, I trusted Finn's instincts. If he said Jo was the best, then she was the best, and we needed the help.

"All right, set up the meeting and we can work out the details," I said. Still feeling pissy, I drained my beer and walked out to my truck without saying goodbye.

FIVE
LINCOLN

Over a week later, Finn had finally set up a meeting with his contact, Jo. I wasn't sure what took her so long. Normally, I'd fully vet any guest guides we took on our trips, but we were short-staffed this season and I was getting desperate. When he said we'd meet back at The Pidge for a few drinks, I wasn't thrilled.

All week I'd been nagged by a bad feeling. Fuck if I knew what it meant, but if the nightmares kept up, I'd go fucking crazy. They still dogged me at least once a week, but this week it was relentless. Every fucking night, I woke up dripping with sweat and panicked. Only bits and pieces would come back to me. Usually, I was chasing someone, or they were chasing me, and I was always in my combat gear.

In one dream last week, I'd been running, my boots feeling like lead. Finally, I'd caught up to them, and when I grabbed whoever I was chasing—when I caught the person's arm, they turned, and I realized I'd been chasing a woman. A beautiful woman with dark blond hair and the most intense green-gray eyes I'd ever seen. Her hair tumbled around her shoulders as the wind whipped past us. I tried to reach for her again, but she brought a finger to her mouth. *Shhh.* She smiled as massive wings unfolded from her back. In an instant, she was gone.

I was losing my goddamned mind.

After my third beer and ready to get the fuck home, I looked back at Finn in time to see his head lift and his eyes light up. I turned to follow his gaze to a woman who walked through the heavy wood door. The warm summer air swept in with her, cutting through the cologne and sweat of the dance floor. Her hair billowed slightly, and a coal burned in my chest.

She started toward us, her dark blond hair swirling around her shoulders, and heat started to spread through me, not exactly panic, but something close. I looked around —could anyone else see her? Was I losing my shit?

I turned to Finn. "Who is that?"

He looked at me like I was an idiot. "It's her. Jo. I asked her to meet us here."

"Where'd you meet her again?" I asked, not believing my eyes.

"Dude, are you ok? We met in college. She lived in Chikalu for like, six years."

With a buzzing in my ears, I let my gaze wander down to see she wore a simple fitted T-shirt, but it did nothing to hide a pair of knockout tits. As Finn stood up, my mouth went dry, and my dick immediately paid attention. I could appreciate beautiful women of all shapes and sizes, but there was something so understated about the way she dressed in nothing more than a black shirt and tight jeans with a tear in the knee.

She moved through the people milling at the end of the bar. Silently, she slipped through the crowd, occasionally stopping to shake hands with some of the men at the bar, giving a smile and a nod to a couple at another table.

As she approached our table, I was hit with the full force of her smile. I stood—Mom would have been proud I remembered my manners.

I had never seen a woman so naturally gorgeous in all of my life. I felt a hot pull straight in my groin and had to adjust my hips to hide my growing attraction.

Finn scooped her up and spun in a circle, earning him a quick and genuine laugh. It took actual effort to tear my eyes away from her. Her tight jeans spread across a full, firm ass. Goddamn, she had a nice ass. As if my dick wasn't on full alert already, I could feel the blood rushing between my legs, and I shifted against the stool to hide my obvious arousal.

"My girl Jo! You made it!" Gently setting her down and earning him a hip check, Finn opened his body and turned to me. "Linc, Joanna—Jo, my big brother, Lincoln. I can't believe you two have never met!" His dimpled grin spread wide across his face.

Holy shit. Jo. Jo . . . No fucking way. Is this Joanna? She lived here for six years—went to college with Finn. Finn's girlfriend is Joanna? Fuck. FUCK!

My thoughts shattered in my brain, with no hope of forming a cohesive thought. I couldn't stand the uncomfortable feeling growing in my chest.

"Hey," I said.

Real fucking smooth. I sat, elbows on the table, and all I could focus on was my beer in front of me and the fact that the woman I hadn't been able to shake for the last seven years was not only possibly standing right in front of me but clearly the object of my little brother's major crush.

"Uh . . . ok." Finn looked at me suspiciously but turned toward Jo. "All right, honey, let's get you a drink. Beer?"

Glancing at the table, she grabbed a shot full of dark liquid and slung it back, without answering. "Uggh. Shit . . . whiskey?" She let out a small cough.

Clapping a hand down on her back, Finn shouted, "Hell yeah!" pumping both fists in the air. "Let's get you a chaser."

With a head nod, Finn caught the eye of the waitress. Misty? Mandy? And she winked as he held up his beer and three fingers.

"Hi, Lincoln, it's nice to finally meet you. Finn's told me a lot about you."

Her easy smile lit up her eyes, and for a moment, I was lost in them. Were they green? Gray? It was hard to tell in the dim lighting of the bar, but in that moment, I wanted to drown in their familiarity. Instead of responding like a normal human, I just nodded and looked back out over the dancers on the floor. I had to stop thinking about what that tight body would feel like underneath mine. I was being such a tool.

Finn pulled out the stool between us, and she slipped onto it, her knee gently grazing my thigh. I couldn't stop thinking about whether Jo had written the letters, and I touched my hand to what remained of the tattered wings tattooed on my forearm. They were barely recognizable, shredded from my injuries, but they were there. The movement of my hand caught her eye, and I took my arm off the table.

Finn kept his hand casually on the back of her chair, and they turned their attention to the dance floor. He leaned in close and whispered something in her ear, and she laughed, shaking her head. It was bubbly and light against the heavy bass of the music. Irrational jealousy flared in my chest. I didn't even know this girl, and I couldn't stand the overprotective way I was feeling right now.

Rubbing my damp hands down my thighs, I stood again to stretch my legs and try to get a grip on myself when Finn grabbed Jo by the hand and pulled her toward the crowded dance floor. She pulled back slightly, laughing, but let him lead her out onto the floor, and they swayed to a slow country song. Finn dramatically twirled her and ended with a dip. She laughed again.

Fucker.

Taking a deep pull of my beer, I let my eyes travel down her body and across her curves. I felt the familiar rush of arousal and couldn't stop myself from appreciating the feminine dip of her waist, the swell of her hips and thighs.

I couldn't help but wonder how her body would feel against me if I cut into their dance. Wrapped my arms around her waist. Took a deep inhale of her hair, my nose grazing her neck, and letting her scent overtake me. Let my hands glide down over her ass. Or the warmth of her skin under her shirt as my hand moved up her back, pulling her in closer to me. The things I could do to this girl if she were mine.

"Got those beers for ya, handsome." Interrupting my thoughts, the waitress set the beers at the table with a hard rattle. She followed my eyes to Finn and Jo.

"Well, they look cozy." She smirked. "She's a lucky woman, that one. Everyone's been dying to get a piece of Finn, but he doesn't seem to have eyes for any of the women around here . . ."

She walked away, her words filling me with a sickening sense of dread as a cold sweat pricked the base of my neck. Even if she was Joanna, which I still didn't know for sure, and the sexiest woman I'd ever laid eyes on, I could see she was already Finn's. I could feel my arousal shift back to the uncomfortable tightness in my chest.

This is wrong. You're better than this. You couldn't do that to your brother, Marine. Get that shit on lock.

Throwing cash on the table, I grabbed my jacket from my stool and headed for the door. I might have promised Finn we'd hang out tonight and figure out our work shit, but I was damn sure not going to torture myself.

Instead, I'd go home, take a cold shower, and get some rest. I had no idea that I'd lay awake in the dark for hours, staring at the black ceiling, thinking about the woman in the letters, Jo, if they were one and the same, and wonder if I'd spent the last seven years attached to a woman who was going home tonight with my brother.

SIX

JOANNA

"You finally met Lincoln?! In person? Were you wearing the dress? Is he as hot as Finn? Did he ask you to dance? Tell. Me. Everything!" Honey squealed.

It was rare that Honey could separate from her busy work schedule, even on a Saturday, but she was always down for girl talk and this. was. *epic.*

Honey knew that when I was in college, I'd become friends with Finn and, as a result, started writing letters to veterans with the rest of the town. She also knew that after seeing some family photos, I'd developed a *major* soul-sucking crush on Finn's older brother, Lincoln. He was fucking hot, a Marine, and there was something about his thick, dark hair and sexy, sweet smile that was no match for an impressionable nineteen-year-old girl.

I'd dropped my letters with the Chikalu Women's Club at every single collection—careful to make sure they knew it was addressed to Lincoln Scott. Every birthday, holiday, special occasion. I'd spent days, sometimes a week or more, writing the letters. I didn't want them to be a standard

"Dear Marine" letter—I hoped to inspire him, uplift him, share a piece of home with him.

I knew there was a good chance he never got some of the letters—we'd been told that the postal service was spotty, and if the troops moved around a lot, many times packages got lost. But after six years of writing and not a single response, I'd chalked it up to a schoolgirl crush that was unrequited. When I'd left Chikalu Falls after college, I'd still drop a letter off during collection—old habits, I guess.

When I'd heard that Lincoln had been wounded in action and was coming home, I was cautiously excited, but Finn was ecstatic. A glimmer of hope bloomed in my chest, and I wondered if he'd ever ask about me—but it never happened.

Pushing away the hurt feelings of a younger, more naïve me, I focused on my call with Honey.

I turned in slow circles in Finn's office chair—I'd checked into the town's motel and come by to talk about the upcoming guide tour. I was still uneasy about the trip, so I wanted a few more details. Finn still hadn't come into the office yet. Figures. He had probably overslept.

I leaned back in Finn's chair as the open window let in the warm summer sun and thought about what to say. Really, I'd only been at the bar a few minutes before Lincoln disappeared, but holy shit. When I caught Finn's eye, Lincoln was sitting at the high-top table, but as I walked up, he'd stood. That simple gentlemanly gesture squeezed my heart—stupid hormones.

He looked different than the photos I'd remembered. His military buzz had grown longer, and his brown hair was tousled like he'd been dragging his hands through it. I couldn't help but imagine dragging my own hands through it, feeling the rough stubble on his face rub against me.

Not quite as tall and imposing as Finn, but years in the service had given Lincoln a hard and muscular body that he'd maintained in the years he'd been home. His dark shirt stretched across his chest in a way that made me want to tear it off him on sight. And his arms? God, that shirt was lucky it was still holding together.

My thighs squeezed together as I thought about how good he smelled when I sat next to him—clean, like pine and campfire and musk only a man could make smell good. I closed my eyes, just thinking about it.

"He's intense, for sure. Quiet. And Finn said he was acting really strange, but he was fine. Kinda . . . I don't know. Cold? He left right after I got there."

I tried focusing on my sister and not on the growing dampness between my legs as I recalled my knee brushing against his thick, muscular thigh. I couldn't help but wonder if he was as thick everywhere else.

"Oh. My. God. Joanna . . . Did he know it was you? Was he hot? That's really what I want to know . . . was he *hot*?"

"Yes! Ok? Yes. He's fucking hot!" I yelled into the air.

At that moment, the door to the office swung open and hit the opposite wall with a bang. Startled, I whipped my chair around, my phone hitting the ground and spinning away from me. I had nearly knocked myself to the ground. I looked up and was face to crotch with Lincoln. He held out his hand to help me up as Finn sauntered into the office.

I placed my hand into Lincoln's and felt lava flow straight into my core. His hands were large and rough, but he gave me a gentle squeeze as he helped me to my feet. My eyes peeked up to see his steely gaze fixed on my face. They were sea-blue, with an outline of navy at the edges. My chest hitched with a sharp inhale—girls like me were not used to getting looks like those.

"Sorry about that." His deep voice rumbled through me, and I nearly moaned. He was even more handsome in the daytime and it left me feeling breathless.

"Sorry, Jo!" Finn's voice cut in and snapped me from my runaway fantasies of Lincoln. "Pack it up, we're going!"

I turned my attention to Finn who'd walked through the door as he'd pushed it open and was making sure he hadn't dented the wall, Lincoln still holding my hand in his.

I looked from Lincoln to Finn. Pulling my hand back, I smoothed my shirt down my hips and cleared my throat. "Hey, what's up?"

"Let's go do some research." Finn's arms opened as if to say "ta-dah!"

I just looked at him, still thinking about the feel of Lincoln's fingers trailing under my palm as he released me.

Blinking and trying hard to regain my bearings, I looked down. "Um . . . ok."

"Jo, what the fuck!" Finn laughed. "Pack your shit!" Without waiting for an answer, he walked out of his office.

In the decade Finn and I had known each other, "doing research" meant skipping out on work to fish together. In reality, it was kind of like research. Two years ago, I'd made the decision to go it alone, and I'd been searching for a place to set up a top-notch fishing guide service ever since. Finn and Lincoln had their family's land for their guides, so he was always keeping an eye out for me.

I looked at Lincoln, and he gave me a small wink before following his brother out the door. Behind his back I squealed a silent, *oh my god!* Honey was not going to believe this.

Oh, shit. Honey!

Looking around the office floor, I found my phone. It wasn't cracked, thank god, but Honey had long since hung up. I'd have to remember to call her later. She'd definitely want to hear about how good Lincoln's firm, round ass looked as he walked out of Finn's office and into the main lobby.

Looking left, then right, I figured I'd need only a few things for our impromptu adventure.

"Finn, are you driving?" I asked through the office door.

"Yup, let's roll," he called back.

I grabbed a thick, gray flannel shirt hanging in the office closet. It was going to be huge on me, but it would keep me from getting a chill. I smoothed my hair, swiped on some lip balm, and stuffed it in my pocket.

Finn and Lincoln kept all of the guide equipment in a row of metal storage lockers in the central main office space. Noticing Finn must have already grabbed the waders from the closet, I grabbed a pole, soft-sided tackle box, and clipped a rag to the outside with a carabiner.

By the time I'd gotten around back, Finn had pulled up in his truck. Since I'd known him, he'd been driving this new, shiny black truck with black rims—it was lifted so high, even my five-foot-seven-inch frame had to clamber up the side to get in. I walked around the back, ready to toss my gear into the bed of the truck when Finn turned the corner to grab my bag.

"I got this. Go on and get in." Finn paused a second. "And, Jo? When we're out there, if the timing's right, I think I'm going to tell him."

I looked up at Finn sharply. Of all the moments I'd known him, he usually chose bravado and cockiness and humor. I'd never seen him scared, but his eyes were pleading with me, begging me to give him strength. I knew that opening up to his brother and telling him that he was gay was something he'd struggled with for a really long time. I wrapped my arm around his waist and squeezed.

"Uh, sorry." Lincoln cleared his throat and looked away. "Do you want to take the middle?" he asked, gesturing a wide palm toward the cab of the truck.

Straightening, I practically pushed Finn away in my surprise. A flash of warmth crept up my cheeks when I felt Lincoln's eyes move with me. Head high, I briskly walked toward the passenger side.

With my left hand on the doorframe and my right on the open door, I went to hoist myself up into the monstrosity of the truck. Right as I pushed off my foot, I felt Lincoln's strong hand curl around my left hip. Surprised, I jumped back, my ass bumping right against the solid length of his body. Both of his hands went to my hips to steady me.

"Didn't mean to scare you," he said in his deep grumbly voice, his mouth so close to me, his breath touched my ear. "I just figured you might need a boost."

I felt a surge of pleasure race down my belly, and I knew my underwear was already soaked through.

Oh, shit. His body is so hard. Oh, shit. Oh, fuck.

Laughing nervously, but not willing to move my body from against his, I said, "Yeah. This thing is ridiculous. Thanks."

Gently pushing off him, I braced myself against the truck again as his hands stayed firmly affixed to my hips. This time, when I pushed up, his strong arms tensed and helped to lift me onto the seat. As I went up, his hands dragged down my sides before dropping. I scooted myself to the center, staring straight ahead, trying to hide a smile.

My heart pounded in my ears, my cheeks burned, and I prayed that neither of them would notice.

Finn buckled, adjusted the mirror, and looked over as Lincoln effortlessly slid into place next to me. My thighs pressed together firmly, but with two gigantic men on each side, I couldn't avoid the outside edge of my thigh touching Lincoln's.

"Let's get 'em, kids." Finn wiggled his eyebrows and grinned as he cranked the engine, the roar of the motor drowning out the release of the breath I'd been holding.

SEVEN

LINCOLN

Turning off Route One, the truck bounced down an old dirt road leading down a winding path through thickets and pines at the base of the mountains. Determined not to stare at Jo's chest bouncing along with the truck, I looked out the passenger window, listened to the low country music from the radio, and the comfortable chatter between Finn and Jo. As we passed near Antelope Creek, it hit me that in the eight years I'd been gone and the two I'd been back, the only thing that really changed was me.

Jo shifted in her seat. Not knowing if she was crowded or just uncomfortable, I could have shifted my body away, but I didn't. I felt her muscular thigh press the full length of mine, and warmth spread through my stomach.

"Sweet, they made it," Finn said as he pulled his truck next to two others—Deck and Colin. As we parked and got out, I held my hand to help Jo step down from the truck and had to rub a hand over my face to hide my smile.

Finn and Jo greeted Deck and Colin with a familiarity that said they must have met before. Deck hugged Jo as

Colin tipped his chin to Finn. I hung back, watching their easy friendship unfold.

How is it that they know her, and I've never met her before?

"Get your ass over here, man," Deck said, holding out his hand. I went to shake it, and he pulled me into a bear hug. "Sorry I haven't been able to stop by lately. Couple of rookies in the department are going to be the death of me."

"I heard you made Detective Sergeant. Congrats, man." I patted his back, squeezed his shoulder.

Cole Decker worked for the Chikalu Falls Police Department—a job he'd known he'd have even in high school. His dad and granddad had been on the force. Serving and protecting was in his blood.

His off-shift hours and my need for space and privacy meant we didn't always hang out together. Deck seemed to understand, and when we did see each other, there was never any weirdness. I thought in his job, he understood what it was like to have to make tough choices, like mine in the Marines, and harder yet—live with those choices. One May after I'd gotten back, we got piss drunk at my cabin on Mr. Bailey's property and we'd gotten to swapping stories. Staring into the bonfire, I'd told him about some of the missions in Afghanistan. In a slurred stupor, he'd gotten real serious and asked if I could keep a secret. I'd said yes, obviously, but we were interrupted by Finn falling into the creek and he never mentioned it again. It had been two years, and I still wondered what it was he was hiding.

Still eyeing Deck, we rounded the bed of the truck to unload our gear. We each stepped into our waders to keep our pants from getting soaked and clipped them at our chest. I'd had to fight the urge to carry all of Jo's gear on top of my own, but before I could, she'd grabbed it all and started walking down the path toward the river.

With a glance over her shoulder, she winked. "Try to keep up, boys."

WHEN FINN SAID she could hold her own out here, he wasn't kidding. The hike down to the river wound through unmarked trails, and Finn took over leading the way to the water. A time or two, she'd stop to get her footing or tuck a hair behind her ear but she never fell behind or needed a boost on the uneven, rocky terrain. When we'd stopped to decide if we wanted to try fishing here or a ways upstream, she swiped a bead of sweat off her forehead.

I knew it was shameful to think of her that way, but I couldn't help imagining what it would feel like to look down at her, beads of sweat at her temples, feeling my body on top of her and seeing pleasure spread across her face as I stretched her open with my cock. How long had it been since I'd felt the softness of a woman's body underneath me? To lie together after we were both spent?

As if he could hear my traitorous thoughts, Finn looked over at me, his brows furrowed. Grunting, I pushed harder up the trail, trying to put a little distance between myself and Jo.

Once we reached a bend in the riverbank, our group spread wide across the shallow section of the river. We spaced ourselves to give plenty of room to cast without driving the fish too far downstream. After a few quick catches, Jo wandered off from the group—hiking the bank, walking the ridge toward the base of the mountain. She looked peaceful, gorgeous, and completely in her element.

Still fishing, the guys and I fell into an easy rhythm—shooting the shit like we'd always done. Deck told us about a few cases of vandalism he was working on. Someone was drawing smiling dicks with little top hats around town—probably local kids who got bored or a senior prank.

"Yeah, I saw one on the side of the Dairy Palace just yesterday," I remarked, laughing.

"Are you fucking kidding me?!" he asked. "God damn it . . ." Grumbling, he pulled out his phone, I assumed to report the new dick in town, and I just laughed.

Colin was working on booking new bands to try to attract more people from the larger surrounding towns. We all talked a little about my time in Kandahar, but they didn't press for specifics, and for that I was grateful.

As the afternoon stretched on, we wandered apart, and I could feel my tension dissolve as I listened to the noises of the riverbank. Water splashed against my boots. Birdsong in the trees. Even the rustling in the woods didn't make me tense. When I saw a small rock bluff up ahead, I decided it would be the perfect spot to sit and think.

What were the odds that Jo wrote those letters? I had to get this timeline straight in my head—Finn said he met Jo during an English lit class at college. She was living here and going to school so it's possible that Finn told her about writing the troops . . . or the Women's Club since it was always a big deal around town. The letters stopped when I'd come home, but I never met Jo? When did she move away? How did this never come up?

The fact that Finn already had a relationship with her gnawed at me. He clearly cared about her. It was a dick move to step in on that if he was trying to take their friendship to the next level, but fuck. I couldn't stop thinking about little details about her—the way her hair moved over her shoulder when she walked. What would it feel like to brush it back off her face or brushing over my chest as she looked down at me?

I could imagine exactly what it would feel like, and my dick twitched in response. I had to force myself to bury those thoughts and stop thinking of her as anything other than Finn's almost-girlfriend. She couldn't mean anything to me.

Finn saw me sitting alone and, with the same unnerving scowl he'd had on earlier, started making his way toward me. I eyed him curiously, not used to seeing those hard lines on his face. Something was definitely up.

Fuck. Had he noticed me touching Jo at the truck? Had he seen the way I kept looking at her? I was such a piece of shit.

I could tell he had something on his mind, and I wasn't entirely ready for this conversation. I had to tell my baby brother that I was hot for his girl. I didn't think we'd start throwing punches, but if he was smart, he wouldn't give her up easily.

As he reached the top of the rocks, he stood beside me, hands in his pockets, shoulders tense. Breathing out a hard breath, he said, "There's something important I need to talk to you about."

I nodded.

"See . . . the thing is," he continued, "you were gone a long time. A lot has changed."

That hit me in the gut. When I'd enlisted, Finn was only fifteen. I never really considered that he felt like I'd left him—not like that, anyway.

Where is he going with this?

"I know you like to be alone—and we try to give you your space, but since you've been living out on Mr. Bailey's property, there's also a lot you miss at home . . ." Finn continued.

Mid-sentence, he shifted his weight. In that moment, a rock rattled beneath him and bounced down toward the river. Adjusting, Finn side-stepped, but the footing wasn't secure. Instinctively, I reached for him but only managed to grab his shirt as he fell backward.

In slow motion, I watched Finn claw toward the rocks, trying to grab anything, but rocks tumbled with him. The drop was only eight feet or so, but as his big frame landed awkwardly, I heard the familiar, sickening sound of bones breaking.

EIGHT
JOANNA

THE MORNING after Finn broke his leg, I had to get outside and work through the jumble of emotions I was feeling. Getting outside and scouting new potential land was the best way to clear my head. I left the Chikalu Rose Motel and loaded Bud up in my old blue Ford I'd named "The Blue Beast" and started driving. I didn't have a particular destination in mind, but I was always hoping to stumble upon somewhere new.

Being mindful of private property or No Trespassing signs, I drove down the winding country roads until I saw a clearing in the tree line to what looked like an established trail. I parked my truck, checked my small backpack for water and a snack, and started walking.

Bud wandered up ahead, smelling the forest floor, stopping to investigate a mushroom or critter that was startled awake. He was used to my aimless hikes, never wandering too far from me. He was such a good, sweet boy.

As the elevation increased, my breath came out harder in gusts. I could feel my blood pumping through my legs as I pushed harder.

My mind wandered to Finn and his broken leg and the relief that washed over me when I knew he would be okay. The truth was, I wasn't nearby when it happened, but had run toward the panicked yells of my friends in time to see Lincoln hoist Finn lengthwise across his shoulders like a fireman.

Deck said that Finn lost his footing on a rock bluff and took a hard tumble, though I was sure he would have preferred if he embellished its height or how very tough he was. Deck kept the details simple.

I wasn't expecting the intense wave of desire that swept through me when I saw Lincoln grab Finn. Damn, he'd looked good doing that. Instinct and training took over—his blue eyes were set as he carried Finn the half mile back to the trucks. I scrambled behind them, grabbing any gear I could as I went.

Lincoln's biceps bulged with the weight, veins popping out of his lean forearms. On his right arm, I could see the scars from the war and remnants of tattoos that had been damaged. My chest got tight thinking about how painful it looked.

Sweat beaded the back of Lincoln's shirt but his breath was steady. With an unrestricted view of his ass as he pushed on ahead of me, I could see his strong legs carrying the weight.

I want to wrap my legs around that tight, muscular body.

In the days since Finn's accident, I couldn't get that thought out of my head. I spent quiet nights in my bed thinking about running my fingers down his abs, lower until I reached his thick, hard cock.

I wanted to know what Lincoln felt like in bed. I fantasized that he was a generous lover, unlike any I'd been with before. I imagined him being assertive, overcome with his desire, and taking me, knowing I wanted it just as badly as he did. I could feel my core tighten just thinking about Lincoln on top of me, pushing his way inside.

I knew it was wrong to think about my best friend's brother like that, but I couldn't help it. I was drawn to Lincoln. I wanted to know more about him, spend time figuring out why sometimes he seemed so lighthearted and other times he grew so quiet and intense.

Finn and Lincoln had some things they needed to work out, but if I could help it, I was going to find a way to see Lincoln again.

Coming to the top of a ridge, I found the landscape open to a clearing. Lost in my thoughts, I wasn't sure how far I'd traveled, so I checked my GPS watch—almost three miles. Bud seemed barely phased by the long hike, but I wanted to take a minute to catch my breath.

I could hear the faint sounds of a road nearby so I knew I hadn't strayed too far from civilization, but getting lost in the mountains of northwest Montana would not be great. I needed to keep my head on my shoulders and stop daydreaming so much about Lincoln.

I looked out over the landscape below and saw a long valley that swept across, bending and moving with the river. It was gorgeous. Wildflowers bloomed along the bank, and the drop-off to the water was gradual, which would allow people to wade into the water to fish. It was the perfect, secluded spot. A ripple of excitement traveled through me.

Marking the location on my watch, I knew I had to find out who owned this section of land—there's no way it was public land. Finn and I had scoured every inch of public land in four counties but hadn't found anything as perfect as this. Flat areas for tent camping, trees for hammocks, easy access to water, not too far from a main road.

Determined, I pulled up a map on my phone. Service was spotty so it took forever for it to load. Scrolling left and right, zooming in and out, I searched the image for any sign of a house or a cabin or anything that would help me get an address. Finally, on the screen was what looked like a small village—a large structure (maybe a house?), a barn, and some smaller outbuildings dotted around it.

Getting my bearings and triple-checking it against my GPS watch, I found it was only about an hour hike from where I was standing. My legs ached at the knowledge that I'd still have to walk all the way back.

"What do you think, Bud? Should we go knock on the door? Can you be charming?" I asked.

Bud, being adorable but also kind of dumb, let out a loud yip and started circling me excitedly.

"Well, you don't seem tired now, but I'm not carrying you back."

Bud barked again, his breath panting. I filled his portable water dish, checked directions again, turned, and headed off in the direction of the house.

An hour later—though my aching legs said it was more like twelve—an old farmhouse came into view. As I walked out of the woods onto the property, a small gravel driveway wound toward the highway to my left. The house sat so far back, it would be nearly invisible to cars passing on the highway, and the only indication I wasn't totally isolated was the occasional hum of a car driving past.

A small creek that led back to the main river peeked out from the backyard. The house itself was a disaster. Broken window shutters hung, their faded paint curling at the edges. A few windows were boarded up with plywood haphazardly nailed over the front. I thought it looked abandoned as I circled the house with its expansive porch, Bud staying tightly at my leg.

The back porch, with two new-looking Adirondack chairs and a small round table, was the only hint that the home wasn't empty. Behind the home, I could see the barn. It looked like a stiff wind would be all it took to set it tumbling to the ground. Farther back, there were what looked like three small log cabins along the creek.

Wanting to make note of the address so I could track down the owner, I started back toward the front of the house. My thighs burned and my feet throbbed. I was definitely not looking forward to the miles between my truck and me.

Before Bud could even bark in surprise, I could feel him.

"Can I help you?" a man's voice asked, laced with irritation. I turned to face Lincoln. "Oh," his voice softened, "what are you doing here?"

A giddy ripple of excitement whirled just under my ribs at seeing him again. I smiled and shrugged a shoulder. "Oh, you know, just in the neighborhood."

His face twitched in a subtle smirk, and I was calling that a win. Suddenly feeling nervous to be alone with Lincoln, I reached out my hand.

Why are you shaking his hand? You're an idiot.

His eyes flicked down to my hand as he hesitated slightly but then reached out to take it. His palm was wide, with long, thick fingers. He was definitely a man who was used to working with his hands, and I could feel the slightly rough callous rub my palm. Our eyes met and I immediately looked down, seeing the scarred tattoos on his forearms again. It made my chest hitch.

Breaking contact, I asked, "So, what are *you* doing here?"

"I live here," he said, offering nothing more, but his brow was furrowed.

I gestured toward the ramshackle house. "You live here? Nobody lives here."

"I don't live here," he mirrored my gesture to the house, "but have a cottage on the property by the water. So again, what are *you* doing here? Did Finn send you?"

"No. Not at all. Bud and I are just out exploring." At the mention of his name, Bud barked happily. Lincoln squatted down, his jeans tightening around his thighs as I tried to look away. Bud eagerly ambled toward him, leaning his stocky weight into Lincoln's legs.

"He's cute. What kind of dog is he?" Lincoln asked.

"Red Heeler, uh, Australian Cattle Dog. He's amazing, adventurous, but also kind of a dipshit. He's always getting stuck in fox holes or up to his eyeballs in fish guts," I shared, smiling down at Bud because he was *my* dipshit.

Lincoln's smile spread across his face, crinkling at the edges of his eyes and softening his normally hard features.

Seeing the door to his resolve crack, I kicked that goddamn door wide open. "Well, since you live here, why don't you show us around?"

He stood, dragged a hand through his hair, and sighed. "Yeah, ok."

His hand dropped with a small smack against his leg. He lifted his arm to lead the way, and as I passed him, I tried not to breathe in the smell of him. Was it cologne? Did he naturally smell like masculine soap and camp smoke? God, it was good.

Out of the corner of my eye, I appreciated the way his jeans hugged the curve of his ass. His waist was trim and the way the hem of his green T-shirt teased at his hips was making my mouth water. Being this close to him, even in the openness of outside, was making me jumpy.

"You really live way out here alone?" I asked, letting my nerves get the best of me.

"Not alone," he replied, and for a moment, my heart sank until he added, "Mr. Bailey lives in the Big House. I've been helping him out, getting it fixed up, making sure he doesn't let it collapse around him."

"That's very kind of you," I offered.

"It's the least I can do, he took me in when I came home."

I recalled that Finn said Lincoln's adjustment to life after the Marines was a challenge. Finn didn't share specifics, but I knew he had struggled with his injuries, life in a small town, and not being with his unit anymore. Living with Miss Birdie and Finn wasn't really working for anyone. Lincoln filled his time with "anger and booze," as Finn recalled. Frowning at that thought, I walked in silence.

Turning the conversation back to safer ground, I looked around the property. "I've got to tell you . . . I'm a little heartbroken. I thought this property was vacant. I was about ten minutes from moving in and claiming it as my own." I smiled at Lincoln but his eyes were fixed on me.

"I'm not sure the owner would mind all that much." Lincoln's voice was just above a whisper and laced with gravel. I felt a hot blush spread across my cheeks.

Lincoln cleared his throat, and I met his eyes as we stopped by a turn in the creek. Heat crept up my neck. He bent to pick up a stick, whipped it toward the creek, and Bud went sailing after it. The sharp splash broke the tension in the air.

"So," he rubbed a hand on the back of his neck, "we're a little screwed with Finn's broken leg."

I nodded.

"Finn suggested that we hire you while he's out." His expression was unreadable.

"What do you mean?" I asked, even though I knew exactly what he meant—Finn had called me earlier in the day.

"I mean, we're already short-staffed and could use another guide. Finn said you usually only do solo guides, but you'd really be helping us out." He took a small step forward and added, "Helping me out."

I tipped my head up as he towered over me, his blue eyes glancing to my lips.

Kiss me. Kiss me. Kiss me.

A small twinge floated over his face but was gone just as quickly as he added, "So it's up to you, but we pay well, meals included. I need to know by Tuesday."

With that, he turned and stomped away.

Following him, I had to practically jog to keep up with his long, purposeful strides.

"Hey, yeah, I'll think about it," I called breathlessly to his back.

"Good."

Feeling dismissed and a little confused—*what the fuck is his problem all of a sudden?*—I whistled for Bud, who turned to follow me back up the path toward the woods. My gait was slow, my legs feeling the ache, and I still had miles ahead of me.

I thought I heard a mumbled *fuck* when he called out, "Hey, I'm headed into town and it's getting late. I'll take you back."

My stomach tightened, and I forced myself to take a small breath before replying, "That's so kind. Thank you."

I walked past him, breathing in his heady scent on purpose this time. His gray truck was newer than mine, but not the showboat that Finn's was. He paused, opened my door, and I couldn't hide the small smile as I clenched my jaw to get myself under control. He double tapped the truck bed and Bud leapt up, curling up into the front corner with a sigh.

The ride was short, and the conversation was light, sticking mostly to comments about the weather, fishing, or the town itself. The dark mood that had settled over him was seemingly gone. I silently cursed how short the drive felt as we pulled up to my truck.

Thanking him for the ride, I quickly grabbed my backpack and called for Bud. I had to put a little distance between us before my panties burst into flames. Clearly, my schoolgirl crush was back with a vengeance.

NINE
LINCOLN

"Dude. You have to cover for me."

With his left leg in a cast, Finn gestured toward it and then put his palms up like, "Well, dumbass?"

"How long is the trip?"

"The guy booked five days, four nights for his group. It's a few corporate guys—you take the group out, camp, fish. It's a dream."

Nodding, I didn't really have a good excuse to turn him down. When it came to guiding, I usually only did small groups, day trips. Being with a larger group for multiple nights didn't give me the space I needed, and it made my skin crawl.

As I looked at my brother sitting on his couch, casted leg propped up with a pillow, he pouted—fucking pouted at me. But with a broken leg, Finn certainly couldn't go. No harm in showing a few yuppies how to fish.

"Besides," he continued, "you'll have Jo and Brandon leading the whole thing. You're just there to help out and show the guests a good time."

Fuuuuuuck.

I'd been finding ways to avoid Jo since Finn's accident, and five days with her on a camping trip would be too much. I still hadn't heard whether or not she was taking the job, but I had hoped she turned it down. Apparently not.

The Marines taught me discipline and restraint, but I was having a hard enough time keeping my dick in check when she wasn't around. Being blessed with a big dick wasn't always a good thing when just the smell of her skin got my blood pumping.

"I don't know, man," I tried.

"Linc. You're doing it. What else do you have going on? I'll text Jo and let her know."

He was right. Once we finalized the details, I left his apartment and headed back to work to gather the gear I'd need, hoping Jo was already out scouting the area. Since deciding to take the job, she had completely taken over Finn's desk.

When I got to our guidepost, Jo wasn't there and I couldn't help the wave of disappointment running through me. My own thoughts were giving me whiplash. It was insane but all I wanted was a glimpse. Was her hair in a ponytail? Was she wearing jeans or shorts? Would she smile when she saw me?

After getting poles, waders, and other basic equipment for the trip, I left a note telling Jo I'd meet her at the drop-off tomorrow morning.

I'D NEVER LOOKED FORWARD to three A.M. before in my life. But when my alarm rang, I popped out of bed, knowing I was going to see Jo.

It was a strange kind of torture, wanting something so

badly but knowing how wrong it was to want it. I knew I had to talk to Finn. I didn't think I could keep myself in check much longer. We needed to have a serious talk about whether or not he was going to pursue Jo—because if he wasn't, game on.

In the early morning light, Jo's beauty was arresting. She moved with strength and grace, unloading and packing tents, hammocks, coolers—she worked with efficiency. I appreciated the long lines of her legs and had to keep myself from staring.

The game plan was to hike, stopping to fish along the shallows of the riverbank, and camp. As a full guide service, we'd have to set up tents, provide the food, help inexperienced fishermen, and keep the pace so we'd make it to the lodge on night two. Once we were at the lodge, we could have a hot meal, hot shower, and resupply for the trip back.

The five men, probably in their late twenties, from a downtown office in Butte, were experienced fishermen, but had never been on a guided trip before.

"Hey, darlin'," one said to Jo, "you doing all the cooking while we're out there?" He gave a playful nod and shove to his buddy.

"Well, I guess that'll depend on whether or not you catch any fish," she shot back. Her face stayed friendly, but her back was straight and tense.

"I'll be sure to call her if I need help handling my pole," another said under his breath. They all laughed and he fist-bumped another. Fist-bumped—what a douche.

I stepped forward, ready to beat the shit out of them for talking about her like that, when I felt her hand on my back, warmth spreading through me at her touch.

"Easy there, tiger. They're harmless." She centered her

pack on her back and started down the trail. "It's not the first unoriginal dick joke I've heard, and it damn sure won't be my last."

"They won't talk about you like that again," I said, fixing my eyes on hers. If they kept that shit up, I didn't care if they were paying customers or not. I'd kick all their asses without breaking a sweat.

She smiled, her green-gray eyes dancing. "I appreciate that." And with a whistle, she walked down the path. Her stocky red dog wearing a hiking backpack with *Bud* stitched on the back trotted happily alongside her.

We hiked, staying together, as we wound around the base of a small mountain range. She asked about how I'd become a medic. I shared with her how I was a Corpsman— starting in the Navy because the Marines don't actually have a medical department. I ate, slept, and shit with the squad and fought alongside the unit until I'd eventually earned the honor of Fleet Marine Force.

"I fired my weapon until someone got hurt," I explained, "and then I switched to medic mode."

"I'm sure it wasn't easy," was all she said. She didn't press, didn't ask me about losing men like people always did, or push to know more than I was willing to offer. Silence with Jo was easy, comfortable. As long as I could stop myself from watching her ass as she bent over to pet Bud, I would be fine.

I tried to bring up the letters, but couldn't find the words, so instead asked about how she ended up in Chikalu Falls, her family, and life in our small town. I learned that Chikalu was actually a Native American Crow word for Honor Song. Jo knew all kinds of random facts about the deep history of the West.

My thoughts briefly flew to Finn. Watching Jo the way I was certainly wasn't very honorable, but she held my gaze as she took a long drink of water, and right then I knew. I would risk everything to be with her.

TEN
JOANNA

GROWLY, protective Lincoln was quickly becoming my new favorite thing. Our group was behaving, and so far, I hadn't heard any other comments about me being a woman. Still, Lincoln glared at their backs all afternoon as we hiked through the trails.

I knew it was likely his training or sense of honor that made him react that way, but I couldn't help but feel a flutter of excitement when I thought about it.

I was never the woman that a man felt protective toward. I was the friend. Little sister. Less sexy girl-next-door and more spinster-librarian.

Considering my sturdy Schnee boots and brown field pants, it was no wonder. I was literally wearing men's boots because they didn't even come in women's sizes. Sure, I loved lacy bras just like the next girl, but out in the mountains, it was always a matter of being practical.

Setting my pack on the ground, I put both hands behind my hips and stretched backward. It felt good knowing the day was behind us. We'd had a solid day of hiking, stopping along the river to cast into the current.

I'd spent most of my time tying and retying flies that got caught in trees, broken lines, or tweaking their arm placements to get a better cast.

Being outdoors, I could breathe. I was meant to do this; I knew it in my bones. All I had to do was be focused, find amazing places to fish, and build trust with people. I did not need distractions in my life right now.

Certainly not distractions that looked like Lincoln Scott.

The group worked on setting up their tents for the night —our stay at the more comfortable lodge wouldn't be until tomorrow. They made a semicircle with their tents. Brandon, another guide who worked for Finn and Lincoln, helped them with the stakes and poles. He'd set his tent up with them, claiming he'd keep them in line, but I knew better. He'd be hungover tomorrow too. I was sure of it.

I'd chosen a spot where I could keep an eye on our group, but far enough away to give them more privacy. They got to have their guys' weekend, and I could sleep without being bothered by late-night, booze-fest campfires.

Unpacking my gear, I saw Lincoln setting up his tent not too far from mine.

"Not hanging with the boys tonight?" I called.

"Not tonight. The view is better up here."

Oh, shit. Did he smirk? Was he talking about me? No fucking way.

Warmth crept into my cheeks, and I tried to tell myself that Lincoln was definitely talking about the actual view. The mountains of Montana were remarkable. While a lot of the state remained large flats, in the mountains, they rose up to bluffs, waterfalls, and pine forests. The air was clean, and you could see for miles. Hidden streams and pools would be covered with pink and yellow wildflowers this time of year.

"Once we're all set up, we can take everyone down to get cleaned up."

"Yes, boss." He smiled as I went into my tent to change.

The creek was about a quarter-mile hike east of camp, not super close, but it was worth it. Finn said on a hike last June, he'd found it. The rocky path gave way to a small, pebbled pool of freshwater, so clear you could see to the bottom. The pool itself was encircled by pine trees on all sides, giving it a private and secluded feel. On one side was a bluff, dropping down into the deepest parts of the pool. Despite the heat, the water was brisk, and as I dipped my hands down into it and sipped, it was cool and crisp.

"All right folks, let's hang out here for a while, take a swim, clean up a little, and then we'll head back to camp for the night."

Before I could even get my speech out, one of the guys was running up the bluff across from me, clambering to get to the top. With a "WHOO!" he cannonballed off the bluff and landed with a splash into the deep pool.

That started a ripple effect of guys dropping the gear and pulling off their shirts to run into the water. Within minutes, a game of chicken had started—one of the guys on bottom claiming that the other should lay off the bratwurst and beer.

I laughed. Men were always boys at heart.

Lincoln stood to my right. I tried not to look at him as he reached behind his back to grab the collar of his tight gray T-shirt and pull it over his head.

Even covered in a shirt and backpack, I knew he looked good, but damn. Seeing Lincoln without a shirt made my stomach whoosh and I felt a warm trickle of wetness between my legs. His arms were tan and sculpted—smooth with only a light dusting of dark hair. His chest wasn't smooth, but rather had a thin layer of dark hair that trailed down his tight abs.

Below his belly button, the hair continued and I imagined licking that exact spot, right below his hip. Panting, I dipped my hand back into the pool and touched the cool water to my face and neck.

Sneaking another peek, I saw dark tattoos that wound themselves around his upper back and biceps, trailing down one arm. Without getting too close, I couldn't tell why some looked broken or incomplete. Then, as my eyes trailed up, I saw pale pink scars marring his torso and arm, breaking into the designs of his tattoos.

Injuries.

It somehow made him hotter, knowing he'd fought for his country, was masculine and strong, but still vulnerable and human.

I let myself stare, pretending to inventory my backpack as I watched him talking with Brandon and another guest. As he gestured with one of his hands, a tattoo down his right forearm caught my eye.

The tattoo had taken a lot of damage but there was no mistaking what they were—Valkyrie wings.

Is that a coincidence? Does Lincoln know that it was me who wrote to him? There's no way those wings had anything to do with me . . . right?

Seeing the Valkyrie wings, vandalized by the effects of war on Lincoln's muscled forearm, spread an ache through my chest. Suddenly, I needed space to be alone. I needed to breathe and get myself under control.

∼

By the time Bud and I got back to the pool after our walk down the trail, the sun was dipping lower into the sky. We'd have to get packed up and back to camp if we were going to make it before nightfall. I caught Brandon's eye and tipped my chin.

"All right guys, time to pack it up," Brandon called to the group.

As the rest balled up their shirts and slipped shoes back on, he said to me, "I'll get these rowdy assholes back to camp if you want to take a minute to clean up. I'll be sure no one stays behind to watch."

Grateful, I said, "You're the best. I've got my flashlight so I'm good. I won't be long."

He walked farther up the trail, the caboose in the douche-train, but stopped to talk to Lincoln. They both glanced in my direction, but then Brandon turned and continued up the trail and Lincoln stood where he was.

"You can go on up, I'm just going to clean up. I'll be right behind you." I smiled, hoping he'd leave before I threw myself at him.

"Sorry, no can do. Finn would kill me if he found out I let you wander around the woods in the dark. And before you stop me," he lifted both hands, "it's got nothing to do with you being a woman."

I eyed him warily.

"Bears." He winked.

I couldn't help but smile back. Being able to take care of yourself and wanting someone to want to take care of you were two *very* different things.

Feeling a rush of nervous excitement, I pulled my shirt over my head and shimmied out of my pants, revealing my black two-piece swimsuit. While it was no string bikini, it was small enough to pack and made my boobs perky and round. I was usually alone when I wore it, not ten feet from Lincoln Scott.

When I noticed the appreciative stare it earned me, I made a note to buy one in every color.

I tentatively stepped into the cool water, sucking in a breath at the cold.

"Just jump in, it's easier that way," he said.

"Easy for you to say, you've got clothes on," I replied slowly, walking deeper.

At that, he held my gaze in challenge and pulled his shirt back off. After kicking off his shoes, he unbuttoned, unzipped, and dropped his pants, revealing tight, black boxer briefs as he held my gaze. With a mischievous grin, he ran up the side of the bluff.

At the top, he inhaled three sharp breaths before leaping off the ridge. With his splash, I was soaked and squealed as I went deeper into the pool of water.

"Oh, FUCK!" He yelled as he broke to the surface "It's fucking freezing!"

Laughing, I pushed a wall of water in his direction. "I told you!"

My teeth chattered as I swam in small circles. The cool water lapped at my shoulders as I watched him. Lincoln's hard body cut through the water as he swam a lap in the deepest section of the pool. His tattooed torso shimmered with water as the rivulets ran between the muscles of his back. I felt a pulse between my legs in response.

He turned, swimming his way toward me. Despite the cool water, a warmth spread inside my body. Closer still, he dove under the water, disappearing in the fading sunlight.

Looking around, I couldn't see Lincoln swimming underneath the water. The woods fell silent, and a wave of unease came over me. My ears prickled. With a "RAAH-

HH!" he burst above the surface, making me scream in response.

We both laughed, breathing heavily. A silence settled between us. My eyes drifted down his face, over his straight sharp nose, to his lips, glistening wet. He sucked his lower lip into his mouth, and I felt a whoosh of breath escape me.

"Jo." His fingertips glided up my sides and moved toward my back.

"Yes, Lincoln," I said, lifting my eyes to meet his. If he didn't lean forward and kiss me, I was going to dissolve in this pool of water.

Lincoln's hands settled on my hips, my legs still softly kicking in the deep water. He gently pulled my hips forward, his fingers digging tenderly into the flesh, until I was nestled against him. I felt the hard length of him between us, and a soft gasp escaped me.

"Joanna," he said, moving his hands over my ass and shifting my legs to straddle him. I wrapped my legs around his waist and instinctively I rolled my hips forward to feel his length against my clit. A tingle of electricity radiated through me as he let out a soft groan.

"No one calls me Joanna," I said breathlessly as my heart pounded in my chest.

"But you are my Joanna, aren't you?" he said, his voice gravely with desire, searching my face for some answer.

My Joanna.

In that moment, I knew. All this time, Lincoln had received my letters. He'd read them and he knew because I always signed each one simply, with Joanna.

ELEVEN
LINCOLN

"Yes," she said softly, and I felt her breath warm my lips.

Before she could even breathe out the word, I crushed my lips to hers. My mouth opened, teasing and tasting her as my tongue slid over hers. I moved my hands down to her ass and pulled her in tighter to my hips, my dick hard and trapped between us.

Alarm bells raged in my head. I knew this was a mistake, but as she wrapped her arms around the back of my neck, I didn't give a fuck. Joanna's body felt warm and hard and amazing against mine, and if this was the only chance I had to feel it, I was taking it.

Her tits pressed against me, and I lifted my hand to find her soft, round breast, her tight, hard nipple. My thumb brushed against it, and her hips jerked in response. She moaned into my mouth, and I took the kiss deeper, teasing her tongue with mine. I wanted to devour her as I let my mouth travel down her neck—licking and sucking and biting her pale skin. At the base of her neck, I felt the thrumming of her heartbeat and dipped my tongue into the soft trench of her shoulder, and she gasped.

"Holy fuck, Lincoln. Yes." Her fingers tugged at my hair.

Her voice snapped my senses back to reality.

You're about to fuck your brother's girl. This isn't right. What the fuck is wrong with you?

Breaking from the kiss, I rested my forehead against hers as I tried to regain my bearings. I breathed heavily, my hands trembling at Joanna's hips.

Camping trip, wading pool, woods.

Camping trip, wading pool, woods.

Camping trip, wading pool, woods.

Fuck.

My old trick of getting my mind right worked temporarily as I felt my breathing slow.

"Hey, come back to me." She dipped her head to try to catch my eye. As she leaned in to kiss me, I turned my head, her kiss landing against my neck. Damn, even that felt good.

"I'm sorry, Joanna." My arms betrayed me as I gently eased her away from me.

We stared at each other, our chests rising and falling. I saw a flicker of hurt pass over her face when her jaw ticked once, and she turned from me.

Sloshing through the water, she made her way to the edge of the pool. I watched her like an idiot as she wrapped a towel around her body, slipped on her shoes, and started to walk toward the trail leading to camp. She grabbed her backpack and, with a whistle to Bud, who'd been snoring against a rock, started toward our campsite.

She didn't look back.

Fuuuuuuuuuuck.

I rubbed my eyes, still feeling the taste of Joanna on my lips, the feel of her body against mine.

You're a piece of shit. You know Finn is in love with Joanna. So much for honor, asshole.

I had royally fucked up. All day, I'd had a growing feeling that Jo was Joanna. There's no way that she couldn't be—her time in Chikalu Falls lined up perfectly, her random knowledge of the Western United States . . . but once I saw the Sharpie marker doodles on her backpack, I knew it was her.

Why couldn't Joanna be anyone else? Finn looked up to me. I was stealing his girl from underneath him, and deep down, I didn't *really* care. What kind of brother did that make me? But, in that moment, I had to have her. Looking at her was like seeing a piece of my soul walking around outside my body.

And now she was walking away from me, into the woods, as it was getting dark.

Muttering under my breath, I hauled ass out of the water, grabbing my clothes as I went and tried to catch up with her. I struggled to get my clothes and shoes back on, and despite my long strides, she was keeping a steady distance between us.

When she rounded the bend, the light from the campfire came into view. Panting, I ran my hands through my hair and took a deep breath as I stepped from the cover of the trees. I looked to my right in time to see Joanna zipping up her tent.

Shit.

Near the campfire, I could hear the laughter and low music from the group. Brandon caught my eye and lifted a beer in invitation. With a glance back at Joanna's tent, I rubbed my palms on my thighs and turned toward the group.

"Hey, boss, come have a beer with us," Brandon called

in greeting as I walked toward them. The fire was bigger than it needed to be, but its heat felt good as the mountain air made the temperatures drop. I grabbed the beer and sat on an upturned log.

I stared into the dancing flames, feeling the heat blast my face and trying to get a handle on what the hell just happened. I'd betrayed Finn. I'd groped a woman I was paying to work for me. I finally found the woman I'd been searching for only to freak the fuck out and push her away.

I felt like I was falling apart at the seams; Joanna pulled at one thread and I was unraveling at her feet.

"You all good, Linc?" Brandon's low voice brought my attention back to the group.

With a swig of my beer, I nodded. "Yep."

I shot a look over my shoulder toward Joanna's tent. It seemed quiet, like maybe she'd just turned in for the night. When I looked back, Brandon was pinning me with a look.

"What?"

"Dude, you've got it bad," he said. He shook his head and laughed quietly.

Bristling, I replied, "Shut the fuck up." But panic stirred in my gut. *He knows. He's going to tell Finn.*

"Hey." I asked, "How long have you known her?" My head tipped toward Joanna's tent.

"Jo? Shit, man, a few years maybe? Fished together with her and Finn a couple of times, that kind of thing . . . Why? What's up?"

Nodding, I kept my eyes down toward the fire. "I know her and Finn have been friends since college, but he's never really brought her around much."

"Well, do you blame him? Jesus, just look at her . . ." he added.

Two of the men at the fire passed a flask between them

when one added, "I'd see if she needed a goodnight kiss but looks like she's got a rabid dog on her heels."

Before I could stand and beat his face in with my fist, Brandon cut him off with, "Not the time, man."

A hot bead of sweat trickled down my back. The thought of anyone, especially any of these candy-ass yuppies, near Joanna made my ears buzz and my pulse skyrocket. My fist curled, denting the beer can. The familiar feeling of rage, the one I hadn't been able to shake since my time in the service, simmered just below the surface.

Look at you, you're a lunatic. A lunatic who's all too eager to cut your brother off at the knees for her. Does he deserve that? Does she?

I finished the beer even though it tasted sour on my tongue. I grabbed another but drank in silence as the rest of the group shot the shit around the fire. Every so often, someone would eye me warily, but they kept mostly to themselves.

Draining the second beer, I stood. "Well, I'm calling it a night. Thanks for the beer."

"Anytime." Brandon nodded. I tossed the empty can into the trash bag and started toward my tent.

When I reached the end of the path, I glanced between Joanna's tent and the fire. I knew the likelihood of anyone messing with her was slim, but I still couldn't get their snide comments off my mind. As I scanned through the trees, I thought of her.

She was so capable—more so than most of the men on our books. She grabbed fish without squirming, tied lines, hiked ravines, and her instincts were spot-on. A few times she'd suggested going upstream or trying a new spot, and when we'd listened, everyone started catching. This woman didn't need my protection.

I smiled briefly. I couldn't stop thinking about how my body reacted to hers. It seemed like she felt it too, but I couldn't be sure. Did she think I was an asshole for grabbing her like that? Was I as bad as the rest of them? I ground my teeth at that thought.

I couldn't let that happen again. I needed to maintain control—of my desire, my temper, my fucking life. If I could prove to be loyal to Finn and forget all about the heat I felt in the water, I could force myself to feel nothing. Stuff it down, ride it out, and forget all of the feelings Joanna had dragged to the surface.

I was still a Marine. Honor and duty were tenets I would always live by.

Nodding in resolution, I reached into my tent and pulled my canvas journeyman jacket out of my pack. Zipping it and tucking my hands into the pockets, I sat at the base of the tree next to Joanna's tent between the campfire and her. It was my duty now to control the situation, and I wasn't about to take any chances with the rowdy group of drunk, horny assholes nearby.

Fuck those guys.

Leaning my head against the hard bark of the tree, I closed my eyes. I had spent more nights sleeping in uncomfortable places than not when I served, but I'd also learned that even if your body rests, your mind does not.

I dreamed of a beautiful and fierce Valkyrie soaring over the lifeless bodies of fallen soldiers. Smoke plumed above the field, curling around the bodies. My broken, charred arms reached for her as I crawled against the dirt in her direction. I begged her to take me with her. Landing, she stood, the armor vest fitted against her muscular frame, hands on her hips—staring at me. With her green-gray eyes locked on me, she smirked. Begging, I continued forward, dragging myself toward her. Unfolding her wings, she turned, leaving my soul behind.

TWELVE

JOANNA

I EMERGED from my tent and felt the cold, damp mountain air run a chill up my back. I blew hot breath into my hands and tried to rub them warmer. I zipped my jacket up, pulled my hair into a messy bun, and headed down to revitalize the campfire so that we could make a decent breakfast.

I looked over at Lincoln's tent. I was still feeling a little raw after making out with him in the water just to have him push me away. Sighing lightly, I closed my eyes and let myself imagine his lips on me again. It felt incredible when his stubbly jaw dragged across my skin. Last night I went straight into my tent, but the truth was that I lay awake replaying it over and over in my mind.

He'd wanted me last night, I knew it, but on a dime, he'd rejected me and I didn't know why.

Because men like him don't go for women like you.

Kicking a pebble at the thought, I watched it tumble toward a tree next to my tent. As it clunked against the bark, I saw that there was an indent at the base and a blanket tightly rolled next to it. Had someone sat there all night? I looked around to see if anyone from our group seemed to have wandered off, but in the dim light of dawn, it was eerily quiet.

Uncertain, I headed down toward the other tents, Bud stretching and walking beside me. Brandon had been hauling our supplies so I would have to get the ingredients from him to make the group a simple breakfast.

As I approached, I saw that Lincoln was already awake.

"Morning," he said gruffly. He didn't look up at me, but continued working on pulling forks from Brandon's supply pack.

Ok, good. Maybe he isn't going to make this weird.

"Morning. You're up early." I smiled, trying to act nonchalant. Lincoln looked rugged and sexy and a little bit tired.

"I don't mind the morning," he said. "It's quieter."

At that, he looked up at me. His eyes looked navy in the dim light, and I wanted to curl into his thick arms, but we both looked away quickly. Swiping a hair away from my forehead along with that thought, I surveyed what we were working with.

Lincoln had added logs to the fire and was already starting on breakfast. He'd made a small space near the coals, close enough to the fire to warm the food, but not so close it would burn.

"What do we have on the menu?" I asked, glancing around and feeling useless.

"Breakfast burritos."

My eyes lit up. I loved a good breakfast burrito. In fact, it was my favorite camping food. My stomach grumbled at the thought. I giggled. "Sorry."

He smiled and looked right at me. "I'll take care of you, Joanna."

I'm sure he meant breakfast, but my body was really

into reading between the lines and warmed at his words. My heart was racing. He called me Joanna last night and again this morning. *My Joanna* he'd said. I smiled to myself and exhaled a slow breath, willing myself to calm the hell down.

Lincoln poked at the small, foil-wrapped packages in the fire with a stick. Reaching his hand down, he picked one up, tossing it back and forth between his hands.

He rolled the little burrito between his palms and turned to me. I reached out my hand to take it, and when he placed it in my upturned palm, he let his fingers drag across the skin on my hand. His hands were warm and rough, and I had to keep myself from moaning out loud.

Taking a seat on a log near the fire, I unwrapped my little burrito baby. Steam escaped from the top, but I was so hungry, I took a generous bite.

"Mmmmmm," I said, closing my eyes. This was the world's most delicious burrito, I was sure of it.

"Careful with those noises," Lincoln whispered deeply, his voice at my ear. My eyes opened to find his face close to mine, eyes smiling as he placed a cup of hot, black coffee on the ground at my feet. My stomach fluttered.

I looked at his full lips. I wanted to ask him about what happened in the water last night. Were we just going to pretend it didn't happen? Was he upset we'd kissed?

Stop staring at him.

As I was gathering my courage, the smell of breakfast and coffee hit the group and they all started to stumble from their tents. Lincoln straightened and moved back to the fire. As I suspected, every one of them was bleary-eyed and hungover, including Brandon. Groaning or rubbing their eyes, they ambled toward us, breaking the spell. I tossed the last bottom bite of the burrito to Bud and stood.

I took one final look at Lincoln to find him staring back at me. I offered him a small smile, but his eyes were hard. The muscle in his jaw flexed. Why was he so tense all of a sudden? Had I done something wrong?

Breathe. Just do your thing and stop worrying about this. He doesn't care about you.

Unexpectedly, my eyes blurred with tears. I had a long day of guiding ahead of me and I couldn't spend it worrying about whether or not a heated moment last night meant anything. It hadn't. Not to him at least. I took a deep breath and turned my back to the group to check our equipment before we headed out.

After the guys dragged themselves from the worst of their hangovers, we packed up camp and headed up the ridge. The plan was to hike along the base of the mountain, stopping to fish along the way toward the lodge. If we wanted to make it to the lodge before nightfall, we'd have to get a move on.

"Ok, let's try the Albright knot. That should keep your line from breaking when you hook a lunker," I said casually to Sean, one of the guys on the trip.

We stood calf-deep in the clear river, water babbling past us over the smooth rocks as he looked on. I slowed my movements intentionally, letting him see how I was tying the knot.

"It's a little heavier, with ten wraps, but when you set it, that fish isn't going anywhere," I continued. I held the three lines between my fingers and wrapped the lines over themselves—a knot I could do in my sleep. Pulling the line tightly, I secured the knot and then clipped the tag end.

"You're all set," I said as I dropped his line and stepped away.

"Thanks, Jo." Sean tipped his head.

I loved this part of fishing. Of course, the thrill of catching would always be there, but what I loved most was teaching people about knots, fish, the land, everything. Bobber and lure fishing in lakes was fun, but fly fishing was an art.

I stepped back to allow ample room for him to practice his casting technique. He was a little jerky in his movements and was having trouble placing the fly in a spot where the migrating fish would see it.

"Do you mind if I give you a few pointers?" I asked. Stepping in to offer help was delicate. Sometimes I was met with indifference, sometimes even anger. Apparently being a woman meant I couldn't possibly be a good fisherman.

"Yeah, that would be great!" Sean replied.

Relieved, I trudged forward through the water. He handed over his pole and carefully stepped back toward the bank so that he could see what I was doing.

"Keep an eye on my stance," I bounced a little on my legs to draw his attention to my foot placement, "but more importantly, watch my arm movements," I instructed, holding my arms out from my body. "It's subtle, but if you think of it as a dance, the line should float out there a little better for you."

Rhythmically, I started moving my fly line back and forth. I moved my body, feeling the weight of the rod in my hands and sensing the ebb and flow of the line on the pole. Teaching fly fishing was so difficult to explain because so much of it was how things *felt*. When I felt the timing was right, I released the fly line into the water, placing it just around a grouping of small rocks that poked above the surface.

I tipped my head to Sean, motioning for him to come forward. "Try that out for a minute. Let it float away with the water and see what you come up with. Then, you can try casting in that spot a few more times."

Sean approached, and I released the pole into his hands, stepping back. Within seconds, a large fish thrashed at the fly, scooping it into his mouth.

"Got him!" I shouted.

Sean set the hook and began reeling it in, his smile wide across his face. His excitement was contagious as he whooped and hollered at the other guys in the group. They all cheered in response.

I was smiling, looking around at the rest of the group scattered downstream when my eyes locked with Lincoln's. He was closer than I recalled, and his deep blue eyes were set on mine. He smiled slightly, then nodding his head, he turned.

I swear to god that man could incinerate every set of panties within a hundred-mile radius with that smile. Dressed in fishing waders, you wouldn't think anyone looked particularly sexy, but damn. My eyes lingered over Lincoln's broad chest, shirt tight around his biceps and chest, and moved down toward his tapered waist and thick thighs. He looked strong and rugged as he walked along the bank, checking in on the other guests.

A flare of heat hit my cheeks, and I felt a pull in my belly. I was thinking of all the dirty things I wanted Lincoln to do with me—hand in my hair, pull me close and kiss the fuck out of me, hot and deep and wet—when my thoughts were interrupted by the buzz of my phone.

Finn: Yo, Banana! How goes it? Tell me everything.

I toyed with the inside of my lower lip as I thought about his text. *Well, maybe I won't tell him everything.*

Me: Hi! It's going good. A few more hours and we'll be at the lodge . . . which is good. I need a shower. You ok?
Finn: Besides bored as FUCK?
Me: You'll live.
Finn: Heartless

I wanted so badly to tell Finn about what happened with Lincoln in the water, but it also felt weird. Finn was one of my best friends, but this was his *brother.* Still, curiosity got the best of me.

Me: Lincoln's been an interesting addition to the trip.

When Finn didn't text back immediately, a tiny alarm bell went off in my body. I didn't know what to think of his silence. Would he be mad?

Finn: Interesting, huh? I find that interesting.

Well, shit. I should have known Finn would see right through me.

Me: Ok, I'm going now. Forget I said anything. Don't make this weird.
Finn: Be good, don't do anything I wouldn't do!
Finn: FYI - lotta leeway there. ;)

Laughing, I put my phone back in my pocket and

thought about how great it would be to have Finn out here with us. He was a great fishing buddy—never crowded my space, was up for anything, and comfortable with silence. The only problem was that Lincoln seemed to get really quiet and broody when the three of us were together and I couldn't figure out why.

They were brothers, but from what I could tell, Finn was closer to me than he was to Lincoln, and that made me ache for the both of them. I knew Finn's secrets and he knew mine. Most of them, anyway. It would be a good thing when Finn could finally talk to his brother. Air everything out. Until then, I planned to keep my growing attraction to Finn's moody older brother to myself.

As the sun moved across the ridge, we made our way to the Chaney Lodge. Owned by a retired couple, it was a bed-and-breakfast geared toward anglers and campers around the river. Finn and Lincoln used the Chaney's property as a midway point in the trip. It allowed the guests to rest, have a proper shower, get a hot meal, and sleep in a cushy bed.

I, for one, was looking forward to melting into the cushy bed.

It had been a great day, overall. The fishing was spot-on, and the group seemed to ease up on the misogynist jokes and comments. All it took was for me to help Sean catch a great fish and they were all eager to ask me for tips and tricks the rest of the afternoon.

After our group arrived, we had decided to eat dinner while it was hot, before unpacking. Mrs. Chaney was adorable, doting on every guest who visited her. For supper, she made beef stew with the softest yeast rolls I'd ever had. She'd even made homemade apple pie for dessert. After living off camping food for the last two days, it was pure heaven.

Once we had full bellies, Mrs. Chaney handed out room assignments. Her beautiful cursive was written on tiny pieces of white card stock. As the guys got their rooms and paired off, my heart sank.

Lincoln and Joe: Stonefly 8

I stared at the small card in my hand and then looked from Lincoln to Mrs. Chaney. "Um, excuse me? Mrs. Chaney? I think there may be some mistake," I said.

She looked at me sweetly.

"Well, you see, I'm Jo . . . no E. As in Joanna," I said with my hand on my chest. "I think I was supposed to have my own room." I snuck another look at Lincoln, but I couldn't read his expression.

Mrs. Chaney looked down at my card as if there was some mistake. "Oh, my," she said. "That would be a problem. When this was booked, it was for eight guests, four rooms."

My mouth opened slightly, and a small sound escaped my throat.

"Surely you can accommodate, Mrs. Chaney," Lincoln said. He glanced at me, only briefly.

"I am so sorry, but we're completely booked tonight," she continued. "We have no available beds."

"Ok. It's no problem, we'll work it out. Thank you, Mrs. Chaney." Lincoln smiled at the sweet old lady, dismissing her. He turned to me.

My face flushed. I wasn't sure what we were going to do because the thought of sharing a room with Lincoln made a wave of desire crash into the wave of panic inside of me.

"I can sleep in a tent outside." His eyes were lowered when he spoke. "It's no problem."

"Don't be silly. We can share the room," I said. The words were out before I could pull them back.

He eyed me slowly and looked unsure of how to answer.

I doubled down and just kept rambling, despite the tingle of energy rippling through me. "It's going to be colder tonight, and it's too late to gather firewood. Plus, who knows if any of her campsites are open. It's just one night, no big deal. Right?"

"Right," he said, smiling.

My body was telling me that was, in fact, a really big deal.

THIRTEEN
LINCOLN

I SHOULD HAVE INSISTED on sleeping outside. Freezing my ass off on the uncomfortable ground had to be better than the thought of Joanna sleeping only feet away from me and having to keep my hands to myself.

I wanted to be a gentleman, do the right thing. When I'd offered to sleep outside, I was fully willing to do it. But once she started rambling about why I shouldn't and that sharing a room wasn't a big deal, I didn't fight it.

Way to torture yourself, asshole.

In a way, this was the ultimate test of will. All day, I'd been watching Joanna. She was a fascinating combination of soft and strong. She'd eagerly helped everyone who was willing to listen. She smiled—god, that smile got to me—and joked. Joanna had such a simple, easy way about her. She got her hands dirty and wasn't afraid to put the work in for her job. She'd worked hard all day, and I respected her so much more because of it.

It also didn't go unnoticed how her ass looked as she climbed ridges and the way her shoulders and arms were lean and strong. More than once, I had to remind myself that Joanna was totally off-limits. I still had to figure out what was going on between her and Finn, and there was the fact that I was fucked up in the head. But I couldn't get her, or her letters, off my mind. My hand moved to the folded paper in my pocket.

Now, standing in the doorway of the Stonefly 8 room, I couldn't help but wonder what the hell I was going to do. The room was small but clean. It had two double beds on opposite walls with matching hunter-green plaid bedspreads. I flipped on the light and saw a small bathroom was the only place either of us would have any privacy here. A wave of unease went through me as I thought of her sleeping so close to me. What if I had another nightmare and she was around to see me panicking and acting like a lunatic?

Fuck.

"Ladies first," I said, motioning her to enter ahead of me. Yes, I was being polite, but not so polite that I didn't also appreciate that ass again with a tilt of my head.

"Do you have a preference?" she asked, motioning between the two beds.

I scanned the room. My instincts were acutely aware of all of the entrances and exits and I knew exactly where she'd be safest.

"I'll take this one," I said, placing my pack on the bed closest to the door.

Sure, I knew Joanna was more than capable, and there weren't any real threats here, but I'd be damned if I wasn't going to put myself between her and anyone coming through that door.

With a tired sigh, Joanna leaned backward and flopped onto the opposite bed.

"Ooohhhh, god, this is comfortable. Just wake me in the morning." She laughed, her eyes closed.

I smiled at her because she was fucking adorable.

"I'm going to go down to the bar for a beer with Brandon to plan out tomorrow and the trip back upriver. I'll take Bud out and he can hang with me. Feel free to clean up or do whatever you need," I told her.

She turned her head toward me and sighed. "Fine. I'll get up." And with a groan, she started getting her clothes together for a shower. "Thank you." She smiled at me again, and it shot me right in the gut. I clicked my tongue for Bud to follow me, and we quietly left the room.

I didn't really need to talk to Brandon. This trip was standard and had been planned months ago, but there was no way I'd be able to be in a room, hearing Joanna showering, with only a thin wall separating us. Just thinking about the warm water running down her smooth muscles made my cock spring to life. I had to get out of that space. I needed to breathe. With a subtle adjustment to my pants, I grabbed my room key and headed to the house bar without looking back at her.

Down the hallway, the main floor opened up with a large bar service. It was an "honor bar," where you took whatever you wanted, but left your room number for it to be charged later. I loved the small-town charm of that and hoped no one was taking advantage of the kindness of Mr. and Mrs. Chaney.

Sean, Brandon, and a few of the other guests were sitting around the bar. Some played cards while others were watching a baseball game on the television. We mainly made small talk that I wasn't interested in, and Bud took all the ear scratches they could give out.

I couldn't get Joanna out of my head.

I thought back to all the years I'd read her letters and the fact that now she was right here. It was a total mind-fuck. Of all the scenarios I'd played out in my mind for how I would find her, this had not been one of them.

She'd literally been on the periphery of my life for years and we'd never crossed paths. All day, I'd been going over and over it. How had we never met if she was such a part of Finn's life? She went to school here, even lived right there in Chikalu for a few years, for fuck's sake. Maybe Finn was hiding her—keeping her for himself.

Taking a drink of my beer, I thought about him. He wasn't a snake—far from it. He was the nicest human on the planet.

Finn and I had slowly drifted apart even in the years I had been home. Sure, we worked together and got along really well, but we didn't hang out. I knew he'd wanted to—he invited me along plenty of times—but outside of the poker games with Colin and Decker, it was pretty limited.

That's because you're a prick.

"How's it feel to be guiding again?" Brandon asked as he lowered onto the stool beside me.

I grunted in response.

"You should do this more often," he continued. "Finn talks a lot about how much fun you two used to have. He misses you, man."

At that, I looked over at Brandon whose attention was on the game. Not sure what to do with that, I took another drink. There was a lot about Finn and his life outside of work that I didn't know. Did that include Joanna? If it didn't, why hadn't he ever talked about a girlfriend or bring anyone home to Mom's for Sunday dinner?

The thought that my own brother was practically a stranger gnawed at me. Feeling restless, I downed the rest of my beer, filled out my slip for Mrs. Chaney, and headed back to the room.

Once I got there, I stood in front of the closed door like a moron. I thought about Joanna just past the door—was she sleeping? What did her pajamas look like? I let myself imagine her draped across the bed, waiting for me.

Slow down, tiger.

I took a breath and quietly opened the door. Bud trotted to Joanna's side of the room and wound himself in circles until he found a comfortable spot on the floor.

I could see her body tucked underneath her covers, her back to me. The lamp on the small table between the beds was left on, and a smile played at my lips. She was kind-hearted and considerate, and just the thought of her this close got me worked up.

All day, I'd tried to put her and her silky hair out of my mind. I wanted to look at her and feel nothing, and all day, I'd failed miserably. Frustrated, I grabbed fresh clothes from my pack and headed to the bathroom to shower. I needed to rinse the day off me.

I was so amped up that I turned the water up as hot as it could go without actually burning my skin. She had no fucking clue what she did to me. Watching her graceful casts, her smile, thinking about how her body responded to me when we kissed in the water. My dick was so hard it hurt.

The steam rose and hot water poured over my shoulders. I rubbed the back of my neck where Joanna had wrapped her arms around me. I could still feel her body entwined with mine, pressed against me as I held her.

Closing my eyes, I grabbed my solid erection. Stroking up and down. I imagined Joanna's soft skin as I pulled her naked body against mine. A tangled mess of limbs as I stroked my tongue against her neck. I could practically feel her hard, pink nipples brush against me. What noises would she make when I took that small, hard peak into my mouth?

My cock throbbed in response. I squeezed harder and stroked faster. Keeping my eyes closed, I let myself have this fantasy—the same one I'd had every day since seeing her in the bar.

Joanna's head back, legs tipped open as I tasted her. I knew her pussy would be the best thing I'd ever tasted. The darkening of those green-gray eyes as I brought her closer to climax before stopping. I wanted to push the head of my cock between the folds of her wet pussy and feel her warmth wrap around me.

Bracing myself with one hand on the tile, I continued jerking my cock harder. I wanted to give in to this and every fantasy I'd ever had about Joanna. The muscles in my shoulders bunched as I drove myself closer. I wanted to give myself to her and feel her come as undone as she made me feel.

I felt the familiar pressure of my balls tightening, on the brink of release. I wanted to come so badly with the thoughts of Joanna under me as I split her open.

A loud, hard *clank* had my head whipping up and my eyes springing open to see Joanna in the mirror through the steam of the shower leaned against the sink, eyes wide, staring at me with my dick in my hands.

FOURTEEN
JOANNA

I wasn't creeping on him, I swear to god.

When Lincoln left and gave me privacy to clean up, I'd done just that. The bathroom was small but tidy, and the hot water did wonders for my tense muscles. I leaned my head against the tiles, letting the water pound the ache between my shoulder blades.

The day was as good as any. The fish were biting, I was able to teach a client something new, and the weather was sunny and warm. I was the best kind of tired—satisfied after good exercise—but the tension I felt in my body wasn't just from the miles we'd put in today. I was keyed up.

Following the water, I let my palms run down my shoulders, over my breasts, down my hips.

Would Lincoln's hands feel like this?

The thought of him running his wide, rough hands over me had me groaning to myself as I caressed my sore limbs. My thoughts stayed on him. I wanted to run my fingers through his thick hair and down his neck. I wanted to see, up close, what the tattoos inked up his arms looked like. I wondered if they were all damaged and if he had any more that I could discover.

I imagined him pressed against me in the shower. Feeling his long, lean body against my back as the water swirled down my thighs. I wanted to open myself up to him, feel naked and exposed and feminine in his arms. My thighs clenched at the thought of his fingertips running over the front of my legs and up, closer to my core.

Get a grip, Jo. It's not like that for him.

Unfulfilled, I sighed and let the hot water run over my face. I turned off the water, toweled off my body and hair. Slipping on a loose tank top and pajama shorts, I exited the bathroom to stand between our two beds. Cuddling would probably be amazing with Lincoln. His strong arms wrapped around me. Shaking my head, I flipped on the small light between our beds so it wouldn't be so dark when he returned and snuggled into the thick blankets of my bed. I breathed deeply.

What was Lincoln doing down at the bar? Was he thinking of me and the heated moments when we caught each other's eye today? Did he want to kiss me again?

Girl, you've got it bad. You're just Finn's friend to him. It was a mistake. Stop reading into it.

Damn, my inner voice was a real bitch sometimes. I rolled over, with my back to the door, and tried to will my body to relax. Deep breaths.

Still reeling from the shower fantasy, I heard the key card for the room click. My body tensed, and I pretended to sleep. Lincoln entered the room so quietly I hardly heard a thing, except for Bud making himself comfortable at the foot of my bed. Seconds later, I heard the shower running and let out a whoosh of breath.

Stop. Picturing him. Naked.

That was impossible. The real-life object of my early twenties crush (okay, fine. Current crush) was naked with only a wall between us and he thought of me as one of the guys. Willing myself to think of *anything* else, it dawned on me that I'd forgotten to brush my teeth.

Damn it. I knew I could wait, but I really didn't want to have to face a hot, wet Lincoln who would likely smell fresh and clean and manly right after his shower.

Just slip in there, brush your teeth, and get back in bed.

My inner voice might have been a bitch but she was a sneaky one. Lincoln hadn't been in the shower long, so the chances of getting busted were low. I grabbed my toothpaste and toothbrush and quietly toed toward the bathroom door. It was slightly open so I pushed it quietly.

Turning the water on a trickle, I wet my toothbrush, added paste, and brushed my teeth as quickly as I could. Rinsing my mouth, I made the fatal mistake of glancing up in the mirror.

Through the haze of the steam stood Lincoln, one hand on the tile, the other on his thick, hard dick. Holy shit, was it big. He was stroking its length, eyes closed. I knew I should turn away, this was an invasion of privacy, but I couldn't. With the steam wrapping around me, I was glued. His back muscles twitched, and I admired the intricate tattoos that ran down his torso and over his back. As I'd suspected, most of them were disjointed and broken with scarring. It was insanely hot.

His round ass and thighs pushed forward slightly as he pumped his fist over and over himself. I had never seen anything so sensual and beautiful in my entire life. My hand found my throat, and my heartbeat thrummed against my skin. My right hand reached back and grabbed the sink

—knocking my toothbrush and paste to the ground with a clatter.

Fuck.

The sound had Lincoln's head whipping up immediately. He pinned me with his stare, and I couldn't move. A small sound escaped my throat, but I couldn't find any words. My eyes raced over his naked body. Everything inside me screamed, "Oh, hell yes," but all I could manage was a meek, "I'm so sorry."

I brushed a hair from my forehead and fumbled to leave when I heard a low grumble of, "Joanna."

I paused and turned to see Lincoln stepping from the shower, water dripping down his body as his abs flexed with his ragged breathing. His dick was still rock-hard.

"Yes," I whispered. It was both a response and an invitation, and we both knew it.

Lincoln closed the gap between us and crushed his mouth against mine, pushing my lower back into the sink. His tongue invaded my mouth, wet and hard as he devoured me.

Lincoln's hand ran down my hip, circling back around my ass to my thighs as he lifted me up to sit on the countertop. I could feel his thick cock push against the flimsy fabric of my pajama shorts, and my body hummed. I wrapped my legs around his trim waist and tipped my hips forward, needing to feel him against me.

I moved my fingers to his hair, gripping his dark strands and pulling his head back slightly so I could lick and kiss the stubble on his jaw and neck. The rasp of his beard against my lips and tongue sent a jolt down to my core.

We were ravenous for each other. Lincoln's hands moved over the silky fabric of my tank top and brushed against my hard nipples, enticing a throaty moan from me.

It felt so good to be wanted in this way. My body was on fire, and I wanted him to touch every last part of me.

Grabbing under my hips, Lincoln effortlessly lifted me off the countertop. He stalked toward my bed as I pressed my body against him. Once we got to the bed, he leaned forward, pinning me beneath his solid frame. He pushed his hips forward, rubbing against me. My clit throbbed in response, begging for release.

"Yes, Lincoln, please," I whispered. I looked down at his solid length, and my chest tightened. *Oh, shit, he's thick.* I was thrilled, but a little bit scared, too.

"Fuck, Joanna, you make me feel so good," Lincoln said, deep and low in my ear. "I want you. I want this."

God, yes, I wanted it, too. Lincoln dragged his hands down my hips, taking my pajama bottoms off as his palms slid down my legs. I reached above me and ripped off my top, tossing it on the floor by the bed. I couldn't get my mouth back on his skin fast enough.

Lincoln held me back, one hand flattened against my ribs, his right fisted around his cock. A surge of desire rippled through me as I saw his scarred and tattooed skin. He rubbed his tip against my wet folds, teasing me. I lifted my hips higher, urging him to enter me. He held steady, his steely blue eyes boring into mine.

"Is this ok?" he asked, gently opening me with the tip of his cock.

"Yes, I have an IUD and I'm clean," I said, understanding his meaning. "Are you?"

"I'm clean. I need to feel you," he said as he pushed the thick length of his cock into me. I gasped at the fullness. He stretched me wide open, and he stilled.

"Are you ok?" he asked, his brow furrowed with concern.

"Fuck me, Lincoln. God, you feel good."

I barely got the words out and he was pumping into me, hard and fast. With long strokes, he filled my wet pussy. He watched his cock push into me, and seeing the dark desire on his face made my body pulse around him, drenching him. The tension in my body coiled.

Lincoln reached out his hand to cup my face as he set a steady, pulsing rhythm. Turning my head, I sucked his thumb into my mouth and bit gently. I wanted this hard and rough, and he was giving it to me. His hand on my hip moved over me, reaching my clit as he began to move his thumb in tight circles. I could feel my body reaching its peak, blood rushing down between my legs.

"Yes, Lincoln. I'm close," I panted.

I leaned my head back, arching my back to feel even closer to him. With access to my neck, he bent down, licking up my neck, sucking, biting. Every nerve ending crackled as he flexed his hips and pushed deeper and deeper into me. His hand found my nipple, and his fingers tugged gently, sending fire to my belly. When he dragged his stubble across my face and kissed me roughly with a growl in his throat, I came undone.

My pussy clenched rhythmically as the surge of my climax flowed around his dick. Lincoln never wavered as he continued to fuck me through my orgasm. He tipped his body forward, pressing me down against the bed as he covered his body with mine.

"Joanna, yes, Joanna." He said my name over and over as his body tightened. Through clenched teeth, he grunted as his orgasm tore through him. I wrapped my legs around him tighter, and I felt his dick pulse as he filled me.

He stilled, then melted his body on top of mine.

FIFTEEN
LINCOLN

HOLY FUCK.

It took several breaths for the white-hot haze in my vision to clear. I'd just survived the most unexpected and intense orgasm of my entire life.

Thinking of Joanna in the shower had gotten me to the edge but seeing her standing there in those thin pajamas—eyes wide and her nipples straining against the fabric—I was so shocked I could only say her name. When she'd responded with a simple "Yes," I'd lost my fucking mind.

Kissing her, stroking her, filling her with my cock was incredible. How many times had I imagined what it would be like when I'd finally found her? How many times in the last *two days* had I thought about it?

My body felt slack with the tension I'd been carrying released, but my dick was still semi-hard and inside of Joanna. It dawned on me that I was likely crushing her, so I shifted my hips and slipped out of her, lying at her side. I rested my forehead against her as I still struggled to regain normal breathing.

I had just fucked Joanna. Bare and completely unexpectedly. I opened my eyes to see hers still closed. I felt *different*. I couldn't explain it. Sure, post-sex relaxation was a thing, but the usual unease I carried with me seemed to dissolve. I thought back on the last time I had felt this way.

Never.

"Hey, stalker, what's up?" I smiled.

Joanna's small hands lifted to cover her face. "Oh my god, stop." She laughed, and it made my heart flip in my chest. I wanted to hear that laugh again—light and breathy.

"I'm mortified," she admitted, taking a peek at me with one eye.

"Fuck, I'm not."

"I totally invaded your privacy. I am so sorry. I swear, I thought I could just brush my teeth without you even knowing." She could barely look me in the eye as she spoke.

"Not quite the ninja you thought you were?" I couldn't help giving her some shit.

"Apparently not." She glanced at me, and I shifted my weight to hover over her a bit.

I leaned down and kissed her lips, then her face, and neck. As I pressed my lips to her throat, I felt a moan vibrate through her.

"That was intense," I said. "I hope it wasn't too rough."

Joanna shifted slightly, and I sensed tension creep into her body.

"Joanna, I'm sorry. Did I hurt you?" Slight panic hinted in my voice.

"No. God, no. It was great. It's just . . ." She looked at me, her eyes searching mine.

I waited, hoping she'd continue because I felt incredible, but her sudden hesitation was making me worry.

Finn.

Thinking of my brother while my dick was still out and

I had Joanna still warm and underneath me made my jaw tick.

When she didn't continue, I asked, "Are you seeing someone?" I couldn't look her in the eye if she was going to destroy me.

"Oh, no, definitely not. I was dating someone a while ago, but it's definitely over. It's just that we didn't use anything, and I've never had sex without a condom before."

A sigh of relief left my chest.

"Me neither," I shared. "I don't know what came over me."

She looked at me skeptically, but a smile crept across her pretty face, making her eyes light up, and I noticed she had a few subtle freckles across the bridge of her nose. So fucking cute.

"A first for both of us, I guess," she said.

I liked the sound of that. Too much. The sudden need to be Joanna's first and last everything felt big.

"Let's get you cleaned up," I tried.

Joanna didn't wait for me, but rather went into the bathroom to clean up. I looked down at the water my hair and body had dripped all over her bed. It was soaked.

From the floor, Bud glanced up at me. His goofy expression looked annoyed that we'd woken him up.

"Sorry, dude," I offered with a shrug. He groaned and looked away.

Moments later, Joanna came out, scooped up her pajamas, and slipped back into them. She glanced from her bed, wet spots and all, to mine.

Pulling the sheets down, I gestured to my bed. "Drier over here," I said, trying to hide the smile on my face.

She nodded and offered a quiet, "Thank you."

I slipped into the bathroom to clean up, and when I

stepped back into the small, dark room, Joanna was tucked under the covers. Quiet, insistent alarms were pinging in my head. I had never slept—actually fallen asleep—with a woman. Ever.

I moved under the covers on my side. Joanna was facing me, her hands tucked under her pillow. She looked tired but content and fucking gorgeous. Her hair splayed over her shoulder as she blinked up at me with wide, steady eyes. I matched her position, facing her with my hands under the pillow. We were only a breath apart, and she didn't move. I breathed her in.

Her smoky green eyes were searching my face but I couldn't tell what she was thinking. I felt like my whole world was tilting. Did she feel it, too?

I reached my hand up to brush a strand away from her face. "You are so beautiful," I said.

She looked down and smiled. Rather than answering, she scooted forward, moving under my chin. I shifted my body to lie on my back, tucking her body against me.

I wanted to be an honorable man. I knew that Finn loved Joanna, but I couldn't help but feel like something was shifting here. Allowing myself this tiny moment, I rubbed my hand up and down the soft skin of her arm. I took one last inhale of her and drifted to sleep with the warmth of her body against me.

THE STENCH of smoke and death curled in my nostrils. The field was black, and the wind kicked ash into my face. I could hear Mendez calling for me, pained screams of "Doc" over and over, but I couldn't find him.

"I don't wanna die out here, man." He sounded distant, but the words clanged inside my head.

Vomit rose in my throat and burned as I choked it back down. I couldn't find anyone who wasn't already dead and broken. Panic made my heart slam against my ribs, and sweat pooled at the base of my spine.

I looked down at my shaking hands. The Valkyrie wings on my forearm burned and before my eyes, began to char and peel away. I tried to cover them with my other hand, but it was useless as the skin deformed.

Up in the distance stood a fierce warrior—her misty green eyes intense as a laugh bubbled out of her.

My body jerked, arms flailing. My pounding heart matched the ringing in my ears. It took a minute to realize I was in bed.

Alone.

Thank fuck she wasn't here to see that. Get your shit together, Marine.

My wave of relief was replaced by surprising disappointment. Her side of the bed still smelled like the citrusy soap she'd used, and being alone, I allowed myself a deep inhale. I didn't want to think about the dreams and why I kept having them. Joanna was my fantasy come to life, but she was haunting me. What the fuck was that about?

I had to stuff it down, control the situation. We had another long day of hiking and guiding today, and I couldn't let my batshit crazy fuck it up for everyone.

SIXTEEN

JOANNA

THE MORNING PASSED in a flurry of fishing and endless fantasies of a repeat of last night's mind-blowing orgasm. I let my mind wander back to the way his hands slid down my hips. How effortlessly he'd grabbed the back of my thighs to hoist me onto the counter.

Damn. I was pretty sure he'd ruined me forever. How could you top spontaneous, rough-in-the-best-way, toe-curling sex like that?

All morning, I couldn't get out of my own head and had struggled to focus on providing high-quality customer service.

You got some high-quality customer service last night . . .

Oh my god, that was exactly what I meant. Focus.

Smiling to myself, I tied a new fishing fly on Sean's line. I hoped the green and purple feathers would give him better luck in this stretch of the river. Looking out onto the water, I could see the current was strong—but Sean was learning quickly—and by listening to my tips, he was becoming the best student in the group.

Brandon walked up, nodding at the fly I was tying. "She's a beaut. That should do you right," he said to Sean.

Sean stepped away, wading his way back into the deeper parts of the water to try casting again. I stayed, mentally critiquing his technique so I could continue to help him improve his casting.

Brandon turned to me. "This is the best guide I've been on in forever," he said.

"We have had great weather," I agreed, tipping my head up and closing my eyes to feel the warm sun on my face.

"That's not what I meant," he continued. "I know we've fished together before and Finn said you were a good teacher, but shit, Jo. You're an amazing guide."

I turned to look at Brandon, who was squinting out across the water. He really was a genuinely nice guy. I was used to hearing things like "You sure can fish—for a girl" or "You can tie a good knot—for a girl" or "You know a lot about equipment—for a girl." It was rare to get a compliment that didn't have the qualifier "for a girl" tacked onto the end. It kind of caught me off guard.

"Thanks, Brandon. That really does mean a lot to me."

"I can't believe Finn and Linc haven't snagged you up before this. Surely he's offered, right?" he asked.

I chewed my bottom lip at his question. Finn *had* asked. Insisted, almost. He'd mentioned me being a partner in the guide service for as long as I could remember. We'd been eating dinner at a dive bar one night when Finn started scribbling ridiculous guide service names on a napkin, like we were a new Hollywood couple.

FinnJo

LincJoFin

FinLiJo

He was truly terrible at it. I laughed to myself at the memory. But he had been so excited about the idea.

"He's asked," I responded. With a lift of my shoulder, I added, "I'm kind of a roamer. I guess I haven't found my home yet."

"Chikalu is as good a place as any. Family isn't always who you're born to," he said and stepped away to help a client, Steve, with a tangled line.

Since when did Brandon become Buddha?

I thought about what he said and of my own family. Relating to my parents seemed hopeless. For people who were born in the mountains, they were terribly buttoned up. Over the past three years, monthly visits had dwindled to holidays and birthday phone calls. I knew they loved me, but they'd given up on trying to understand me. Honey was my only real tie to them. No matter how dissimilar we were, she tethered me to my parents, never allowing me to drift too far.

Thinking of her, I decided I'd text her a quick picture. Turning my camera to selfie mode, I snapped a portrait of me against the curving river with the large pines dotting the shoreline.

Me: Don't you wish you were here?
Honey: Not unless there's a spa.

She was hopeless and perfect and I loved her so much, despite our differences.

"You know, in this light, your eyes are a beautiful shade of moss green." A deep voice had my head shooting up from my phone. Lincoln.

My tummy dropped at the sight of him. His tattoos peeked out from underneath his T-shirt sleeves, and I briefly remembered how soft his skin felt under my fingertips last night.

"What are you up to, Joanna?" He ignored, or at least didn't seem to mind, my obvious ogling.

"Checking in with my sister. She appreciates a status update—knowing I haven't fallen into a ravine."

"Can I see that?" he asked, motioning to the phone in my hands.

I warily handed him my phone. I was mid-text, and I wasn't sure what he was doing, but the way he smelled and the intensity of his blue eyes had me handing over my phone without question.

Still looking up at him, he pulled me in close to his side, outstretched his arm, and snapped a picture. He looked down at my phone for a second, tapped a few buttons, and handed it back to me with a simple, "There you go."

"There I go what?" I asked, looking at my phone to see what he'd just done. He had texted the picture to Honey—me tucked under his arm, his handsome face smiling into the camera while I looked up at him. He looked happy, and I looked like a love-struck moron.

"Just sending her a status update," he confidently answered, and with that, he walked away, me still gaping after him.

Of course, my phone blew up after that. In a flurry of texts, Honey demanded every detail, but I had work to do. I gave her the basics and promised I'd catch her up as soon as I could. I also needed to talk with Finn. He'd probably be surprised, but I hoped he was happy for me and not too upset that Lincoln and I had hooked up. I knew their relationship leaned toward complicated, and I just hoped I wasn't making it worse for either of them.

For the better part of the afternoon, I tried to convince

myself that what had happened between me and Lincoln was nothing more than the heat of the moment getting the best of us . . . twice.

I listened to the river lapping my legs while I rhythmically whipped the line over the running river water. Lincoln's playfulness and eagerness to cuddle after we had sex were surprising. Mostly he seemed serious, stoic, and intense. The way he had tenderly stroked my arm and back until I fell asleep was not at all what I had expected.

I want you. I want this.

My stomach tightened at the memory of those words. I had never felt so desired in my entire life. Lincoln's sheer manliness and control ignited the most feminine parts inside of me. A flutter ran through my body.

I had opened myself up to him, completely and without hesitation. I was afraid that in the morning light, things would get awkward and I really didn't want to endure another "that was fun, you're a nice girl, but we're better as friends" conversation. Especially not coming from him.

That's why when I'd woken up, limbs still tangled around Lincoln, I'd only allowed myself a moment to appreciate the hard lines of his face and the earthy pine-smoke smell of his skin. I snuggled my face against him a moment longer, breathed him in, and quietly eased myself out of the bed. There was plenty to get ready for our trip back to town, and I was determined to save myself the embarrassment of Lincoln's rejection.

Now, with playful Lincoln back—taking selfies and texting my sister—I was more confused than ever. Beneath his growly, moody exterior, he was actually really fun. It was a shame that he and Finn had such a hard time connecting. They were more alike than either of them realized.

Perched on a fallen tree along the riverside, I tied tiny

feathers to a hook, creating a sparkly new fishing fly. I looked out over the water, watching the sunlight wink and shimmer, and thought about the brothers.

Between classes, and sometimes instead of them, Finn and I spent hours on the river. There was an easy rhythm to our friendship. He was loud and charming and always joking. I was quieter and more studious, and I think Finn secretly loved getting me to play hooky. Most people assumed we dated, but after I'd asked about girlfriends, Finn confided that he had known he was gay since he was seventeen, though he'd suspected for far longer than that.

Lincoln had already been overseas by that point, and it was an easy secret for Finn to keep. No one seemed to suspect that one of the most eligible bachelors in Chikalu Falls had a reason for turning down so many girls. Sometimes, Finn would visit me in Butte, and at the bar, I'd see him flirt with men he was into. It was nice to see him shed the façade. Finn feared telling Lincoln would change their relationship, and I'd promised to protect his secret. Although, at that time, keeping the secret from a man I'd never actually met seemed so much easier than the situation in which I was now living.

Blowing a wisp of fallen hair out of my eyes, I refocused on what I was doing. Any feelings for Lincoln that resurfaced after so many years were not going to work. This trip would be over tomorrow, and I'd go back to my regular life—building clientele, finding new places to fish, wandering wherever the water took me.

So why was the thought of my dream life giving me a stomachache?

～

Dinner was a success. All five guys were proud to try fish fresh from the river that they had helped catch. Lincoln surprised me again by adding lemon and fresh herbs to the fish, taking it from good to exquisite. The fact that he was a decent cook was not helping me put him solidly into the friend zone, but I tried my best to keep my stolen glances to a minimum. The mood was light, and as the fire crackled, the stories and beers came out.

"Jo! Take a load off, have a beer," Steve called as I started to head toward my tent. Apparently, I had proven myself capable of hanging with the guys tonight.

"Just one," I said. "Long day back to the trucks tomorrow."

I sat again, popping the top off the not-cold-enough beer that Sean handed me. As the fire crackled between us, they told stories about each other, pranks they'd pulled in college, typical fire talk.

Lincoln sat quietly next to me. He didn't engage with the group but sometimes would quietly chuckle at their ridiculous stories. The whole while, his head was down, and he was weaving something with his hands.

Once curiosity got the best of me, I leaned my body toward him and whispered, "Whatcha got there?"

He flicked his eyes to my face, and as the fire danced in those pale blue eyes, he said, "Just keeping busy."

Undeterred by what felt like a brush-off, I continued, "Macramé?"

"Am I supposed to know what that is?" He didn't look up again.

"You know, macramé. Don't tell me you didn't have a grandma with a macramé plant holder. Everyone did!" I smiled at him, hoping my casual banter would show him that I was okay with us acting like what happened between us was fine, normal.

At that, he did glance up, and I couldn't help a smile from blooming across my face. The tension in his shoulders eased, and he tipped his head lower. I leaned my body closer to him to hear his deep, low voice.

"Actually, that's not too far off," he whispered, opening his hands to show two long strands of olive-green rope. "Paracord," he continued. "You know it."

I couldn't help the spread of pleasure at his assumption that I knew that parachute cord had all kinds of uses—from tying gear to being used as an emergency rope. I actually always carried several feet of it in my backpack. It was handy.

Lincoln shifted his body back to his space. I watched him as his long fingers deftly maneuvered the cords. One strand, wrapping behind the others, tucking the end through itself in a small loop, pull. He worked quickly, too quickly for me to accurately figure out how to do it. He worked his way down, methodically creating repetitive knots along the length.

Once he reached the end, he made a final knot. Lincoln took a small pocketknife and snipped the end. Leaning toward the fire, he held the knotted cord to a flame. My breath hitched as I thought he was going to toss it into the fire. Instead, as the heat slightly melted the cut end, Lincoln licked his finger and swiped it onto the cord, sealing the end. I glanced away at the thought of Lincoln's tongue in other places, feeling the heat of the fire prickle and flush my skin.

"Here," he said, reaching one hand out to mine. I looked down at his hand, confused, but placed my hand in his. "Happy Birthday, Joanna."

He released my hand, but wound the cord around my wrist, a bracelet. I stared down at it. *How did he know I just had a birthday? Had Finn said something? The letters?*

My eyes swept up to his, and a smile played on his soft, full lips, turning up at one corner.

The bracelet fit my small wrist perfectly. Little criss-crosses of identical knots wound around, and it felt like the cord was tightening around my heart instead. I swallowed hard.

A small "Thank you" escaped as a whisper as Lincoln finished connecting the knot. His fingers grazed the sensitive skin on the underside of my wrist as he stood.

I stared as the most handsome, thoughtful, confusing man stepped away toward the fire.

SEVENTEEN
LINCOLN

THE FIRE BURNED down to embers as our group continued swapping stories. I was sure most of them were total bull-shit, but the usual sense of unease I felt was gone.

I sat looking around at the group, waiting for the prick of tension and panic to burn through me. For my ears to hear a sound and my eyes to dart around, looking for the danger. My acute awareness of the surroundings was still there, but gone was the blade-sharp edge of stress I usually carried with me.

Thankfully, there wasn't enough beer for anyone to get shitfaced, and they mostly seemed like a happy-drunk kind of group, if a little loud. Joanna had stayed with the group, so I'd chosen to stay up, too. Twice I'd caught her touching the bracelet I'd made for her and I thought I had seen a flash of a dimple.

God, she made me feel like I was twelve years old again. I hoped she liked it. It was rugged and simple, but it matched the bracelet I always wore. The warmth that spread in my chest at the sight of her wearing it was not just from the fire. This girl was changing things for me, and I didn't know what I was going to do about that.

I had decided that tomorrow, as soon as this trip was over, I was going to talk to Finn. Man to man. I was going to tell him about the letters, Joanna, how I'd pursued her, broken his trust. He would finally see that I was a shitty brother.

A flare of anger rose inside of me. I hoped Finn would hit me, scream at me, beat the shit out of me. I wouldn't fight back because I knew I deserved it. I'd always been a man with honor, but now I'd have to answer for this.

When I left for the Marines, Finn had made me promise him that I would come back and take care of him and Mom. I took that promise seriously, even then.

I had made a complete and total mess of this.

Why did this woman have such a hold on me? Why couldn't the woman from the letters have been *anyone* else? She was confident and beautiful and capable. She was the last one who needed saving, and yet I was drawn to her. I looked at her and felt an overwhelming need to protect her.

But she didn't need my protection. She didn't want it either. Joanna had made it clear that she was a talented and proficient woman. She certainly didn't need a fucked-up mental case mooning over her when she had Finn, the younger, mentally healthy version pining for her at home. I absently touched my pocket, feeling the edge of the letter inside.

Aggravated, I flipped a stick into the fire and watched it be consumed by the flames. I would come clean to Finn and then no longer stand in the way of whatever relationship they would develop. I didn't need a flag on my shoulder to know it was the right thing to do, but goddamn, it burned a hole in my gut just thinking about it.

~

As MUCH AS I wanted to invite Joanna into my tent and worship the long lines of her body, I couldn't bring myself to do it. She had lingered slightly outside of her tent after everyone else went to bed. It was clearly an opening, but I'd made my mind up and didn't take it.

Now, hours later, I was staring at the ceiling of my tent, mentally kicking my own ass.

I swear to god, if he marries her and they have a million babies, I'm moving to the East Coast.

The image of Finn and Joanna together made me seethe with jealousy. The snap of a twig pulled me from my murderous thoughts.

Alert, I silently tugged on my boots, grabbed my knife, and crouched at the zipped entrance to my tent. Someone was outside.

I listened carefully, breathing my way through the initial rush of panic. The hairs on my neck stood up, and my ears pricked. Slowing my heart rate was something I had learned to do, and it was useful in clearing my mind before a raid.

Silence.

Silence.

Snap.

There was definitely someone walking around the perimeter of our campsite. Where the fuck was Bud, and why wasn't he hearing this, too? Clearly, he was a terrible guard dog.

Slowly, I unzipped the tent as quietly as I could manage. My eyes were already adjusted to the dark, and I peered into the dense woods, searching for any movement.

Aside from the rustle of the pines and a quiet crackle from the fire, more silence.

Flashes of memories in Kandahar clicked through my mind, and I had to stuff them away to focus on the threat at hand. Someone was moving in a slow arc around the outside of Joanna's tent. I steeled myself with the knowledge that no one would be allowed to hurt her.

Crouching, I exited my tent, moving silently along the outer edge. A flash of light had me turning my head and flattening my body against a tree.

Joanna.

A wave of relief washed over me as I sighed. I saw her up ahead on a tramped down path about thirty yards away from the campsite. Bud at her side, she was walking down the narrow path toward a clearing. Bud trotted alongside her, sniffing at the grasses, and he never wandered too far from her legs. All right, I'd give him points for that—he wasn't a total dipshit.

Afraid to startle her, but unable to let her wander alone in the dark, I quietly followed behind her on the path. Once she reached the end of the trail, it opened into a wide meadow. The moonlight washed away the purples and yellows of the flowers, but a silver halo radiated around her. For a moment, I just stared at her, struck by her beauty. The moon illuminated her as she tipped her head up, eyes closed. She stood in total silence and raised her arms at her side, palms up.

My Valkyrie.

My heart hammered in my ears. I shifted, and the slight movement caught Bud's attention. Her eyes whipped open as a low, protective growl rumbled in his chest.

I stepped out of the shadow, palms up. "Easy, boy. Just me."

"Shit," she exhaled, her hand clutching her throat. "You scared me."

Bud recognized me and ran forward, rubbing his body against my leg. I reached down to scratch between his dark red ears.

"Who's the stalker now?" she joked, her gentle laugh dissolving the tension in the air between us.

"I heard someone outside," I admitted.

"I didn't mean to freak you out. I just couldn't sleep, and all my tossing and turning in the tent was making Bud restless."

I moved toward her, unwilling to accept the distance between us. "I haven't slept either. Want to go for a walk?"

Joanna's eyes lit up the darkness. Her pretty face hurt to look at so instead of kissing her like my body was screaming at me to do, I turned and motioned toward the path. We walked together, side by side, around the wildflower meadow. Joanna was quiet, and I listened to the steady whoosh of her breath as we walked.

Reaching my right hand down at the edge of the path, I plucked a long flower. Holding its stem, I ran the flower down her forearm. She looked down, and when her eyes lifted to mine, I offered her a small smile. I was out of my depth here, drowning in the big feelings I had for her.

She reached for the flower and pressed the small bud to her nose. When she smiled at me again, I nearly crumbled to my knees. As we walked the wide loop in companionable silence, my blood thrummed. My fingers tingled with the need to feel her skin. Despite the warnings of honor and brotherhood in my head, I let my hand bump gently into hers.

Being brave always came easily to me, but in this moment, it took everything inside of me. I moved my hand closer again, brushing the side of my hand against hers. Feeling her silky skin against me, I wound my pinky around two of her fingers, lingering at the touch. When she didn't pull away, I allowed myself more.

The width of my hand was easily twice that of hers, but when her palm connected with mine, I gave her a gentle squeeze. She turned her head to look at me, eyes wide, and I held her gaze. Everything inside of me wanted to wrap her in my arms. I had finally found her.

When we'd closed the loop of the path, I walked her back toward the campsite. I wanted nothing more than to spend the next few hours wrapped in darkness with Joanna against me. At her tent, I leaned my forehead against hers.

"Lincoln," she said quietly, "stay with me."

A war inside me waged with the desire to give her what she needed and the duty to do what was right.

"Goodnight, Joanna," I replied. I leaned down, brushing the stubble of my beard against her. I paused, kissed her cheek, and turned from her, slowly retreating to my tent.

EIGHTEEN
JOANNA

Apparently, I was supposed to pretend the sexiest, not-sex of my life never happened.

When we broke camp the next morning and started the long hike back to the trucks, Lincoln kept a noticeable distance. Apart from when it was absolutely necessary, he didn't speak a word to me. What started out as an optimistic morning quickly soured when he barely grunted at my cheery "Good morning!"

Never being one to miss a hint, I steeled myself against the cold shoulder I was getting from Lincoln. If he wanted to act like nothing happened, fine.

Fuck that guy.

I frowned when I looked down at the bracelet he had made for me. I could talk a good game to myself, but I still hadn't been able to take it off. Running a finger over the bumpy surface, I couldn't help but soften—just a bit.

I used the thin mountain air to distract me from the uncomfortable feelings pushing up against my ribs. One minute, we're kissing in a pool of water, and then next, he stops it. I'm his friend, then his lover. He's tender and sweet and taking charming walks at midnight and the next morning, a total asshole.

It's vacation sex to him. Men like him don't choose girls like you.

Was that it? Was what I thought to be a spark between us nothing more than the fact that I was the only woman on an all-male trip?

Pushing my body harder than necessary, I trudged up the ridge. I had to get more distance between myself and the rising feelings of disgust and disappointment. Disappointed in myself for mistaking hot sex for a connection. For wondering if the scarred Valkyrie tattoo on his forearm was about me, but being too afraid to ask. For letting myself think one walk in a wildflower meadow under the stars could be the start of something different.

Knock it off. You know better.

After we got back to the trucks, I helped Brandon and Lincoln unload, but I couldn't get out of Chikalu fast enough. The exercise from the hike and the sunshine didn't do anything to lift my dark mood.

Back at the Chikalu Rose Motel, I gathered the few clothes I had left behind and stuffed them unceremoniously into my suitcase. I'd worry about laundry once I got out of there. I blinked back the tears that threatened to fall and cleared my throat. I had absolutely zero reason to be this upset.

My phone chirped with a message.

Finn: There in five.

Oh, for fuck's sake.

True to his word, and never one to be late, Finn knocked while opening the door before I could even say "Come in."

"Hey, Banana! I heard you were back already." His boundless energy was truly astounding. Even the cast on his broken leg didn't seem to slow him down. He hobbled over to the bed.

"Hey, Finn," I said without looking up from the mangled mess of my suitcase as I pushed on its bulging top, tugging at the stuck zipper.

"Whoa, whoa, whoa. What's going on?" He scooted closer to me, but rather than look at him, I continued waging war against the cheap suitcase. When he realized I was trying to ignore him, he laid his gigantic, muscled body across the suitcase, looking up at me with his brown puppy eyes. "Jo . . . what's up?"

"You really are an idiot," I said, but I couldn't help the small laugh that escaped me.

"But I'm *your* idiot." He blinked up at me.

I sighed. Years of experience taught me that it was useless to resist Finn. He was relentless when he was determined to get information or cheer me up. His life was fueled by the need to help other people feel as positive and upbeat as he did. "I am a disaster with men."

"Girl, same." Finn winked at me, and I burst out laughing.

Finn being gay wasn't something that really defined him or our friendship. He certainly didn't fit into any stereotypes, and sometimes, I wondered if he even noticed how amazing and special that made him. He was *so comfortable* in his own skin.

I flopped down on top of him with a groan, and he

wrapped his arms around me and rolled so we were side by side on the bed.

"I screwed up, Finn," I said. "I got ahead of myself and got my hopes up and now I'm just . . . ugh. I feel awful."

Finn eyed me carefully as I spoke. Finally, he said, "What happened? Did you hook up with a client?"

"Worse," I started. This was hard to admit to him, and I was afraid he was going to judge me. Taking a breath, I closed my eyes and said, "Lincoln."

The look of surprise on Finn's face was a dagger, and my insides burned with regret. "I'm so sorry, Finn," I continued. "I don't really know what happened. There were all these glances, and smiles, and little touches, and then there was the shower . . ." I couldn't help myself from rambling. The words tumbled out of me. It was cathartic, and I couldn't stop.

"One minute he's all, '*My Joanna,*'" I said in a deep man-voice, a bad imitation of Lincoln. "And the next he's completely ignoring me. I don't understand him *at all!* He has got to be the world's most confusing human."

"Ok, Jo, ok. You're going to have to slow your roll so I can catch up. You? And Lincoln?" he asked.

I folded my lips in and nodded, trying to read the varying expressions flitting over his face. "Do you hate me?" I asked timidly.

"Hate you? I could never *hate* you, Jo." I waited for him to continue, but he seemed to be mulling something over in his mind. Finally, he added, "Wow."

"I know. I swear I didn't mean for this to happen. But I promise you, Finn, I didn't tell him. I would never betray your trust . . . I mean, besides the having sex with your brother part."

At that, a smile widened across his handsome face. He

had a boyish grin, deepening his dimples. "This is wild. I can't believe I didn't see it coming, but I think I love it."

Groaning, I leaned toward him, and he wrapped me in a hug. "You are literally no help. I'm relieved you're not mad at me, but what is with him, anyway?"

"Linc's been through some shit. Hell, I don't even know the half of it. He doesn't open up to *anyone*. I think the Marines made sure he mastered the art of burying emotions." Finn continued, "But you know that's no excuse, right? I mean, I love him, but if he doesn't see that being with you would be, like, the greatest thing to ever happen to him, then he doesn't deserve you."

Hearing Finn say such kind things about me made me slightly uncomfortable, but it was nice to hear. I hugged Finn tightly. "Thank you."

"Do you want me to talk to him? Kick his ass or something? I mean, I'm not sure I can take him, but I'll give it a shot." Finn eyed me carefully. I knew he was dead serious.

"No, of course not. I think this was just a blip. A mistake. I think I'm going to go back to my sister's place in Butte, figure a few things out, and then get on with my life." I sighed.

"All right, but the offer still stands," Finn said. "I can probably get a few good shots in—maybe knock that scowl off his face or something." He sat up and looked around the sad motel room. "You deserve better than this, Jo."

After I walked Finn to the doorway, he wrapped me in a tight hug. "You're the best friend a guy could ask for," he said, kissing the top of my head. "You're sure I can't convince you to stay?"

"You're pretty okay yourself." I smiled at him. "I'll call you next week."

As Finn backed out of the motel parking lot in his shiny,

black truck, I waved and my stomach rumbled. I determined that I would get some food, maybe a stiff drink, and a good night's sleep. In the morning, I was going back to Butte to forget about Lincoln Scott.

NINETEEN

LINCOLN

I SPENT the afternoon after the trip cleaning gear, replacing lines, and making an inventory of anything that needed to be replaced. Brandon tried to help, but after I'd snapped at him—twice—I sent him home so he wouldn't have to deal with me. I preferred to work alone, anyway.

I also texted Finn and let him know the guide was successful. Everyone left happy, and two even asked about a repeat trip in the spring.

I needed to figure out a way to tell Finn about what went down with Joanna this weekend. I still didn't know how to tell him without sounding like a total douche, but that was a risk I was going to have to take. Finn deserved to know the truth, and it was my job to face it.

Frowning, I looked out the window at the fading sunlight. I wanted nothing more than to head back to the cottage on Mr. Bailey's property and nurse my foul mood. Unfortunately, I hadn't planned ahead and was going back to an empty fridge. I decided I could spend an hour at The Pidge, get some food, and share a beer with Colin. Maybe Deck would even be there, and I could forget all about

Joanna, the way her skin felt beneath my hands, how her laugh bubbled up and made the hairs on my arms stand on end.

When I passed the Chikalu Rose Motel, I didn't want to glance over, but I couldn't help myself. I wondered if Joanna was still there or if she'd left town as soon as she could get away. My question was answered when I saw her standing in the doorway to a room, with her arms wrapped around my brother. My gut burned. Finn had his arms around her, wrapped in an embrace, and he kissed the top of her head.

Of course, they were together.

I needed to steel myself against the reality that Finn and Joanna would likely end up together. If I were to be in his life, that was a fact I would need to accept. Hammering the gas, I stared ahead as I drove down the block to the bar.

A burger and a beer later, I was still nursing my sour mood at a dark corner table. Colin was busy setting up the next band, but I'd promised him I would stick around long enough for a drink with him.

The moment she walked in, I felt it. Static electricity crackled in the air. My head whipped up to see her pushing the door to the entrance open, scanning for an empty table.

Maybe she won't see me. Make an excuse to Colin and just leave. You can't trust yourself around her.

The way her hair billowed from the breeze outside as the door closed had my pulse galloping. I couldn't tear my eyes away from her.

There was a decent crowd to eat and enjoy the band, but not a few steps into the bar, she saw me. Joanna stopped abruptly. Something flickered over her face, and she looked down, but then suddenly back up and stared directly at me.

With purposeful strides, she walked straight to my small table. *Fuck.*

"Fancy meeting you here."

Ignore the tightness in your chest. Breathe. "That's small-town life for you. Not a lot of options on a weeknight." I couldn't seem to look at her.

"Apparently." At that, she smiled. "I was just popping in to get a bite. Can you keep me company?" she asked, already pulling the chair from under the table.

I just looked at the chair, and she paused. *Don't be a dick.*

"Of course. I already ate but you can have the table." I shifted to stand.

"Please don't go because of me," she said, looking down. "If I make you that uncomfortable, I can eat somewhere else."

I recovered from the citrus scent of her hair long enough to realize how much of an asshole I was still being. Clearly, she was trying to make things less awkward and I wasn't letting her.

"No," I said, sighing. "Of course not. It's fine."

Joanna sat, looking around and tapping her finger on the scarred wood top of the table. The corner section was tight, forcing us to sit side by side, knees nearly touching. I stared at the beer between my hands and focused on breathing rather than how soft her hair looked as pieces of it fell from her bun.

As the silence stretched, she added, "I'm sorry if I made things uncomfortable on the trip."

"Oh." I turned to finally look at her. Her eyes were cast down, and her fingers picked at an imaginary something on the wood. "No, it's fine. It was . . ." I didn't know how to do this.

"Well, I thought about it and I think we should just let this be . . ." she waved a hand in the air, "whatever it was. Friends?" She reached out her hand to me.

I looked down at her slim hand. It looked so small compared to mine, and I couldn't help but remember how it felt when it had run up the muscles of my back as I drove into her.

Focus. Breathe.

Pushing the thought from my mind, I slid my hand into hers, and she pumped it once and nodded her head.

"Friends," she confirmed. She seemed to relax a little, letting herself lean against the back of the chair. She looked around the bar again, her eyes settling on the stage. "Does he play?" she asked, nodding toward Colin as he fitted a guitar strap over his head.

"Yeah. Really well, actually. He pursued it seriously for a while, but then some family stuff had him coming back," I said. It was the truth. Colin had learned to play guitar when we were kids, and he was incredible. Had a good voice, too. But he'd made it pretty clear that he had no intentions of ever leaving Chikalu Falls again. I shook my head slightly in disbelief at the thought. When I looked back at her, she wasn't looking at Colin anymore, but had her eyes roaming over me.

"Can I get you something, honey?" the waitress asked her.

She cleared her throat and looked away, a blush rising to her cheeks. I smiled at that and took a pull from my beer. "Burgers are good," I offered.

"Yes. Perfect," she said, still a little flustered. "I'll take a cheeseburger, everything on it. Fries. And the amber lager, please."

Colin and the house band started a new song, and she

focused her attention on the stage. I used the opportunity to peek at her. She was freshly showered—that's probably why I could still smell that damn citrus shampoo—and had changed out of her guide clothes. She wore light jeans, the kind that were tight all the way down her legs, that were cuffed at the bottom. Her hiking boots were replaced with Converse sneakers that matched the snug black V-neck top that plunged dangerously low. I wanted to run my tongue down her neck and dip into her cleavage. Her clothes were casual, she wasn't trying to be noticed, but the firm lines of her body made any man within a five-mile radius take notice. As my eyes traveled over her, they paused on the bracelet she still wore. My heart thumped and a rush of pride filled me when I realized she hadn't taken it off.

"Did Finn ask you to guide for him next week?" I asked her, trying to get an idea of how long I would be torturing myself with her around.

"He did." She smiled at the waitress as she dropped off her beer and took a long pull. "But I'm not going to be able to fill in again, so he's calling around." Her finger picked at the label of the beer bottle.

I knew it was best for me that Joanna not be in Chikalu. It made things less complicated for everyone involved, but the idea of her not being around when I had spent so long looking for her created a dull ache at the base of my skull.

"Finn told me what you said about Mr. Bailey's property—about the access point and using it like the Chaney's," I said, trying to change the subject. "It's an interesting idea. I'm talking to him about it this week."

Joanna's eyes flew to mine, lighting up. "That's amazing! I could see it all when I was hiking there that day . . . the river, cottages, the Big House. It could really be something."

I liked seeing her this excited. She buzzed with energy. "Mr. Bailey's a piece of work. He doesn't really like change, but it may be a way to convince him to use the land for the community. He's big into conservation. He would never admit it, but he's lonely too. I think having people using his land in that way would actually make the old bastard pretty happy."

She perked up at the table, and I could see those magnificent eyes turning over all of the possibilities. She played lightly with her lower lip, and my thoughts immediately went to my mouth on hers.

Fuck. She is so kissable. Maybe no one would notice in the dark corner of the bar.

My jaw clenched. I had to put those thoughts out of my head.

Surely by now, people knew Joanna was here, and if they saw Finn's brother making out with her, I'd have to deal with that in a matter of minutes—that's just how small towns worked. Honestly, the rumor mill was probably already buzzing, just because we were sitting here together.

I drained my beer and let the moment fade. Even though I knew better, I caught the eye of the waitress and signaled for another beer. When she came back with Joanna's food, she placed my beer in front of me.

Joanna took a generous bite of her burger, a drop of ketchup plopping onto the plate. "Oh my god . . ." she said, eyes closed, mouth full.

I couldn't help but laugh at her enthusiasm. "That good, huh?"

"You weren't lying. These are damn good," she said, scooping the dripped ketchup with a fry and licking her fingertip with a pop. My eyes watched the movement as if it were in slow motion, and my body stiffened in response.

Act normal. You're friends now, remember?

Joanna noticed my stiff movements and grew a little quiet. As she looked down, I saw her eyes settle on the tattoos that trailed up my forearm.

"Can I ask about those?" she asked, pointing to the scars and ink splayed across my skin.

"Shit. These I've had for a long time. They used to look pretty good, once upon a time. None of them are special," I lied. I didn't notice that I'd covered the scarred wings with my opposite hand until Joanna laid her hand on mine lightly.

"You don't have to cover them," she said softly. "They tell your story."

I stared at my arm, her soft hand covering mine. I wanted to turn my hand over to hold hers, but instead, I slipped my hand into my lap. "Well, that's a story no one wants to hear," I said. "It's kind of a bummer."

Joanna wiped her hands on her napkin and took a sip of her beer. I watched her lips again. "I'd like to hear it some-day," she said. "But just the parts you want to tell me."

Really? She was willing to listen to my story and not press for details I didn't want to share? Not that I'd had many girlfriends, but most women I'd met wanted to know every detail—especially the stories I didn't want to tell. There was something about dating a Marine that seemed to make women care more about the Bronze Star and less about the work it took to stay sane afterward or the hollow-gut feeling whenever I thought about the men I'd let die in the field. "There's not much to tell. I signed up, fought hard, got hurt, sent home."

She nodded. "Not really according to plan, then, huh?"

"Nah. I was a lifer. Just didn't work out that way, though."

Joanna picked up that I was done talking about it, and to her credit, she didn't press. "So what's the new plan?"

I looked at Colin playing on the stage, and a strange, yet familiar bubble of humor rippled through me. "Rock. God."

I was rewarded with a fit of giggles from her, and making her laugh made my stomach flip. I tried to hide my reaction with a sip of my beer. She just made me feel so damn good—like the old part of me, before the death and the pain of my life overseas hardened me, was coming back.

"So tell me about you," I said, wanting to shift the focus away from me, my tattoos, and the fact that I somehow had to be friends with the perfect girl.

"I'm not sure there's much to tell. I'm kind of boring, to be honest."

"I don't believe that for a fucking second," I said. "How'd you get into guide fishing?"

A warm smile spread across her face. "Pop. My grandpa." She told me all about her grandfather and how he'd taken her under his wing. She shared that her parents wanted her to be a teacher, but that never quite felt right. I understood how it felt to be an outsider in your own family, but I didn't share that with her.

I learned that she'd been visiting Chikalu Falls since she was a kid, and I couldn't help but think how different my life could have been if I'd met her first. I warmed at the thought of meeting her when we were kids. I could picture a cute little girl with cool gray-green eyes and dirty hands splashing in the river.

When she'd broken the news to her parents that she wasn't going to school to be a teacher, but rather the community college in Chikalu, they'd been upset. She'd moved anyway, met Finn in a college class—I was already overseas—and started guiding full time. She never brought up the letters—though I did catch another glance at my forearm—and neither did I.

"So your parents don't realize you're still a teacher, then?" I asked.

She made a small face. "No. Not at all. You see, Mr. and Mrs. James have *very* specific ideas about what it means to be a lady. Fishing definitely does not fit into that. They don't really see it as anything more than a tomboy's hobby. My parents don't really get me."

"James? Your name is Joanna James? That's an amazing name. Like an outlaw." My chest hitched at the smile that spread across her face.

"Pew, pew." She shot finger guns, and I fucking lost it. Together we laughed. I loved that she had such an easy way about her. I caught myself looking at her again. Her eyes turned toward me, and I got lost in their warmth, delight, and affection. I loved that I could make her laugh and that just the sound of it made me feel lighter.

Why the fuck couldn't things be different?

Talking with Joanna was easy, natural. I felt more relaxed than I had in months. I didn't want to break whatever spell we were under by putting her on the spot, and something about her relationship with my brother gnawed at the back of my mind. I needed to remain in control and get a handle on it myself. If we avoided talking about Finn or the letters or my unrequited feelings for her, I could do this.

"So what's next for Joanna James, outlaw? Roaming the West?" I asked.

She dragged the last of her fries through the ketchup and gave my question some thought. "That," she responded with a sigh, "is the million-dollar question."

"I don't know, Joanna . . . you don't seem like a marauder to me."

"I haven't had roots in a long time. But I know I want to find my home, where I'm supposed to end up. Honestly, I thought I might already have kids by now, but that's just not how things worked out." She shrugged her shoulders lightly.

She shifted uncomfortably and I knew I was playing with fire by asking her about her plans to stay, but I couldn't help myself.

"What about you?" she cut in. "I imagine you have your pick of the single ladies around here?"

Fuck. The conversation took a left turn, and I did not want to talk about this.

I mirrored her shrug. "Nah. I'm not the marrying kind." I tapped my temple. "Too much shit up here. My temper's unpredictable, and I'd rather be alone. I'm gearing up to be the next Mr. Bailey. Someone will have to be the next town crab-ass eventually."

She laughed a little *hmph* but didn't say anything more.

Joanna changed the subject, and we spent the next hour talking about the town, small towns versus big cities, travel out east. She asked about Colin and his almost music career. Once, she and Finn had tried to surprise Deck for his birthday but ended up almost getting arrested instead. I laughed, never having heard that one before, but also a little sad that I'd missed it.

Joanna filled the space with easy banter. Lulls in the conversation weren't uncomfortable, and I was mesmerized when she would hum and sway to a song she liked. Once an old, upbeat country song played and her eyes danced along with the couples two-stepping on the dance floor.

I wished I had the balls to ask her to dance. I knew how. Hell, I was a great fucking dancer, but I couldn't do it. Just the thought of my arms around her again shifted my thoughts into dangerous territory. My hand flexed at the image of it wrapping around her small waist.

Joanna was the kind of pretty that was understated, uncovered, and real. She had no fucking clue that the curve of her ass down to her strong legs made me want to burn every bridge I had, throw away any relationship, just to be with her. But now that we'd agreed to be friends, I'd blown my chances.

Why hadn't I worshipped that body when I had the chance? Stroking my dick in the shower and thinking of her, only to find her *there* with the hot look of desire on her face unraveled me. I was hurried and frantic and didn't take the time to show her how gorgeous she truly was. So fucking selfish.

Her sigh broke me from my trance. Joanna gently rubbed her palms on her thighs. "Well . . . I should call it a night."

At that, I frowned but nodded. I knew she was right, but it physically hurt to think about watching her walk away. Somehow, in this dim little corner of the bar, it felt intimate. Before I could stop her, Joanna was standing, ready to walk out of my life for good.

TWENTY

JOANNA

ALL I WANTED WAS to get a quick dinner and spend the night wallowing in my dingy motel room. Seeing Lincoln perched on a stool in a dark corner of the bar was a shot to my system.

Once our eyes locked, I knew I couldn't hide from him. I quickly decided I was just going to face him head-on. It wasn't the first time I'd been friend-zoned, and it wouldn't be the last.

As it turned out, our conversation was easy, natural almost. Though I felt a tingle every time I heard Lincoln's deep laugh—it rumbled through me and a warmth spread down between my legs. I tried to push those warm feelings away. He agreed that we could be friends . . . We even shook on it.

But damn. He looked *so* delicious. There was something about his dark, moody, scruffy exterior that just worked for me. It worked for the majority of the women in the bar too. I wasn't a fool and could see the envious glances that were shot my way. God, why did I suggest we could be friends?

I tried to focus on the band—Colin was impressively talented, and I couldn't believe I never knew that about him. I hummed along to the cover songs I knew and willed myself to just enjoy the moment and completely ignore the desire to crawl into Lincoln's lap in the dark corner of the bar. But I loved the way his T-shirt fit tightly across his muscular chest. His dark hair, short at the sides but longer at the top, was begging me to run my fingers through it, pull just a little. If our time after his shower was any indication, Lincoln liked his sex just a little rough. Every time he took a sip of his beer, I had to look away and not think about his full lips as they found the thin skin on my neck.

I couldn't help myself, and I asked about his tattoos. I had to know if the wings on his forearm really had been Valkyrie and if there was any connection to the letters I had written him so many years ago.

None of them are special.

Those words gutted me. I tried to hide the tears that burned at the corners of my eyes. When he covered them with his hand, I couldn't help but share the sadness that crept into his eyes. There was something there—deep and dark—that was haunting Lincoln Scott.

A rolling ache spread across my chest. I wanted nothing more than to take away the sadness that darkened his expression. I was relieved when the moment passed almost as quickly as it had come.

A silent war waged inside me—I was supposed to be his *friend,* but all I could think about were the stolen moments we'd shared this weekend. Lincoln was still a mystery to me. He was dark and moody but also had a witty sense of humor and wasn't afraid to laugh at himself. I craved more of those moments where he shed his tough exterior.

A bubble of anger developed when I thought about how

natural and easy our conversation was and how it could never be more than a friendship. I wasn't one to pout, but the irrational side of me wanted to stomp my foot, shake him, and show him how much *fun* we could have together. Not to mention how hot it was when we'd had sex. A repeat of that would definitely be welcomed.

Feeling resigned to live in the desolate land of *friends*, I knew it was time to make a clean break. "Well . . . I should call it a night."

As I shifted on my stool, Lincoln stood. I watched him pull out a few bills from his wallet, and I got a quick glimpse of his incredible ass.

"My treat," he said as he put the bills down on the table. He really needed to stop being such a gentleman. Him paying for my dinner made it feel more like a date and my face warmed, a blush creeping across my cheeks.

"Thank you," I said, looking around. "And thank you for keeping me company tonight. I've got a little walk back, so I'll leave you to it." I moved away from the table.

"Joanna," Lincoln growled. The intensity in his eyes was back, and my breath hitched. "I'll drive you back to the motel."

He wasn't asking. My gut told me it wasn't a good idea, but if it meant even a few more minutes with Lincoln, I was taking it. Friend zone be damned.

He walked quickly through the bar, and my legs burned trying to keep up with his long, quick strides. When we reached the door, he pulled it open, placing a hand on my lower back and guiding me through. His fingers lingered on the dip of my back, just a moment, and I could have melted into a puddle right then and there.

"I'm parked this way," he said, motioning toward his gray pickup. The air in the truck had shifted from the last time I was here, electrified. Tension felt heavy in the small cab. I watched Lincoln as he opened my door. Did he lean in, just a little bit?

My mind was racing. I didn't want to read into anything, but he was definitely still throwing out mixed signals. We'd decided to be friends, but he had paid for dinner and offered to drive me back to the motel. What was with him?

The motel was only a few short blocks away, and Lincoln stayed quiet and intense the entire ride. His eyes never left the road. When he pulled into a parking space, he put the truck into park and shifted in the seat, finally facing me.

"Thank you for the ride. And for dinner," I said. *Why was I acting like such a robot?* The confines of the cab were filled with his masculine scent, and I knew exactly why I was having trouble forming coherent thoughts.

"You should really consider filling in for Finn while his leg heals," he said, surprising me.

I sighed. "I have. I'm just not sure now is a good time. Things got . . . complicated this weekend and I need to be getting back to reality." I couldn't bring myself to look Lincoln in the eye.

I felt his finger under my chin, tipping my head so that our eyes could meet. Lincoln's molten, deep blue eyes burned into me. "I'm sorry if I made your life more difficult," he offered.

His hand slid back, moving around the base of my neck, kneading gently. I locked my eyes onto his. *Pull me close, Lincoln. Kiss me.* I tipped my head forward slightly.

"Goodnight, Joanna." His voice was a low, rough whisper. His hand gently squeezed the back of my neck as he released me. Lincoln's large frame shifted back, facing forward. His eyes turned hard, and I knew that was my invitation to leave.

Disappointed, I turned the handle and paused. "Thank you, again, for dinner. Goodbye, Lincoln." With that, I hurried out of his truck, embarrassment burning through my veins.

I quickly opened the door to my room and closed it without looking back, slumping against the doorframe.

He turned you down twice. Get a damn clue, Jo.

I closed my eyes as I heard the rumble of his engine pull out of the motel parking lot. The lump in my throat threatened to turn into full-blown sobs.

Bud whined at my return, so I grabbed his leash and took him for a short walk on the small patch of grass behind the building. It was quiet, and judging by Bud's soft brown eyes, he seemed to know that my spirits were low.

After our quick walk, I stood in the dim, cramped motel room. *This is not the life I imagined.* If I was going to move forward with owning my own guide business and having any measure of success, I needed to make some serious changes. In the morning, I planned to head out early, scout a few potential properties, and call my sister. She was always good for a pep talk and would help me figure out where to go from here. I just really hoped I didn't have to end up on her couch again. So humiliating.

I knew one thing for certain—I was clearly not meant to be tethered. No more consideration of a business with Finn, no more wondering if my life would have been different if I had listened to my parents, and definitely no more thoughts of Lincoln Scott.

I tapped my wet toothbrush on the sink and turned toward the bed when I heard two sharp knocks on the motel room door. A low growl formed in Bud's throat, and I rested my hand on his furry head with a "Shh." My pulse hammered as I crossed the room but paused at the door, listening.

"Joanna." Another three bangs.

I slipped the bolt unlocked and yanked the door open. Lincoln stood in front of me, fists clenched at his side, the veins bulging in his forearms, his body filled with tension.

Oh, shit.

TWENTY-ONE
LINCOLN

I MADE it about as far as the county road before I'd stopped. *What the fuck are you doing, asshole?*

Everything inside of me screamed for Joanna.

I stared at the blinking light at the four-way stop.

Turn right and you're a good brother, an honorable man. She doesn't need you in her life.

The center of my chest physically hurt, the more distance I put between us. I closed my eyes. The darkness of the road enveloped me. I thought of Joanna's sparkling green-gray eyes, the way my hand had felt in hers as we walked in the meadow.

If she were any other woman, I could walk away. But with Joanna, whatever this was, it was cellular—not a choice I could make. Her presence shifted my life, and I felt like everything had suddenly clicked into place.

A quick *beep beep* from a car behind me snapped me back to the moment. Without hesitation, I whipped my truck forward and pulled hard into a U-turn.

Barreling down the two-lane highway, my brain filled with nothing but thoughts of her. I couldn't let her go tomorrow until she knew. About how I felt when she was near, the letters, Finn—she deserved to know all of it.

My palms felt damp, and a nervous twitch ran up my arm as I rubbed it against my thighs. I had royally fucked this up with Joanna, sending her nothing but mixed signals all weekend. What if she didn't feel the way I felt? What if I had pushed her too far, too late?

Arriving at the motel, I slammed the truck into park and stalked toward her motel room door. I opened and closed my fists to release the energy and tension that built in my body.

I knocked twice on her door. Nothing.

"Joanna," I ground out. Three more hard knocks.

The door flew open, and the gust of wind twirled Joanna's hair around her face. Her eyes were wide with shock, but she looked like a goddess standing before me. She was so pretty my mind went blank.

Unthinking, I stepped forward, and our bodies crashed together.

My mouth took hers, and I wound my arms around her slim body, lifting her off the ground. Her lips slanted over mine as my tongue swept over hers. As I set her down, her arms ran down my chest and I gripped the back of her shirt, pulled her into me.

I stepped forward into the room, taking her with me. I paused to kick the door shut behind me, and Joanna pushed forward, pressing me against the closed door. My hands reached down over her round, firm ass and I squeezed.

Joanna kissed my face and moved down my neck, licking and sucking. I groaned with pleasure. My cock throbbed with the need to be free. With one hand, she moved down my chest, palming my thick erection through my jeans. A low growl escaped my throat.

My hands dipped low, finding the hem of her T-shirt. I moved my palms up her back, dragging my nails softly against her silken skin. She lifted a leg in response, pressing herself into me. I shifted my hips forward, pressing my hard length against her, giving her more of the friction she craved.

We grunted and moaned as our fingers roamed over each other's bodies. I reached back and pulled at the collar of my T-shirt, stripping it from my body. Joanna's hands moved over my bare skin, and her nails raked my chest. She paused slightly at the scarring across my ribs and torso. With both hands on her face, I tipped her head back and kissed the pulse that hammered in her neck.

All I could feel was the desperation to have her. Where words failed me, I wanted to show her how completely undone she made me. Her response to me was undeniable. I knew she wanted this too, and that knowledge unleashed something primal inside of me.

My palm dipped down her back and inside the waist of her jeans. I gave her round ass another squeeze, and a moan escaped that sexy fucking mouth of hers. She was willing and eager and pliable in my hands. Still palming my cock, she moved one hand to fumble with the button of my jeans. Our arms tangled as we clawed at the clothing separating us.

She peeled her jeans down. When she hooked her thumbs into the top of her underwear, she bit her bottom lip and gave me a flirty look that caused a surge of anticipation to run down my body. I gripped myself as I watched her.

After pulling off her top and tossing her bra to the side, Joanna moved forward again, her naked body pressed against mine.

Knowing she felt the same pull toward me as I did to

her stirred something deep inside me. As my hands moved up her sides and found the stiff peaks of her nipples, I had to show her.

I pressed my mouth to hers as I quickly walked Joanna backward toward the bed. Still frenzied, we tumbled onto the mattress. She rolled, seating herself across me, and I could feel a warm, slick wetness rub the length of my cock. I sat up with Joanna straddling me, taking her hips in my hands.

"Wait . . . wait . . ." I said, pressing my forehead to hers. My breath was ragged with desperation, but I needed to slow us down, savor and stretch this moment. I searched her eyes to see if she was feeling the same overwhelming longing I was feeling.

I touched my palm to her face, sweeping a loose strand of hair away from the soulful depths of her eyes. Joanna's skin was radiant. In one fluid movement, I lifted her from my lap and turned, stretching her on her back across the bed. I settled my hips between her thighs.

Joanna tipped her head and arched her back. I lowered my mouth to her breasts, taking one soft, rosy tip into my mouth. I dragged my thumb over the other hard peak and pinched it slightly between my thumb and forefinger. Her breathy gasp urged more, and I took the other side into my mouth—kissing, licking, sucking.

Still teasing her nipple, I moved one hand lower, feeling the curve of her ribcage under my broad hand. Lower still, I moved my hand across the soft, round swell of her hips and squeezed. Joanna tipped her hips forward.

I gently moved one hand across her slit, feeling it already wet with pleasure. I slipped one finger inside of her, then two. Joanna moaned as I fingered her pussy and licked up the side of her neck, nipping slightly. My thumb pressed against her clit in slow circles. My cock begged to be inside of her, but feeling how wet she was, I had to taste her.

I moved down, kissing the soft skin of her belly and hips. I nestled my head between her soft, muscular thighs. I started slowly—soft strokes of my tongue from base to top, swirling my tongue around her tight bundle of nerves.

"Fuck, Joanna. You taste so fucking good," I ground out between long, soft drags of my tongue.

I was rewarded with a moan, louder this time, as I went back to tasting her delicious pussy. Teasing her clit with my tongue, I slipped one finger inside her. When I felt her drag her nails through my hair, I moaned into her center.

"Yes." I craved more of her.

Tasting her on my tongue, feeling her hands in my hair, hearing her moan with pleasure—I could have come right there. She was everything, and I needed her to feel as good as I felt in this moment.

I had searched for her—for years—hoping she wasn't a figment of my broken mind, and now I had her, ready and eager in my arms. *Finally,* I thought. *Fucking finally.*

She bucked her hips and pushed toward my mouth as I sucked and licked harder. I could feel her warm, slick heat against my tongue. I ached to be inside of her, but she was so close. With one hand, I reached up and palmed her, taking her hard, stiff nipple between my fingers. As I pinched, I sucked her clit and felt it throb against my mouth.

The muscles in her legs went tense. She was a coil ready to spring loose. I moved my tongue faster, adding more pressure. My left hand grabbed at her thigh, pushing her more open to me so I could devour her pussy. Suddenly, she was crying out and I felt her orgasm pulse against my mouth. My cock throbbed in agonizing response.

Still kissing between her thighs, I felt her pull up on my shoulders.

"I need you inside of me," she said hastily.

I moved carefully up her body and kissed her glistening skin until I was hovering over her. I fisted my cock in my hand, dragging the tip against her folds.

"God, yes, Lincoln. Give it to me."

I traced slow circles with the head of my dick, pressing into her only slightly. I watched her eyes flutter closed and her head tip back. The long lines of her neck begged to be licked, nibbled. I dragged my tongue up one side as I pushed in slightly deeper, stretching her open.

"More," she demanded.

I moved slowly. Shallow thrusts in and out of her.

"You want this, baby?" I asked, still holding my thick cock.

She tipped her legs wider, offering more of herself to me. "Yes, Lincoln. Yes. I want you to fuck me."

Hearing those words from her pretty mouth made me ravenous for her. With a deep thrust of my hips, I pushed into her, bottoming out. I held here, feeling warm and tight as she surrounded me. We groaned in unison.

Slowly, I made deep, long strokes as she gasped and arched, her hands clutching the sheets beside her. As I started to pound into her at an increasingly steady rhythm, she hooked her legs around me, heels digging into the backs of my thighs. I shifted forward, tilting my body so the base of my cock pressed into her clit and rubbed as I slid in and out of her.

My body tingled, and her moans of my name had my head swimming.

"Don't stop," she begged into my ear, taking it into her mouth and sucking.

I wanted to tell her right then. The unfamiliar swell in my chest was like a vise. This woman was different than I'd imagined, better, and I felt the stony interior of my heart start to crack.

This girl is it for you.

Pushing faster, harder, I chased away any thoughts other than her in this moment.

Joanna was begging for hard and rough, and I was going to give her everything she needed. She grabbed my ass and pulled me into her, matching my steady rhythm.

"Fuck, Joanna. This feels incredible."

"Yes, Lincoln. Don't stop," she whispered.

I leaned my body forward, looping my arms under hers and pressing her into me. I was probably crushing her, but the need for every part of me to be touching her was over-whelming. I pressed my body into her and felt her tighten around my cock. She wound her arms and legs around me as I brought her to the edge with me.

I pumped my hips forward, and she kissed my neck, bit my shoulder. The intensity in my chest moved lower, tight-ening in my balls as I teetered closer to the edge. I moved one hand down to her breast and squeezed her hard nipple between my fingers. With a high moan, she tightened around me and then exploded as her orgasm tore through her.

Unable to fight it any longer, completely overwhelmed by her, I let go, pumping furiously into her. Hot streams of my desire filled her. My hips jerked, and I ground my teeth —the intensity of my orgasm was shocking.

I dropped my head to her hair, taking in her citrus shampoo mixed with the intoxicating, heady scent of our sex. I breathed deeply. After a few craggy breaths, I tried to slow the uncontrollable drumming of my heart.

After a moment, I lifted my weight off of her and looked down at her face. She was flushed, glistening, but with a dreamy look and a soft smile.

The tightness in my chest returned. I stroked her mussed-up hair away from her face. I wanted to tell her everything.

"You are so beautiful," I said to her. After I could gain my bearings, I lowered my lips to hers and said the only words my mouth could form. "I lied to you."

TWENTY-TWO

JOANNA

"You are so beautiful . . . I lied to you."

I blinked at Lincoln, still trying to get my mind and body on the same page.

Holy shit, did that just happen?

Lincoln Scott was still hard inside of me, my body humming with the aftereffects of the best sex I'd ever had. The hard lines of his body were still pressed against me, making it difficult to form a coherent thought.

"Wait, what?" I started, eyeing him carefully. I tried to level my breathing.

Lincoln shifted, gently pulling out of me, and rested his hips beside me. "Please don't go back home, Joanna."

My face flushed at his words, and the flutter in my belly returned at the use of my full name, as it always tended to. "Let's back up a little," I said. "You lied to me?"

Lincoln's eyes flicked down. "I lied to you," he said again. "When you asked me if any of my tattoos meant anything."

A crashing wave of relief washed over me at his admission. As he spoke, he lifted his forearm slightly, revealing his marred and broken tattoos. "This one here," I glanced down at his arm again, "used to be Valkyrie wings." His eyes were searching my own as a warmth bloomed in my belly.

I reached my hand up, running it along the bumpy and uneven surface. What once were likely gorgeous, well-defined tattoos were now blotchy, broken, and nearly unrecognizable. Swirling emotions of sadness and desire pooled in me.

"So you read them? My letters?" Tears pricked at the corners of my eyes, and my voice got thick with emotion. I swallowed back the lump that had formed there.

"It's why I only call you Joanna and not Jo. That's how you signed every letter." Lincoln ran his hand down the length of me, settling it on my hip.

My eyes roamed over his chiseled face—his stubble, his straight nose, his sharp jaw, his sea-blue eyes. Overwhelmed, I still couldn't speak and swallowed hard again.

"I wondered if it was you when we met at the bar," he continued. "But I knew for sure once we talked on the trip. Everything about you drew me in and I just knew."

Still stroking his arm, tracing the outlines of his faded, pink scars and ink, I asked, "And the letters meant so much to you that you got a tattoo of Valkyrie wings?"

"Joanna, those letters meant everything."

My body tingled at his words. "But you never wrote me back. The return address was the Women's Club. I could have gotten them."

"I know," he said with an exhale of his breath. "I can't explain it." Lincoln shook his head slightly. "At first, I thought your letter was a fluke—just a nice one-off that made that week feel a little less lonely. But then . . . they kept coming. I looked forward to them, craved them."

The intensity in Lincoln's eyes was fierce, and my

nipples stiffened in response. Was a man like him really talking about a girl like me?

When I stayed quiet, he continued. "I looked for you when I got back. I looked for a long time. When I couldn't find you, I almost had myself convinced that I'd made you up somehow—that I really was even more fucked up than everyone knew."

I shifted and placed both of my hands on the sides of his face. He breathed deeply, closing his eyes and leaning his head into my hands. "Lincoln, I'm here."

He lowered his body and kissed me as he shifted his weight toward me again. "Please tell me you aren't leaving, Joanna. I know things are complicated."

"I'll stay," I whispered, brushing my hands over the back of his neck and into his thick hair. I smiled, still not quite believing that this gorgeous man was asking me to stay. I had no idea where I was going to stay—I could probably afford a week or so at the motel—and what staying *really* meant for Lincoln. I was not the woman who men pined for, devoted themselves to, but for however long Lincoln was willing to give, I would stay.

"THIS BED FUCKING SUCKS."

At Lincoln's words, a giggle escaped me. After cleaning up, we'd laid down together on the small motel bed. Lincoln on his back, his arm tight around me, tucking me into his side. He was quiet. Something was *definitely* on his mind, but I pushed that nagging thought away and focused on the way his fingertips dragged slow circles on my shoulder. We tried to sleep, but every shift made the lumpy bed push against us.

"No, I'm serious. I have slept in some pretty shitty conditions, but this bed is like the seventh level of hell," he continued.

"It's not ideal," I conceded, still fighting the bubble of giggles rising in my throat. My smile grew as I tipped my head up to him. I wiggled my body to try to find a more comfortable position. It didn't work.

"That's it," he said. "Get up. We're out of here." Lincoln popped off the bed, and I got a glorious view of his ass as he went searching for his boxer briefs.

"Where are we going?" I asked, sitting up.

"My place." He continued scooping up his clothes without looking back at me.

I scooted off the bed, tracked down my bra and underwear, and hastily threw on my clothes. "So . . . your place?" I asked.

"Yup."

"All right," I said, tucking a loose strand of hair behind my ear. *Oh god, I'm sure I have "just been fucked" hair.* I smoothed my hand over the rest of my ashy blond hair, trying to untangle it.

When I moved toward my shoes, he added, "Grab all of it. You and Bud aren't staying in this shithole anymore."

I raised an eyebrow at that.

"Listen," he added, "there are other empty cottages on the farm if you don't feel comfortable staying with me. But tonight, we're going home."

We're going home.

The words he used buzzed in my head and made me feel dizzy.

TWENTY-THREE

LINCOLN

My truck seat squeaked as I bounced along the dimly lit highway. I kept glancing into the rearview mirror to check on Joanna and make sure she was safely behind me as we made our way to the farm. She'd packed her things quickly and Bud loaded up into the cab of her truck.

I hadn't intended to invite her to stay with me, but lying in the shitty motel with its lumpy, worn bed and the musky old-lady smell overpowering the lush, citrus scent of her shampoo, I just couldn't stand the thought of her having to stay there a minute longer. There was an overwhelming desire to protect her taking root inside of me, and I wasn't sure what to do with that.

Leaving her in the parking lot after dinner was an idiotic thing to do, but now I was faced with the consequences of going back. I realized I had not only upended Joanna's plans, but my entire fucking life. Breathing heavily, I pulled into the gravel path that served as a driveway to my small cottage.

The farm was dark, making the Big House look a little more menacing than it did in the daytime. A small light in the window indicated old man Bailey was still awake. I would have to talk with him in the morning about our new guests.

Joanna's truck pulled up alongside mine, and she hopped out, Bud trailing happily behind her. I moved to the bed of the truck and hoisted her duffel bag and backpack out, carrying both.

"I can get those," she said.

I pinned her with a raised eyebrow.

With both hands up, she laughed. "Ok, ok." She laughed again, and my heart took a tumble in my chest. "I appreciate it."

I walked up to my front door and dug the key out of my jeans pocket. Once the door swung open, I realized that maybe I should *ask* her if she wanted to stay the night. Shifting on my heels, I said, "Uh . . . I haven't been in the other cottages in a while. I know for sure there are no clean sheets right now. We can stay here tonight, if that's okay with you."

"Great!" Her eyes beamed in the darkness. "I'm low maintenance. This works."

Low maintenance.

In my experience, most women who claimed to be low maintenance were the exact opposite of that. My eyes drifted up Joanna's shape when she walked past me into the darkness of the room and I actually believed her. I smiled to myself.

I'll take care of you.

I wasn't sure where that thought came from, but it wasn't entirely unwelcome. A tiny bud of warmth spread through my chest.

We settled in, and I gave her the grand tour, which

included me sweeping one arm wide and saying, "This is it."

Joanna chuckled softly. "It's great. Cozy."

"Can I get you a beer? Bourbon?"

"A bourbon on the rocks would be perfect," she said.

As I moved to the kitchen to pour us each a glass, I flipped on a radio—old country classics played quietly through the speakers. She moved toward the small wood-burning stove in the corner of the living room.

After tilting her head, Joanna started stacking wood inside the stove and gathered the tinder to start a fire. I loved that she was able and confident as the small flames flickered and splayed shadows across the walls.

After I handed her a glass, we sat on the couch near the fire, Joanna's legs tucked underneath her, her free arm propping her head up as she looked at me. My arm was stretched across the back of the couch, but we were at opposite corners and I fucking hated that.

I reached my hand toward her, and she stretched hers to meet me. "Get over here," I said softly.

Joanna scooted closer to me. For a few minutes, we were quiet, listening to the low hum of cowboy songs on the radio. My fingers traced the long line of her neck. I could feel the songs vibrate through her as she hummed along. She watched the small flames dance in the fire, and I took in her beautiful face. Her long lashes, full lips, hints of freckles across the bridge of her straight nose. I couldn't believe she was really here. This night had been incredible, and she was so much more than I could have ever imagined.

For years, I had been chasing a ghost, but here she was. *Real.* It felt overwhelming, confusing, and a little unsettling to think that a search I couldn't seem to get past would simply fade away.

But then there was everything else. *Everything* with Joanna was easy. I could talk to her, and I didn't really like talking to anyone. Feeling her body against mine felt like second nature. I found myself twirling a strand of her hair, listening to her humming when she tipped her face toward me and smiled.

"Can I ask you something?" she asked. When I nodded, she continued. "Do you ever get lonely out here?"

Taking a sip of my bourbon, I thought about her question. "Mostly I like being alone. But I do have Mr. Bailey to take care of. He's capable, but getting on in years. He needs help with maintenance around here, so I stay busy, and some nights we'll sit on his back porch and visit."

"He's lucky to have you," she added. I watched her mouth as she tipped her glass, the bob of her throat as she swallowed.

"I'm the lucky one," I said. "He let me stay here when I was determined to fuck up my entire life. He wouldn't let me bail on Mom or Finn but gave me a safe place to go crazy." I shifted uncomfortably. That was something I never talked about—I wasn't sure why I had just shared all of that —and part of me didn't want Joanna to know about the darkness that still crept over me at times.

She didn't press for more information. Instead, she smiled gently, inched a little closer to me, and we let the moment pass—for that I was grateful.

The music turned to a familiar honky-tonk ballad. The singer crooned a warning about not turning her blue eyes his way for fear she'd see how in love he was. That song got me in the gut every time I heard it.

I stood, holding out my hand to her. Joanna's elegant fingers slid across my palm as I pulled her into an embrace. I hovered over her, but dipped my head low and pressed my temple to hers.

We stood, swaying to the music, with the length of our bodies pressed tightly together. My hand on her lower back traveled lower as I began to murmur the words of the song in her ear, of course, changing the "blue eyes" lyric to green.

I tried to ignore the gnawing guilt as my thoughts flicked to Finn. I pushed it down and focused on the woman in my arms.

Her skin was warm and soft as I slipped a hand beneath the hem of her shirt. My cock pulsed to match the uptick of my heartbeat. She shifted her hips, pressing herself closer to me, feeling my length against her hip.

"Lincoln, I have to tell you something." Her voice was breathy and soft. "I've never been with anyone like you. It feels so good to feel you against me right now."

The corner of my mouth tipped up, and I gently pressed her against me. Her breath hitched. "Tell me."

Still swaying, she reached up to move her arms around my neck. Joanna dragged her fingertips across the backs of my shoulders. "These shoulders."

Her fingertip trailed a vein running down my bicep. "This vein." She continued burning a path of desire down my arm.

Yes. More.

"These forearms." When her hands met mine, I closed my eyes and breathed her in.

"These hands. I want your thick, rough hands all over me." She twined her fingers with mine. Hearing her give voice to her desire sent a flood of heat to my cock. It did not go unnoticed.

Joanna shifted her hips, pressing herself into my thickening erection. Her hand moved to find me hard and aching. She squeezed my cock through my jeans, and I nearly came.

Fucking rookie.

Her fingers moved to the button of my jeans, unfastening it. Her eyes flicked up to mine. "But this," her green-gray eyes never left mine as she slowly lowered my zipper, "this is what I want right now."

As Joanna slipped both hands around my ass and pushed my jeans down, I reached back to pull my shirt over my head. She toyed with the band of my boxer briefs before lowering them. My cock sprung out, and she filled her hand with me.

I moved my hand to her breast, finding her nipple round and hard. I grazed my thumb over the hard peak and she moaned as I pushed my hips forward, thrusting my cock into her hands.

"Fuck yes," I rasped, tilting my head back, enjoying the sensation of her strong hands gliding against my dick.

My eyes snapped open when I felt her move down, lowering herself to her knees. Joanna's eyes were full of mischief.

Holy shit. Yes, fuck, yes.

She nestled herself on the ground, and I shifted my weight, widening my hips for her. One hand raked up my stomach, teasing the trail of hair that extended from my belly button down to my cock. A tingle ran through me, and my dick jerked in response.

Joanna wrapped one hand around the base of my erection and leaned forward. Licking the crown, she swirled her tongue and then made one drag of her tongue up the base of my cock.

"You want that?" I asked, my voice low and deep.

"Fuck yes, I want this." She stroked with one hand as

she moved her tongue along the other side.

Taking me into her mouth, she moaned an *mmmm,* and the vibration radiated through me. I watched as she stroked and sucked. Seeing her lips wrapped around my cock was like a drug. I had to hold myself back from fucking that pretty mouth of hers rough and hard like my body was begging me to.

Joanna worked my dick. Too small to fit all of me, she licked and sucked and swirled while keeping a firm, pumping grip at the base. When she took me as deeply as she could and the tip of my cock hit the back of her throat, a rumbling moan escaped me.

She looked up at me again and licked my tip. One eyebrow raised, she took my hand in hers and gently guided it to the back of her head.

Oh, fuck.

Careful not to hurt her, I pumped my hips and held her head as she sucked harder and faster. I was rewarded with whimpers of pleasure. On the brink, I could feel my body tighten. I didn't want her to stop devouring me, and I also didn't want this to end. Joanna took me deep again, eyes up as I fisted her hair, and I felt her tight mouth around my cock.

I snapped.

Shifting back, I pulled my cock out of her mouth with a pop. Moving fast, I dropped down and shifted her kneeling body toward the couch.

Behind her, I pinned her upper body to the soft fabric and nipped her ear. "You like it rough and dirty? Or are you a good girl?"

"What do you think?" Challenge glowed in her eyes as she looked over her shoulder.

I moved my hands up her sides, pushing her shirt up so I

could lick and kiss and nibble the skin on her back. She groaned, encouraging me to keep going.

Removing her shirt and bra, I cupped her breast and pushed my dick into her jeans, pinning her body against the couch. I moved to push the jeans down, along with her underwear but didn't bother to take them completely off.

I grabbed the base of my cock and ran it up her seam. She was already wet, glistening against my taut skin.

"Take me, Lincoln. Own me." Her voice was thick.

I moved my cock down again, pressing the hard length against her clit, and it throbbed in response. Dragging it up to her entrance, I spread her open with the tip.

"More."

I gave another inch. Backed out.

"More, Lincoln."

Giving more, I teased her. She was primed and ready, and I wanted her to come before I completely unleashed on her. I used a finger to rub small circles around her clit, and her breath quickened, back tightened.

I pumped in a steady rhythm, but still not giving her my full length.

"Is this what you want?" I surged in and out.

"No. I want it all. I said give it to me."

With that, I pushed farther, spreading her pussy open and filling her with my cock. We both moaned in ecstasy. I watched my cock slip in and out of her while I played with her clit.

She panted and I stroked. I felt her muscles squeeze me tightly and release once. She was almost there. I was learning the rhythms of her body. Steadying my pace, I drew out her orgasm. When the clenching of her pussy was rhythmic and tight, I pumped harder, deeper.

"Yes, Lincoln, don't stop."

With one hand on her hip and the other between her legs, I pinched her clit between two fingers. A surge of wetness surrounded my cock as she came. She pulsed around me.

"Yes, Joanna. Fuck, yes." I came, surging into her until I was emptied. My body doubled over her back as we both regained our breath.

~

IN THE DARKNESS, the dying light of the dwindling fire spread a warm glow over Joanna's body. We'd never quite made it to the bedroom—instead, wrapped in blankets, we had fallen asleep on the couch. Well, she had, at least.

Joanna's warm body was tucked next to mine, and I traced circles over the curve of her shoulder. She drew deep, slow breaths, and the rhythm matched my own.

How easy could this be?

Joanna there with me felt so natural, but the buzzing just under my skin didn't let me rest. I couldn't risk falling asleep, having a nightmare, and scaring or even hurting her as I jerked awake, arms flailing. I wanted at least one day where she wouldn't see I was a total fucking lunatic. I wanted to live in this fantasy—where I was normal, and Joanna was mine.

I wondered if the nightmares would stop now that she was here. Breathing deeply, I brushed my lips over her hair, taking in her scent. I tilted my head backward, allowing rest, but not deep sleep, to take over me.

Stay here, in the moment, remember your training. Breathe. Once a Marine, always a Marine.

For the first time in my life, those words felt a lot less like a comfort and more like a curse.

TWENTY-FOUR

JOANNA

WITH A STIFF UPPER BACK, I shifted my weight on the couch.

Alone.

I knew Lincoln wasn't there as soon as I had enough sense to remember where I was at. I swung my legs over the side of the couch, sitting up and feeling a soreness between my legs that brought a playful smile to my lips. It had been the most incredible night.

Realizing I was awake, Bud yipped his usual "get your ass up and feed me" greeting. I kissed his sweet face, rubbing his ears, and stood.

In the small kitchen, I saw an empty coffee cup and underneath it, a little, handwritten note on a torn scrap of paper.

Went up to the Big House. Didn't want to wake you—you sure looked pretty.

-L

The flutter in my stomach danced, and I tucked the

note into my pocket. I made myself a hot cup of strong coffee, slipped on my boots, and wandered down the property toward the riverbank.

It was early, puffs of smoke rose from the house's chimney, and I pulled my jacket a little tighter across my chest. The wide expanse of the land hugged the farmette and sloped downward toward the river. It was peaceful, quiet. The call of a loon echoed across the water, adding an element of eeriness as the morning fog still clung to the water.

I found a large group of rocks by the water, sat, and hugged my legs to my chin as I sipped my coffee and looked out over the land.

This is the perfect spot.

A tug of envy pulled at me as I thought about how rare it would be to find a location like this—access to the river, space for lodging, a big, beautiful house. The large house here was far from beautiful, but beyond the chipped paint and busted windows, the large wraparound front porch reminded me of how grand it must have been in its former glory. With enough patience and love, it would have made an incredible location for an all-inclusive guide service.

I knew that soon I would have to decide where I was going to land, but Lincoln's words from last night echoed in my memory.

Please tell me you aren't leaving.

When he spoke those words, desperation thick in his voice, I couldn't deny him. I knew that staying was only temporary—temporary was all I ever had with men—but I was willing to see what staying with Lincoln meant.

"So, you're staying around then?" A gravelly voice from behind my back made me jump, and a splash of hot coffee plunked on my thigh.

Rubbing away the burn, I turned to see the hard lines of Mr. Bailey's face.

"Oh! Good morning," I fumbled. "Uh." I cleared my throat. "Yes, sir. If that's all right with you, that is."

He peered down at me; his green eyes were clear but held a hint of suspicion. "Makes no difference to me."

"Thank you, sir. I do appreciate it."

Mr. Bailey eyed me again before looking out onto the river. "You're Steve's granddaughter. Is that right?"

"Yes, Pop and I were very close." My voice was laced with sadness.

"He was a good man, honest. I recall a little girl following him around every summer with dirt on her hands and skinned knees. I figure that was you?"

At that, I laughed. "Sounds about right."

With a nod of his head, the conversation was over, and he turned to leave. I watched the man walk away slowly. Time had made his movements jerky, but he was still strong. Proud. My heart warmed to the crabby old man who remembered my Pop.

Pulling out my phone, I sent a quick text to Honey. We had *so* much to catch up on. She was expecting me back in Butte, but I had let her know that it would be at least a few days.

"There you are." Mid-text, Lincoln's voice had the tiny hairs on my neck standing up.

I looked up from my phone to see Lincoln, coffee in his hand, a smile on his lips, and his hair disheveled.

"Good morning." I arched my back to stretch again. Lincoln's eyes flicked down to my chest, but then he quickly found a stick and started tossing it to Bud, who happily retrieved it.

"I talked with the old man this morning." His eyes

tracked to Mr. Bailey who was almost to the Big House. "I let him know you and Bud will be staying on the property until you get settled. We're on our own for sheets though."

"That's not a problem. I can go into town and get anything I might need. I really do appreciate it." I toyed with the inside of my lip, looking down.

"What's wrong?" He took a tentative step toward me.

"No, it's nothing. I'm just wondering what rent might be to stay at the cottages. I have some money saved up, but wanted to be sure."

"Joanna, you're my guest here. No charge. As long as you'll stay."

It didn't go unnoticed that he'd used the words "as long as you'll stay" and not something like "as long as you need" or "for the weekend." Curious. Lincoln wasn't giving me much to go on so I would do what I could to be a good guest and not overstay my welcome. After all, he wasn't asking me to move in *with him*. He was just being kind and helping me so that I didn't have to stay in the dusky Chikalu Rose Motel longer than necessary.

"I have some things to take care of at the office. I need to see Finn . . ." Lincoln wasn't looking me in the eyes.

"Of course!" I said, my nerves making my voice a little too cheery. Clearing my throat gently, I took a breath and continued. "I have some things I need to take care of. I'll also get settled in one of the cottages. Does it matter which one?"

Lincoln reached into his pocket, revealing a small, brass key. "Cottage Two." He placed the key in my palm, letting our fingers touch, and a zip of heat ran through me.

"Neighbors, then." I winked at him.

He leaned down—arms at each side, caging me in—his delicious, masculine scent wafting over me. "I'm not sure you'll get a whole lot of use out of that cottage, but it's there if you need it."

I paused, breathing in his pine-and-campfire scent, closing my eyes. He tilted his head, kissed my cheek, and slowly retreated.

In a daze, I watched him swagger back up toward his cottage, admiring his thick legs and round ass. Damn, that man could wear a pair of jeans. I shook my head. So much had changed in just a few days. I brought my attention back to my text to Honey. Knowing I wouldn't be able to hide from all of her questions and that it would be easier to explain than text, I pressed *call* instead.

Honey was going to be more surprised than I was that I'd finally had the toe-tingling sex she was always bragging about.

WALKING down Main Street in Chikalu Falls, Montana was a masterclass in small-town living. From the old ladies in the beauty parlor to the coffee clutch of men outside the diner, the town swirled with charm. Whether it was my upbeat mood or the innocence of the kids zipping down the sidewalk on their scooters, I had a little pep in my step.

I had talked with Honey for a solid *hour* where she made me rehash the events of the past few days. I left out a few of the more intimate details. Barely.

After we chatted, I looked into Cottage Two and realized I was going to need a few things to make it habitable. A broom, for sure. And sheets. And disinfectant.

It was neglected and needed a deep clean, but overall, it was just as cozy as Lincoln's cottage and it was free. The fact that it was only steps away from Lincoln was also a major plus. I wondered how invested I should be about this cottage—would I be staying with Lincoln or expected to sleep at my own place?

Unsure of the details, I made my way down to the general store on the main drag of downtown. Sure, it would be a little more expensive than the big box store just outside of Chikalu, but I didn't mind if that meant I could meander through town at my own pace. Mr. Richardson, the elderly owner of the general store, even insisted his bag boy carry all of my items out to my truck. It was a simple, sweet gesture that kept the smile on my face all morning.

My thoughts kept returning to Lincoln. Jesus, that man could stir up all kinds of lustful feelings. Not really sure what to do with the rest of my day, I popped into a ladies' boutique on the corner.

The bell dinged at my arrival, but the only greeting I received was a "Morning, hun!" from somewhere in the back. The entire store smelled sweet but spicy, like a mix of vanilla and cinnamon. My tummy rumbled, and I wished for one of Honey's cinnamon rolls.

A woman in her sixties with permed brown hair and navy-blue eyeliner walked up as I softly touched a few silky, delicate blouses. Nothing in here was even close to the tees or canvas work shirts that lined my drawers.

"Hi and welcome to Blush Boutique. I'm Trina. What brings you in today?"

I smiled, nervously tucking a lock of hair behind my ear. "I'm really not sure, just browsing? You have lovely clothing."

"Well, I'm right around the corner. If you need anything, just holler."

I smiled politely, unsure of what I was even doing in a store like this. It was an eclectic mix of blousy tops, jeans with bedazzled back pockets, and chunky silver jewelry. My mother would be in heaven here.

A woman browsing clothes across from me caught my eye. I'd recognized her face, but couldn't place her name. She was around my age and lived in town with her daughter, who looked to be deep into the awkward phase of a preteen. When the woman caught me looking over, she smiled.

"Hey there," she said, moving toward me. "I'm Maggie. You're Finn's friend, right?" She walked to me, her daughter staying behind to look around.

"Jo." I smiled back. "Yes, Finn and I went to school together."

"That's right! You two were thick as thieves back then. Have you moved back to town?"

Her genuine warmth and kindness warmed me.

Yes.

The thought surprised me, unnerved me in such a simple moment.

"Oh, um, no," I stumbled, unsure of where that thought had come from. "You probably heard that Finn broke his leg. I'm just helping out while he's out of commission."

"I did hear that! It caused quite a stir around here. Ms. Millie said that she heard Finn broke it saving a baby who'd fallen into the river."

I had to laugh at that. "Fortunately for any babies around here, it was far less dramatic. He slipped." I shrugged.

We shared a laugh. "I figured as much. It was nice running into you, but we should get going. Good seeing you, Jo."

As Maggie left, a small pang of jealousy crept through me. Longing, maybe? I had never had many girlfriends and

Maggie seemed so nice. I knew she was a single mom, and if she was shopping here, maybe we didn't have that much in common, but simply talking with another woman felt really enjoyable.

I was ready to turn and leave when a small table of lacy lingerie caught my eye. It was tucked away in a back corner of the boutique. Moving closer, I eyed a few things, running my fingertips over the delicate edges.

"New love or old love?"

Blinking, I looked up at Trina.

"It'll influence what I recommend. Are you newly in love or looking to rekindle an old flame?" Trina winked at me.

A ribbon of heat wound around my chest.

"New," I answered. I glanced around to make sure that no one could hear me refer to Lincoln as a "new love."

"Well, then time for him to get to know you!" She laughed. "Don't be shy, honey, it's why I'm here. What are we going for? Sweet and sexy or red-hot heat?"

"Red hot," I blurted before I could even think about her question.

"That's my girl! You're going to want something over here then." She moved left. In front of her were tiny scraps of fabric, little bows, and straps that I wasn't quite sure how I'd get into.

A black lace balconette bra caught my eye. I picked it up and checked the sizing. Trina held up the matching panties—a tiny triangle of fabric with three thin black straps on each side that connected the front and back. Nothing but a slim line of black ribbon went up the back.

Desire pooled between my legs when I thought about Lincoln looking at me wearing nothing but the set. My ass would be out. *My whole ass.* I squeezed my thighs together to give myself a little tingly pressure.

"I'll take it."

After I paid, Trina folded the items in delicate tissue and tucked them into a small Blush Boutique bag. A trill of excitement ran through me—I couldn't wait to try them on.

"Have fun." She winked again. "Hope to see you soon, honey."

Clearly, I was being charmed by this small town, and I had forgotten how warm and welcoming it had always felt. It reminded me of what grandma Nana used to say—there were no strangers in Chikalu Falls, only friends you hadn't met yet.

After dropping off my bags, I spent the next hour or so tidying up the cottage, washing the new sheets, and arranging the bed. I bounced on the edge a few times—it squeaked a little, and I laughed to myself. I bet Lincoln and I could make a racket.

When I realized the fridge was unplugged, I was glad I hadn't gone to get groceries yet. I plugged it in and figured I could keep myself busy until it cooled down. I grabbed my fishing pole and walked a stretch up the river and tried my luck in the fading afternoon light. I still hadn't heard from Lincoln, so I decided to text Finn instead.

Me: What are you up to?

Finn: Slowly dying of boredom

Me: k

Finn: WOW

Me: haha. I'm out fishing by Mr. Bailey. No lunkers yet.

Finn: I thought you left town?

Me: Yeah . . . about that . . .

My phone immediately sprang to life. "Hey, Finn." I smiled into the phone.

"Dude."

"I know, I should have told you. Some...things... happened yesterday."

"Sounds like it." He didn't sound annoyed or upset, but curious.

"Lincoln and I ran into each other last night at the bar. We had dinner together." He didn't respond, so I kept going. "He insisted on driving me back to the motel. He didn't stay...but then he sort of came back?" The end raised like I was unsure.

"Huh. Well, that explains a lot, actually."

"What do you mean?"

"Lincoln's been completely out of his gourd today— walking around whistling, saying hi to people, being *pleasant*." The thought of Lincoln in a good mood because of me sent a ripple of goosebumps up my arm. "I swear to god that fucker has been mooning over you all day. I've been giving him dirty looks and mumbling shit in his direction because I thought the fucker was *happy* that you'd left town!"

A laugh bubbled out of me. "You're a good friend, Finn, but you can let him off the hook. We had a good time."

"So, now what?"

Yeah, Jo. Now what? Play house? For how long?

"Well, I'm not really sure. Lincoln talked to Mr. Bailey, and he's letting me stay in a cottage for a few days instead of the motel. Beyond that, I'm not really sure. But if you still need me, I can help with a few guide tours."

"Fuck yeah, I need you! I'm pumped you're staying around! Let's do dinner tonight, we'll plan it all out."

We hung up, and I spent the next several casts thinking

about what Finn had said. Lincoln was happy because of *me*? How long could I stay right next door to him and pretend I wasn't totally falling for him? Moody, broody, sexy guys were way out of my depth. What if this was just a weekend fling for him? Pushing away the nagging thoughts, I was determined to relax and enjoy my time in Chikalu.

I refused to think this oddly felt like coming home.

TWENTY-FIVE

LINCOLN

ALL DAY I FELT GREAT. Fucking *fantastic*.

The sun was warming the mountain air, and the skies were clear. It would be a great day to help outfit some new fishermen. Fisherwomen. All people interested in fishing.

I'd even booked a guide tour when a dad came in with his two sons, looking for some new equipment. They'd just moved to Canton Springs, a town over. I popped my head into Finn's office to tell him. He looked up from his phone, mumbled something that sounded an awful lot like, "Big fucking deal," and continued working.

What the fuck was his problem?

Maybe he knows.

I swallowed hard, knowing I needed to clear the air with my brother. I was determined to tell him I had very real, very deep feelings for the woman he was in love with. Finn didn't make it easy on me—he'd been giving me the cold shoulder, hobbling around me in his walking cast, barely making eye contact. When he did, he could have frozen hell with the glares he shot my way.

Work consumed me all day. Energy buzzed through me,

making me more productive than I had been in months. Files that needed to be made, calls to vendors, follow-ups with potential clients. When I sat back from my desk, I breathed out. I felt good—productive and content. I was also really fucking excited to see Joanna again.

I was about to call her and see if she wanted to have dinner with me when Finn's large frame filled my office door. His face was noticeably kinder.

"Hey, Linc. I just got off the phone with Jo. Wanna grab some dinner later?"

"Uh, yeah, of course." I frowned a little at my phone. I was really hoping to take her out on a real date, but Finn and Joanna were close, and if I was going to make this work, I had to accept that.

"I was thinking maybe tacos at Robles, yeah?"

I nodded at him, still unsure about this Jekyll-and-Hyde routine he was putting me through.

He moved to leave but paused. "Sorry I was pissy today. Misunderstanding." He stepped away with a soft *thunk* of his walking cast.

Misunderstanding? What had he and Joanna talked about?

Unsure if I was supposed to drop it or mystically know what the fuck he was really crabby about earlier, I decided to let it go for now. Finn and I could work out our bullshit over a few beers. But not tonight.

"HOLY BALLS, THIS IS GOOD," Finn mumbled around a mouthful of tamales. Robles hummed around us with the chatter of a busy restaurant.

"Mmm-hmm," Joanna agreed with a closed-lipped

smile. A little mouthful of food pushed out her cheek, and she nodded in agreement. *So fucking cute.* She had ordered tacos al pastor. And beans and rice. And a tamale. I smiled to myself, loving that she had an appetite.

The place had a steady business, but we were able to get a small booth within a few minutes. Finn had folded his large frame, tucking himself into one side. I slid in across from him.

Without hesitation, Joanna leaned left, scooting herself next to me in the booth. My body warmed at her closeness.

Joanna and Finn started working out some details about the upcoming guided tours. None of them were particularly demanding—all were easy day trips along the river.

I usually didn't handle the customer side of guiding—I was much happier handling the business and limiting my interactions with the public. Finn's personality was much better suited to schmoozing guests. He cared a lot about making each trip memorable, and he was the face of the business, without a doubt.

Leaning over their plates, they conspired over secret access points along the river, new places they needed to check out, where fishing had been hot in the weeks before.

Finn slid his leg out, rubbing his calf against mine. My eyes flicked up, meeting his as we both jerked our legs back.

"Sorry, dude." Finn tipped his chin and cleared his throat. A smile quirked the corner of his mouth.

Is he trying to play footsie with Joanna?

I sat up a little straighter in the booth, tilted my body slightly closer toward Joanna as she stifled a small giggle.

"I can pay a visit to Mr. Johnston. Maybe I can sweet-talk him into letting us try his leg of the riverbank. With only three people, I don't think he'll put up much of a fuss," Joanna said.

"That's brilliant." Finn's eyes sparkled at her.

As they continued plotting, I was happy enough to get a good look at this beautiful woman beside me. Even in a whisper, her voice was confident, strong. I watched her full lips as she conspired with Finn. Enthusiasm radiated through her, and the buzz it gave her had a leg bouncing under the table. Unable to resist, I tipped my hips open slightly, allowing my thigh to rub against the outside of hers.

She stilled, without breaking the conversation, and pressed her leg into me. A ribbon of heat wound up my leg and settled between my thighs. I could feel my cock thicken.

Heat crept up my neck as I tried not to think about how Joanna's trim body felt pressed under me. With Finn here, and in a public restaurant, I needed to focus on something other than the way she made my blood run hot.

Feeling bolder, I scrubbed my palms over my thighs, leaving my right hand below the table. I slowly moved it over, finding the outside of Joanna's thigh. Gently, I inched my fingers over her muscled thigh and slowly dragged my hand along the outside edge of her leg. When I glanced at her, I saw the pulse in her neck quicken and felt her leg press farther into my palm. With a squeeze just above her knee, I ran my hand up her delicious thigh again before bringing my hands above the table.

This incredible woman is going to be the death of me.

That was for damn sure.

Needing to stretch, I excused myself to use the bathroom.

Walking back, I noticed that the restaurant's dinner crowd had filled in and the ambient noise was rising steadily. Forks clanked, glasses wobbled, a barking laugh from a table in the back. Without warning, tension wound around my neck, and a buzzing filled my ears. I suddenly felt hotter, and my chest got tight. Behind me, a server bobbled her tray, and when it came crashing to the ground, I almost fucking lost it.

I stormed past Joanna and Finn in the booth, bumping into Fred Castle as he was standing, and headed straight outside to the truck without a word to anyone.

Don't let her see you lose your shit.

Sucking in air, I was bent over, hands on my knees behind my truck. I felt like I was trying to breathe through a straw, and panic rose in my gut.

Don't let her see you lose your shit. Don't fucking do it.

My heart was pounding, and small black dots began to fill my vision. My feet felt tingly, and I knew if I didn't get myself under control, I would pass out in the middle of the parking lot like an asshole.

I felt a wide palm between my shoulder blades and heard Finn's deep voice in my ear. "Breathe, two-three-four. Hold, two-three-four. Out, two-three-four. C'mon, man. You gotta do it with me. Breathe, two—"

I focused on Finn's voice, trying to follow his commands. This wasn't the first time Finn had been around when I lost my shit. He knew that the breathing technique was about the only thing that was going to pull me out of it. My chest heaved and finally—*finally*—I got a breath that felt deep. After a few more rounds of breathing with Finn, the spots moved out of my vision, and I didn't feel like I was quite so deep underwater.

I straightened with Finn at my side.

"You got it, man. You're all right," he said.

I nodded as he pulled me into him, clamping down hard on my shoulder.

"I left Jo inside," he said. "I figured you didn't want her seeing this if it got really bad."

Really bad. Finn had been around enough to see a full-fledged panic attack, and it wasn't ever pretty. Usually, it meant me freaking the fuck out and tearing out of wherever we were, desperate to get away. Once, it'd happened at The Pidge and I ended up coldcocking some guy who didn't move out of the doorway fast enough. Definitely not one of my finer moments. Thankfully, these episodes were pretty rare.

"I appreciate that."

"What happened, Linc?"

"I'm not sure. I just wanted to stretch my legs and then everything seemed really loud and close and...fuck. I don't know, man." I hung my head. A tension settled between my shoulder blades, and I knew I'd be tight for a few days after that.

"All right. You good?"

"Yeah, thanks."

"'Course. You know I've got you."

A rocky lump formed in my throat as I looked at my little brother, and I fought hard to swallow it down. When I left, he'd been such a wide-eyed little kid. In the years I'd been back, I realized how much he'd grown, changed. That little kid was gone, but in his place stood a man who was strong and kind and loved by everyone in this town.

I was the damaged one—too fucked up to manage even a simple dinner in town. Plus, the fact that he'd protected Joanna from my meltdown had grateful tears burning at the edges of my eyes. I squeezed my hand tighter on Finn's shoulder and cleared my throat.

Another few deep breaths and I saw Joanna push the

door open and walk out into the parking lot. Her brow was furrowed, and she searched my face for answers. I couldn't look her in the eye—fucking coward.

"Hey." Her eyes were still seeking mine. "Toss me the keys. I'll drive."

TWENTY-SIX

JOANNA

THE ENTIRE CAR ride back to the farm, Lincoln quietly stared out of the passenger window. I flipped on the radio to break the silence and give him a little space.

From the restaurant window, I had seen Lincoln bent over near the back of his truck. When I sprang up to go to him, Finn pleaded with me to stay behind.

"Let him save face," Finn begged me.

Afterward, I wasn't sure exactly what happened, but I assumed it was a panic attack. Did he get those often? Was this a bad one or did they get worse?

A tug at my heart had me chewing my lower lip. Assuming Lincoln didn't want to talk about it—he definitely seemed like the "bury that shit and pretend it didn't happen" type—I hummed along to the radio and moved my right hand absently up and down his muscular forearm.

It took until the turn into Mr. Bailey's expansive driveway to feel the tension drain from Lincoln's body.

Parking his truck next to mine, I flipped the key to off and turned my body toward Lincoln. "Want to see what I did to Cottage Two or did you want some time alone?"

Lincoln looked at me like he was confused. His cobalt eyes roamed my face, and when he cleared his throat, a little playfulness was back in his voice. "I'd love to see it."

Together we walked toward my cottage, and Lincoln surprised me by running his hand down my forearm, twining his fingers through mine. The warmth of his palm coursed through me, and I felt my center tighten. I leaned my shoulder closer to him.

I unlocked the door and let Bud zip past us, barking wildly. I laughed as he yipped and circled the cottage. He really loved exploring the open space here.

Stepping into the cottage, I flipped on the small kitchen light. It illuminated the tiny space, and I smiled widely. The floors were peeling at the corners but shined, and there wasn't a speck of dust anywhere. I had even found a small mason jar and filled it with white and purple wildflowers to put on the table. Although it was quaint, I found it quite charming.

"This looks great, Joanna." His voice was still thick and slightly heavy.

"I think so," I breathed out. "I love the bay window that looks out onto the water. That's definitely my favorite part." I moved toward the window to see Bud chasing a squirrel, and I stifled a laugh when he stumbled over his own four feet.

Lincoln moved behind me, pressing his muscular body against my back. The hard ridges of his abs and hips pushed against me as I leaned back and tilted my head to the side.

His nose moved up my neck, taking in my scent. A warmth pooled between my legs, and I pressed my thighs together. This man, with his earthy, pine scent, was heaven.

"You turned a dirty, dark space into something beautiful. Do you always see the good in everything?"

I considered his words. "There's always good inside." I shrugged. I wasn't sure if we were still talking about the cottage, but the words rang true.

"I hope so," he whispered. Lincoln moved his mouth over my neck, pressing soft, teasing kisses against my skin.

A gentle groan escaped me as his kisses ignited my desire. I turned to face him. His large frame loomed over me in the dimly lit cottage, and I could see his dark brow was still tight and furrowed. His shoulders hung heavy. Lincoln pressed his forehead to mine.

"My second favorite part of the cottage is the tub," I said. "You look like you could use a soak."

"Hmmph. Is that right?" His voice was low.

"Let's start a fire here, maybe have a little wine, and take a dip. What do you think about that?"

Lincoln pulled his arms tighter around my waist, breathing deeply. A rumble rolled through his chest, and it vibrated through me.

I lifted my hand to his face, searching his eyes. I brushed my thumb over the crease in his brow and placed a kiss on his cheek before moving toward the bathroom.

With the water as hot as I could stand it, I added the Epsom salts I used to ease my achy muscles and some bubble bath I picked up earlier in town while Lincoln let Bud back into the cottage.

I slipped out of my clothes, desperately wishing I had changed into the sexy lingerie I had purchased. As I was pulling the shirt over my head, Lincoln stepped into the bathroom with a bottle of Shiraz and two plastic cups. His hungry eyes roamed over my body. The intense stare should have made me feel self-conscious, but from him, I felt beautiful, desired.

Without taking his gaze from me, Lincoln set down the

wine and unfastened his pants. He let them slip to the floor. The intimate gesture of undressing while I watched him had a bead of heat trickling down between my shoulder blades.

His wide palms ran down the hard edges of his abs as he slipped them below the waistband of his black boxer briefs. His thick cock sprang free, and it took everything inside of me not to break down right there and beg for it.

Finding my courage, I walked toward him and lifted a hand to his chest. Circling around him and getting more than an eyeful of his glorious, muscular body, I asked, "Big spoon or little spoon?"

His head turned to the side, and he looked at me quizzically. "Um...I don't think I've ever been any kind of cutlery." He groaned as my hand flitted over his hard length but not giving him the grip he desired.

Clearly, this man had never been cuddled, and that was a travesty.

"Ok, big guy, get in. You get to be the little spoon." A smile played at my lips as I slapped his ass. I had no idea where this brazen, confident woman was coming from, but I loved her.

With a hearty laugh, Lincoln carefully stepped into the warm, bubble-filled tub. The tub itself was old and tiny, his large frame taking up most of it, knees poking up out of the water. I slipped in behind him, settling into the back curve of the tub.

I reached forward, pulling the expanse of his torso against my breasts. My nipples peaked with pleasure, and the sly smile he shot me over his shoulder let me know it did not go unnoticed.

We sat in comfortable silence for a few moments, letting the heat and steam soak into our bodies. Lincoln ran his hands up the sides of my calves while I leaned my head against the back of his shoulder. I felt his body release more of the tension he had been carrying, and I breathed in his masculine scent.

I trailed my wet fingers up the side of his torso, and he sucked in a quick breath, his abs flexing tightly.

"Ticklish?" I grinned.

"Maybe just a little," he admitted.

I continued tracing the broken lines of the tattoos and scars that wrapped around his ribs and up his back.

"You can ask about it, you know." I could feel his deep voice rumble through his back and into me.

I thought carefully. His ribs, torso, thigh, back, and arm were dotted with long, deep linear marks and even more short, oval scars. In the closeness of the bathtub, I could see how the scars even ran up the side of his neck, disappearing into his hairline. I pressed a kiss to the back of his neck at one of the deepest marks.

After a moment, I answered. "I only need to know what you want to share."

He exhaled deeply. "That's the problem," he said. "You make me want to tell you everything."

At his words, I pulled him closer into me, wrapping my legs around his trim waist.

"Ok then." I circled a finger around the unreadable script running down his bicep. "What did this say?"

His hand covered mine, pressing it into his skin. "It's actually something my dad said to me once." His voice was quiet, and I stayed still, hoping he'd continue.

"It used to say, 'Nothing you could ever do.' Once, I had talked to Dad about some of the shit I had gotten into overseas. Nothing really specific, but he knew it was hard on me, on all of us. He once told me, 'Nothing you could ever do would make me love you any less.' I don't know...that just really stuck with me."

"That's beautiful." Hot tears filled my eyes, and I pushed my tongue to the roof of my mouth to keep them from spilling. "I met him, you know. He was such a kind man." I turned my cheek onto Lincoln's shoulder.

When he tilted his head toward me, I continued. "When I was in college with Finn, the year before he died, I was over a lot for dinners and we'd go fishing, that kind of thing. Your dad was the one who taught me the Albright knot. I use it all the time and think of him. He was so proud of you, Lincoln."

He rubbed my arm, pulling it closer to his body. "It helped to have a piece of him with me, especially after his heart attack. That's what most of these tattoos were— symbols, words...pieces of people important to me, people who helped me get out of there alive."

Lincoln's soapy hand covered mine, sending a warm flutter across my chest. Then, he flipped his hand over, resting his exposed forearm across mine on his stomach.

"This one," he tipped his head toward the marred, barely recognizable Valkyrie wings tattoo, "meant the most to me." He shifted his body slightly so that he could look right at me.

"Joanna," he continued, "I kept every letter that you wrote to me."

"You did?" I could hardly get the words out—hardly believe them—but my heart beat faster at his words.

"I did. But when you wrote and told me the story of the Valkyrie, I knew I had to keep a piece of you with me. The first leave after that, I found a tattoo shop."

Biting my lip, I summoned all of the bravery I could. "Why haven't you gotten any of the tattoos fixed?"

Lincoln breathed out. "I looked into it. Tattooing over scars can be difficult and spotty at best. But now, I figure it's just a reflection of who I am."

"It's not your whole story, Lincoln. You need to remember that," I said. With every wet kiss along his neck, I needed him to feel the emotions pouring out of me. I couldn't keep telling myself that this was a girlhood crush anymore. I was falling hard and fast for this man and I wanted all of him—broken, scarred, funny, kind—all of it.

Lincoln moved his hand to my face, kissing me gently. His kiss deepened, and my entire body lit up with desire. Who was this woman? This woman who had a sexy-as-hell man *naked,* having a hot bathtub make-out session? Grabbing my newly found boldness, I moved my hips to the side so I could slide myself out from behind Lincoln.

I shifted my leg over him, straddling him. Through the warm water, I felt the thick length of his cock move between the lips of my pussy. I shifted, dragging my slit against him, and was rewarded with a deep moan while he deepened the kiss.

I may not have been the kind of woman that men desired, but I had him here now and I was damn sure not going to spend time thinking about that.

"Lincoln," I breathed, "I want you inside me."

On a growl, he dragged me up with him, out of the bathroom, and tossed me on the bed.

"We really need to start thinking about drying off before we have sex again." Playful Lincoln was back.

I looked around at the soaked-through sheets and

touched my wet, matted hair. Laughter rippled through me. "You're probably right about that."

Still out of breath, Lincoln rolled onto his back, taking me with him. Our wet bodies were still pressed together, and I felt his hard length against my belly. Insatiable.

"Good thing we have my place," he said. "Want to get some rest?"

I nodded, gathered up my clothes, and followed Lincoln back to his cottage. All the while, I couldn't wipe the love-struck grin off my face. I could get used to being tucked under his strong arms every night.

With the tension from the day finally gone from Lincoln's body, I listened to his slow, steady breaths as he fell asleep. I tightened my eyes, wishing this moment could stretch on forever.

TWENTY-SEVEN
LINCOLN

I WOKE UP WITH A START, my skin hot and sticky. I hadn't remembered falling asleep, but Joanna's soft, steady breathing was a stark contrast to my short, rasping breaths. At my jolt, Joanna shifted slightly, but didn't awaken.

Thank fuck.

The delicate strands of her dark blond hair were splayed out behind her, and her cheek was pressed against my shoulder. Her skin felt warm and smooth against me, her thigh hitched up across my body.

I had never had a woman draped over me—I had never been a cuddler—and I couldn't help but feel like it wouldn't feel right unless it was with her. I pushed that thought down, stayed focused on the present. If I was going to make it through every day, I couldn't focus on her leaving or, worse, wanting her to stay.

Despite my restlessness, Joanna stayed tight against me, her hand across my chest.

This woman was definitely getting under my skin. I could feel something creeping in. For years, she took up space in my brain, but now she was in my work, my home—

and fuck—rooting and taking hold in my heart. When I thought about meeting Joanna from the letters, I never expected *her*.

Not only was she a knockout—her green-gray eyes and full lips always seemed to be smiling—but she was capable and strong and sweet. She had no use for a fucked-up basket case who felt an overwhelming *need* to protect her. She could do just fine on her own. And soon she would be leaving, back to her old life, once Finn was healed up.

I clenched my jaw and worked my fist open and closed, trying to release the building tension. Anger bloomed in my chest at the thought of her leaving. I took a deep inhale of her citrus scent and willed myself to get a grip. This incredible woman deserved so much more than I could ever offer her.

But right then, in that moment, I pulled her even closer to me, nuzzling my nose into her hair. I may not be able to have her forever, but I could pretend tonight that I could.

THE WEEKS PASSED SWIFTLY as we settled into a comfortable routine. Most days, Joanna filled in for Finn—guiding groups and keeping customers supremely happy. Recently, people started asking for her by name, and I felt a swell of pride every time that happened.

Nights were always spent together, either her cottage or mine. After two weeks, we stopped pretending like we weren't going to end up falling asleep together, and that was the end of that ridiculous nightly discussion.

Every morning, I made us coffee before my run, and by the time I got back, Joanna had made us both breakfast—

usually eggs and toast or muffins she said her sister taught her to make.

I tried to ignore the nagging shadows that hung in the corners of my thoughts. Finn was cleared from his walking cast on Thursday, and once he was up and moving, Joanna would be free to leave. We both avoided that conversation completely, pretending everything was normal. She stole the breath out of my lungs without even trying, and I walked around with a hole in my chest, pretending it wasn't there.

The more I pushed it away, the darker and more frequent the nightmares became. Acrid smoke filled my nose and lungs, choking me. Just out of reach, always, was Joanna—my Valkyrie. In my dreams, I strained, begged for her, but she would never take me. In the darkness, when I tried to calm my breath without waking Joanna, I thought back to her letters. It was only then I realized exactly why my dreams were playing out in a horrible, repetitive pattern.

The Valkyrie only take the *worthy*.

"Hey, handsome." Joanna ruffled my hair and dropped a kiss on the top of my head.

Before she could get away, I grabbed her wrist, pulling her down onto my lap with a squeal from her. "Not so fast, sugar."

My hand moved to her hip, squeezing her ass, and my dick got hard under her weight. Joanna tipped her lips down to mine, her hands on the sides of my face. I wrapped my arms around her torso and pulled her closer to me. Deepening the kiss, I swiped my tongue over hers and groaned. I could taste the cinnamon-flavored coffee on her lips.

"Fuck, you taste good. Let's play hooky today."

"Mmmm." She groaned through our kiss. "Can't. My boss is a real grouch."

I shifted my weight and pulled Joanna across my lap so she was straddling me. Tilting my hips up, I showed her exactly why I wanted her to stay home with me today.

"You are a hard man to say no to." She circled her hips into me.

"I can show you hard." I stood, keeping my mouth on hers, and lifted her with me. I turned and placed her ass at the edge of the countertop, spreading her legs wider with my hips.

Joanna wound her arms around my neck and arched her back, flattening her breasts against my chest. God, I loved how she responded to me.

I moved my hand up, my thumb brushing against the curve of her full, round tits. Slanting my kiss over her neck, I brushed my thumb against her hard nipple. My cock twitched in response.

"I need you, Joanna." My words were barely out before she pulled open the front of her shirt, exposing her bra. Through the flimsy material, I sucked one hard, pebbled nipple into my mouth and was rewarded with her throaty gasp.

Needing pressure, I stroked my rock-hard cock through my jeans from base to tip. Everything inside of me wanted to be buried in Joanna, but I urged myself to slow down. I wanted her to feel the incredible power she held over me.

Trailing wet kisses down her ribs and over her exposed belly, I licked and sucked a path to her center. With a tug, I pulled her pants down her hips. I nearly lost my fucking mind when I saw that her underwear was already wet with her arousal. Teasing the edge of the fabric, I brushed my fingers against her sensitive skin.

Slipping my middle finger under the edge of the fabric, I caressed her folds. Teasing her slit, I kissed lower, finding her apex through her underwear. With a gentle nibble, I teased her clit, and she grabbed my hair with a gasp.

Smiling, I looked up at Joanna—her mouth was open, entranced, and her eyes were filled with desire. "Let me taste this pretty pussy, baby. You have no idea how badly I want you."

I slipped one thick finger into her center and felt her walls clamp down on me. My dick was begging to slam into her and chase its release, but I had the overwhelming desire to taste her orgasm on my tongue.

I grabbed the waist of her underwear and slid them down her legs. "Keep your legs here," I instructed, placing her legs on each of my shoulders. "Hold on."

With that, I lowered my head again, breathing in her heady, sensual scent. With a long, flat drag of my tongue, I stroked up her pussy. She tilted her hips forward, begging for more.

Giving my girl exactly what she needed, I devoured her. My fingers played with her folds before pushing into her center as I sucked on her throbbing clit. Her grip in my hair stung but sent a hot bolt of heat between my legs. I needed her to come.

Like a starving man, I reveled in her taste—teasing, sucking, groaning into her. When her legs stiffened, I knew she was at the peak. With two fingers, I pushed into her again, crooked them forward, and stroked her. Joanna pulled my face deeper between her legs. I happily lapped at her clit and gave it a gentle bite. She exploded around me. I continued my assault as her pussy pulsed against my tongue and I nearly came right there with her.

Joanna was panting, and her body went slack. I stood, wrapping her legs around my waist.

"I got you, baby," I said as I held her to me. With one hand, I pulled down my jeans and rubbed the tip of my swollen cock up and down her soaked folds. The tension rising in my balls was too intense, so I surged into her and ground out her name.

"Yes, Lincoln. Fuck yes. Please."

With a steady rhythm, I held her—one arm around her waist, while the other held her legs to me. Pumping into her, I felt her tight, slick walls squeeze me over and over. With long, hot spurts, I emptied myself inside of her as she clung to me.

I love you. I love you. I love you.

Over and over, the words tumbled through my mind. I would never be the same without Joanna.

TWENTY-EIGHT

JOANNA

BLOWING out a breath that lifted the front tendrils of my hair, I looked down at my buzzing phone. Finn was late—again—so I wasn't entirely surprised. I tapped my phone and placed it to my ear without a greeting. A smile played at my lips as I wondered what random excuse he had today.

"Banana!"

"You are entirely too chirpy for this early in the morning. Plus, you're late."

"I know. I got tied up. Literally."

"Literally?" I asked.

"Well, I was doing the tying but yeah. It was a good night." His deep laugh ended with a sigh.

I rolled my eyes. Only Finn could find yet another kinky hookup *and* manage to keep it a secret in this small town. "Ok, stud. Can you at least bring me a fresh coffee on your way out?"

"Here's the deal, babes...Linc texted me after you left and asked if I could swing by the office. Can you handle this morning solo?"

I closed my eyes, feeling a small build of tension behind

them. It was hard to get enough sleep when you were next to someone who smelled and felt as good as Lincoln. I was insatiable and constantly ravaged his willing, eager body. But I couldn't take my lack of sleep out on my best friend.

"Yep. It's a twosome. I'll manage."

"Thank you, Joanna Banana. You're the best. And hey..." He paused. "I think it's time to tell him."

"He loves you. It'll be a good thing—for the both of you. I promise," I reassured him.

We hung up, and I couldn't help but be proud of Finn. Telling Lincoln was the last step in coming out completely. He was utterly comfortable with who he was, but there was still a large part of him that was nervous to talk to his big brother. Lincoln was stoic and could be intimidating, for sure, but I could see how much they loved each other. I knew in my heart that Lincoln was a good man who would only want his brother to be happy. It would be fine.

What was not fine, however, was the fact that I had to solo guide two of the most obnoxious guests I'd had in months. Pulling my ponytail through the back of my cap, I breathed out, "Here we go."

"Hey, check out that ass," one mumbled under his breath to his equally foul friend.

With my back to them, I rolled my eyes so far up into my skull it was a wonder they could look straight again.

"See if she needs your pole," the second responded with a snicker and a tug at the front of his pants.

Standing, I chirped, "Ok, fellas, we're all set!" I handed each of them a newly strung fishing pole, quickly explained a basic cast—again—and stepped back.

First of all, they were disasters, unwilling to listen to any of the advice I was trying to dole out. If I suggested a step upstream, Todd didn't like the rocks. If I wanted to try new bait, Stan didn't like the color. I seriously could not win with those two.

As the morning dragged on, my jaw ached from clenching my teeth. I glanced at my watch. Less than an hour or so to go.

The sun was rising higher, slanting warm afternoon light onto the river and making it too bright for decent fishing.

"We might want to call it a day," I offered, my hand shielding my eyes from the glittering sunlight. "Without any cloud coverage, the fish tend to go into hiding. It'll be a hard go from here on out."

"Are you fucking serious?!" Todd responded.

"Yeah, that's the way it goes sometimes. But we had some decent catches, don't you think?" I was determined to stay upbeat.

"Man, this is fucking stupid," he replied. Todd took a deep pull from a flask I hadn't noticed earlier and passed it to his friend.

My ears pricked as I glanced around our very hidden, very remote setting.

Fuck. Why did I agree to let Bud stay with Lincoln today?

"I'm sorry if you're unhappy with how it went today." I bent down to remove my waders and gather our gear into my backpack. As I glanced over the clear riverbed, I could see Todd's reflection on the water. He was standing behind me, too close, pretending to grab my hips and thrust himself forward and back.

I stood and pinned him with a glare. "Time to go."

"Aww, come on, sweetheart. Don't be like that." He stepped forward, and I instinctively mirrored his movement backward. Stan moved right until he flanked me. My spine stiffened, and my heartbeat ticked up.

"I said it's time to go." I willed my voice to be steady and strong, but it betrayed me and cracked on the last syllable. Clearing the tightness in my throat, I moved to push past Todd.

As I side-stepped him, he reached out a wide, dirty palm and wrapped his calloused hand firmly around my upper arm, pulling me into him.

"I'll say when this is over." The sharp liquor smell rolled off his tongue and burned my nose as he brushed the back of his hand up the side of my breast.

Stan scrubbed his palms up and down his thighs, grinning, as I tried to yank my arm free.

"Get your hands off of me." My voice raised in panic with every word, but I couldn't wrench my arm from his tightening grasp.

"Stan, you keep an eye out, I'm gonna teach this girl some manners." The gleam in Todd's eyes as they moved across my body rolled my stomach. He yanked my arm again as I strained away from him.

Ears ringing and my vision going hazy, I brought my knee up and swiftly connected with his balls.

Todd let loose a guttural heave and doubled over in front of me. Without looking back, I tore down the path, running as quickly as my legs could carry me.

My boots felt like they were filled with cement and my lungs burned sharply, but I didn't stop. I ran and ran until the glint of the afternoon sun winked off the bumper on my truck.

Pulling open the door, I got in, closed the door, and

slammed my hand down on the lock. I tipped the visor down and dropped the keys into my lap. With shaking hands, I fumbled, dropping them to the floor.

"Fuck!" I shouted.

I glanced at the rearview mirror but didn't see anyone else exiting the wooded path leading to the river. Taking one steadying breath, I tried the keys again, and when the truck roared to life, I slammed it into reverse, tearing across the grass toward the road and out onto the highway.

"GLAD YOU COULD FINALLY grace us with your presence."
I smirked at my younger brother as he sauntered into work,
hours late.

"I had some things to work out. Besides, Jo said she
could handle the morning tour."

I nodded, but something pricked at the back of my neck
that I couldn't quite place—an itch that you couldn't find
when you went to scratch it. I lifted my phone and tapped
out a message to Joanna.

Me: All good?

I frowned at the screen when several minutes passed
without a reply. Something gnawed at my gut, so I flipped
back through the books to see who was scheduled for today.

"Todd Bender and Stan Ellis. You know 'em?" I asked,
tapping the names on the ledger.

Finn shook his head. "Nah. I don't think so. One's a
mechanic over in Canton Springs, maybe? Why?
What's up?"

I shook my head again and flipped the book closed. I recalled the men who checked in at the office. I gave them directions to the meet-up site and didn't give it a second thought.

"I don't know." I rounded my desk and walked past Finn to the coffeemaker. I poured myself another black cup and stared into the inky liquid, leaning against my desk.

I pushed the uneasy feeling away and focused on my brother. Today was an important day. I needed to tell Finn that I was falling in love with Joanna.

And while I wasn't sorry about it, I wanted to acknowledge his feelings. I wanted us to be able to move past it. I knew I didn't deserve her, but I would try like hell to be a good and honorable man for her. Part of that meant facing my brother, his crush on her, and probably taking a fist to the jaw over it.

"Lincoln. There's something we need to talk about." When Finn started with my full name, my thoughts stuttered.

"Yeah, I think so too." I felt my chest whump once as I placed my coffee cup down with a hard snap and stood—chin up, chest out, shoulders back, stomach in.

"Ok, so here's the deal," Finn started as he ran a hand across the back of his head. "I realized a few things while you were gone, and I've never had the balls to talk to you about it, but—"

Our heads flicked toward the entrance as a wild-eyed Joanna bustled through the main door. She looked at me, then Finn, before leaning hard against the wall.

Instinctively, I moved for her as her legs wobbled. I wrapped my hands around her arms to steady her and pulled her into my chest. I could feel her heartbeat rabbiting against her ribs.

"Baby, what's wrong?" I demanded.

"I...I don't know. I just..."

Finn moved to her side, placing his palm between her shoulder blades. "Jo, what happened?" Finn's voice was laced with panic as he searched her face.

Joanna huffed out a breath in an attempt to steady herself. She didn't lift her eyes from my boots. "Something happened," she started.

Alarm bells clanged in my skull, but I leveled my breathing.

She continued. "I don't know. I just got scared."

I tightened my grip on her, and she winced. I lengthened my arms so I could look at her and swept my hands inside her jacket, pulling it down her arms. Just above one elbow, a fresh, angry bruise bloomed. Clear indentations of fingertips dotted her inner arm.

"Who the *fuck* did this to you?"

"Holy shit, Jo."

Our voices tangled over each other.

Crimson seeped into my vision as I stepped away from her and yanked my keys from the top of my desk. Finn pulled Joanna into him, running a comforting hand down her back as I strode past them, my mouth in a hard line.

Finn shouted something at me, but I didn't listen. There were only a few places a piece of shit could go in the middle of the day in this town. If they were still there, I would find them.

My truck came to a grinding halt, hopping one wheel on the curb as I slammed my foot on the brake and shoved the gear shift to park. I didn't bother to take my keys or close the door as I tore across the sidewalk.

A thick, pounding heat coursed through my veins. I pushed open the heavy wooden door to The Dirty Pigeon bar, spilling afternoon sunlight into the dim interior. Alert, I scanned the dusky room for my targets. When my eyes found the two motherfuckers I had come for, my spine turned to steel.

As my long strides ate up the space between the door and the bar, one of them—Todd, I recalled from when they checked in this morning—lifted his head. His dull, heavy-lidded eyes met mine in the mirror behind the bar and went wide.

My lip twitched with a menacing smile as I barreled toward him, fists clenched.

Someone moved to my left, and with a shove, I sent him stumbling backward. Before Todd could react, I lifted my boot and kicked the wooden barstool out from beneath him, sending it squealing across the floor. His half-drunk body crumpled to the ground.

My boot connected with his side in a satisfying crunch, and in one fluid movement, I was straddled over his coiled body. The force of my fist connected with his face as I hammered away at him.

Tugs at my shirt and the shouts that encircled me did nothing to stop the punishment I delivered. My collar tore as Todd's friend clawed at me. He got one good pop in—his elbow connecting with my eyebrow as he tried to disengage me. My head flared back, but I recentered myself quickly.

He wound his arm around my neck, but I grabbed his elbow and pulled, shifting my weight to the side, and sent him careening over my shoulder. His thick body slammed into the ground next to me.

I trained my eyes on him and delivered a fresh set of punches to his face, ignoring the splits in my throbbing knuckles and the blood that burbled out of his throat. I looked up, only briefly, to see Colin as he vaulted the bar against the back wall, shotgun in hand.

A low thump hammered in my head, drowning out the commotion of the gathering crowd. I couldn't stop, didn't want to. These assholes had touched what was mine, and they were going to pay for it.

Colin reached us within seconds. I had discarded Todd and had his friend pinned against the base of the bar.

"Back up, Lincoln." Colin's voice was hard.

My breath came out in explosive bursts as I continued my assault.

"Jesus, Lincoln. Enough!" Colin shoved a hand in the center of my chest, putting himself between me and my mission.

My head snapped up as he shoved me backward onto my heels. Ragged breaths pounded out of me. I looked down to see my hands, split and swollen, covered in blood.

Three men dragged the moaning Todd and his friend toward the center of the dance floor. I gnashed my teeth together and fought to quell the rage that still bubbled inside of me.

Colin passed his shotgun to the bartender and grabbed the tattered edges of my collar. "What the actual *fuck*, Linc?" he shouted into my face.

The urge to surge forward and continue my decimation of those two pieces of shit was undeniable.

"Fucking look at me, man. What the hell is going on?"

"Those assholes attacked Joanna today." The words were acid in my mouth.

The audible gasps rumbled through the small crowd.

Todd and Stan were moaning and grunting as they were helped to their feet.

I unfolded myself, standing tall and leaning forward with my fists clenched at my sides.

Wanna go again?

Colin's hand stayed planted against my chest. "We'll take care of this. You need to calm the fuck down and go into my office before I make Deck arrest your ass."

I darted my eyes in his direction. *Fucking do it. I dare you.*

"I'm serious, Lincoln. You need to back up."

"I'm not fucking leaving until those assholes pay for what they did to her."

"All right, I hear you, brother. We'll figure this shit out. But I need to know you aren't going to go apeshit again if I walk away." Colin's eyes pinned me in place. I trusted him, and his words were the first to crack through my rage. I took one step back, bumping into a barstool, and sat.

Colin paused, still assessing, before he stepped over to a heaving Todd and Stan. "Get the fuck out of my bar." Colin's gravelly voice enunciated every syllable.

"Someone call the cops!" Todd shouted. "I'm pressing charges against that animal!" He was looking around frantically as the local crowd began to shake their heads and turn away.

"I don't know what you're talking about," Colin continued coolly. He crossed his arms over his broad chest. "I saw you trip and fall."

Todd's swollen eyes widened. "Is that how it's gonna be?" He could barely lift his arm as he pointed in my direction. "This guy comes out of nowhere, starting shit. He attacked us!"

"Like I said," Colin's voice dropped an octave and he

glared at the two of them, "all I saw was you trip and hit your head. I sure hope you're okay."

"This is some bullshit," Stan said, straining to breathe. "Let's get the fuck out of here, man."

Todd spat a bloody wad across Colin's boot as they staggered toward the door. My jaw ticked, and my fist itched to connect with their swollen faces again.

With them still struggling to open the door and leave, Colin turned to me. "My office. Now."

"Jesus, fuck, dude." Colin reached into the mini fridge behind his desk and tossed a water bottle at me from across his office. "What the *fuck*?"

Without answering him, I uncapped the bottle and brought it to my parched lips, downing half of it in one go. My hands ached, and the swelling across my eyebrow made it increasingly hard to see out of my right eye.

My leg bounced with unspent adrenaline. I was dying to get back to Joanna. I needed to check on her, check every fucking inch of her to make sure she was safe.

The image of the bruising on her arm flipped through my mind, sending a fresh wave of fury coursing through me. I couldn't sit still so I stood abruptly, the backs of my legs pushing away the chair behind me. I paced in Colin's office and ran every possible scenario in my head. I hadn't even gotten any details from Joanna before I barreled out of the office and into the bar. My phone was still on my desk so I couldn't even call her to make sure she was secure.

"All right, boss. You need to calm the fuck down before you throw yourself into a panic attack." Colin's eyes never left me as I etched a path on the faded carpet, and he caught the glare I shot from the side of my purpling eye.

"I don't need a fucking caretaker." I spat my words at him, and my gut clenched, knowing full well I was being a total prick.

"Yeah, well, someone needs to make sure you don't use all that military training and pent-up rage to kill someone."

His words slammed into my chest. I scrubbed the drying blood off my hands as the truth settled into my churning gut.

It wasn't that I could kill them. It was that I *wanted* to.

The tenets and rules that structured my entire life crumbled around me. In one instant—without even knowing the facts, without hesitation—I was willing to end someone's life.

The years that I had been back home came into startling view. God and I had developed an understanding—I was an imposter, and I knew that he knew I was not a good man.

A sharp rap at the office door dragged my attention away from the spiraling chaos that was my life.

"It's me." Cole Decker's voice was all business as he pushed open the office door. Deck stepped in, dressed in his uniform.

Colin tipped his chin in greeting, and the three of us exchanged glances.

"Look, Deck," I started. "Joanna took those guys out fishing this morning by herself. I don't know what happened, but she came home with bruises."

"Finn already called me," he said. "I met them at your office, but when I saw her arm, I took her in so we could take some pictures. He stayed with Jo."

I nodded slowly. Joanna deserved a man like Finn. He was steady and strong and there for her when she needed it.

"I took some pictures at the station and got her report."

"Is she all right?" Colin asked.

"She's pretty rattled. I guess those two fucks had been sneaking whiskey, and she didn't know it. At the end of the morning, one of them started to get aggressive. She said he grabbed her arm and..." His voice trailed off as his eyes swept between Colin and me.

"And what?" I demanded.

His large chest expanded beneath his police vest as he weighed how much to tell me. "She said he got handsy—felt her up a little, and when she resisted, he went for his belt buckle. She was pretty convinced he was going to take it further."

My jaw tightened so fast it hollowed my cheeks.

Deck lifted his hand. "Listen. She's all right. After a shot to his balls, she was able to run to the truck and headed straight to you. I take it that's when you decided to block a sidewalk with your truck and go all Rambo in here?"

I squared my shoulders, hands behind my back, and leveled my gaze to his. I nodded once. I would take my punishment.

Colin leaned a hip against his desk. "So what's our move?"

"Well, we're lucky this town loves him." He jerked his head in my direction. "No one in that bar is talking...at all. You beat the shit out of two people in the middle of the day with a dozen witnesses, but when I came in to ask questions, most people acted like they didn't know what I was talking about." His head shook in disbelief. "We have a man out to round up Todd and Stan, but even if they want to press charges, there's no one to corroborate what happened."

"Well, all right." Colin walked up next to me with a

smile, slapping a hand down hard on my shoulder. "I'll get shit cleaned up here. You go get your girl."

My girl.

The past several weeks flickered through my mind. The shotgun bubble of her laughter at her own terrible jokes, her fingertips dragging a tingling path up my forearm as she read her book, the way her face lit up when she reeled in a monster fish, how she hummed—completely off-key—to any song she half knew. Everything about her was painfully perfect. She deserved someone who wasn't a walking disaster, someone who was sane. A man with honor who wouldn't steal his brother's girl or lose control and nearly kill a man.

In one rage-fueled outburst, I had successfully ruined everything. The thought of me touching Joanna after what I had done had guilt and shame skittering in my stomach. My chest felt like it was going to cave in. Once she truly knew what I was capable of, she would never look at me the same way again. I would lose Joanna, and it was my own fucking fault.

I hated myself. She was too kind and good to ever leave on her own so it would be up to me to build the wall between us. Trudging to my truck, I knew exactly what I had to do to make sure Joanna would have the life she deserved.

The smoldering coals did nothing to warm the chill in my bones. Late afternoon was transitioning to early evening. The orange-and-purple-tipped clouds slanted warm light through the bay window. I still hadn't seen Lincoln since he'd stormed out of his office.

My insides felt hollowed out. It was humiliating telling Decker what the men had said and done in the confines of the forest. He insisted on taking photographs of the bruising on my arm. His unwavering professionalism did little to comfort me, but when he was done taking my statement, he brushed a tendril of hair from my eyes and gently squeezed my hand. Deck was a kind man and a good friend who was doing his duty. My humiliation stretched on as Finn followed me around like Bud's clone, insisting on staying within three feet of me at my cottage.

"Tea or coffee?" Finn held up a chipped floral mug and a spoon from the cottage kitchen. His eyes hadn't left me since I fell apart in his arms in the doorway of his office.

"Coffee would be nice." A small smile hitched at the corners of my mouth. "Cream, no sugar, please."

I smoothed the coarse auburn hair along Bud's neck. My furry companion hadn't left my side either. Despite the love radiating from both of these adorable men, the one man I wanted—needed—with me wasn't here.

"Any word from Lincoln?" I asked Finn.

He sauntered to the couch, placed my steaming mug on the side table, and rubbed his expansive palm across my shoulder, kneading a small line of knots with his thumb. "No word yet." His typical wide grin was set in a hard line. "I did hear from Decker, though," he went on. "I still think you should press charges."

I stared into the depths of my biscuit-colored coffee. My eyelids felt heavy, and my thoughts were scattered. I wanted to curl under a blanket, preferably with the safety of Lincoln's strong arms around me, and sleep and sleep. A lackluster shoulder lift was all I could muster.

Finn sat opposite me on the couch, but his long legs ate up most of the space between us. He picked at imaginary lint on his jeans and said, "Decker also said that Lincoln ran into Stan and Todd. They got into it at the bar. I didn't get all the details, but he said it was pretty brutal."

"Brutal?" I sat up. "Is Lincoln hurt?" The flustered edge in my voice expanded.

He shook his head. "Lincoln can handle himself. I just wish he'd answer his damn phone." He tapped the screen again, frowning at the lack of messages.

Bud looked up at me with his warm, honey-flecked eyes and let out a small whine. I leaned closer to him, feeling the soft fur of his ears against my cheek. "I know, buddy. I'm worried about him, too."

At the rumble of a truck engine and the familiar crunch of gravel, Bud's whine flipped to a soft staccato whimpering.

My heart ticked up and my breath hitched. I stared a hole into the back of the cottage door.

Lincoln did not saunter into my cottage with his familiar pine-smoke smell that warmed my senses like so many nights before. Instead, I heard the brakes whine and the engine cut, but then, silence.

Finn loped into the kitchen and peeked out of the gauzy curtains at the window above the sink. He walked to the door and poked his head outside. "Hey, man," he called. "She's insi—oh, fuck."

At his words, I shot to my feet, feeling a prickle of worry inch up my back. Finn stepped back, making room for Lincoln to walk through the small front door.

His head hung low, shoulders slumped, but he still managed to take up most of the entryway. My eyes fluttered over the expanse of his body, taking in the chaos of his appearance.

His shirt was bloodied and torn at the collar. Deep maroon smears climbed up his forearms as the roped muscles twitched with every flex of his hands. Lincoln's hard, chiseled face was puffy and angry across an eyebrow, and a circular bruise the color of rotting eggplant along one side of his jaw.

I moved toward him, but he raised his hand, fixing my feet to the floor.

"Are you all right?" Lincoln's voice felt cold and distant.

"I should ask you the same thing. Lincoln, what happened?"

"It doesn't matter," he said, shaking his head.

"*Okay.*" The word dragged out as my mind raced to piece together what was happening. "Well, get in here. You're bleeding. Let me help you."

I started to step forward again when he raised his blue

eyes to mine. Something swirled in them, making the tiny hairs on my arm feel tight. He stared at me a beat longer but then nodded his head slightly. I took the invitation and stepped into his space. I slipped my arms around his trim torso and pulled him into me. I didn't care that he was bloodied and smelled like sweat. I needed to feel him envelop me and tell me everything was going to be okay.

Instead, he stood, a monolith—hard and unmoving. My hand rubbed up the center of his lower back. My mind screamed for him to hold me as tears welled under my lids. His heart hammered against my ear.

"I went back to where you were on the water. I think I was able to get all of your gear, but you'll have to check for yourself." He stood unwavering, but I clung to him, digging my fingertips into his back.

Finn cleared his throat. "I can take it all back to the shop. You two should take it easy tonight."

He moved behind me, circling his arms around us both in an awkward Jo-sandwich. Finn placed his palm at the back of my neck and gave it a gentle squeeze.

Finn and Lincoln's eyes met, and they gave each other a curt nod. Without another word, Finn left us in the dim fluorescence of the cottage kitchen.

My hands moved up the hard lines of Lincoln's abs, floating over the stained fabric, unsure of where to touch him. I settled my hands delicately at the sides of his bruised face. Lincoln's eyes were fixed to the floor.

"Hey," I said softly. "Please look at me."

He closed his eyes on a sigh. Lincoln worked his jaw but didn't speak. I felt a chasm opening between us, and the uncomfortable frenzy of panic vibrated through me.

With the tip of his head, Lincoln finally—*finally*—lowered his head and leaned into me. The breath I didn't realize I was holding whooshed out of my lungs as I squeezed my eyes closed even tighter. A hot tear slipped beneath my lashes and trailed down my cheek.

When I lifted my head, I could see that his right eye was swollen nearly shut. I touched a tentative fingertip on its outside edge. A soft grunt was the only reaction to my touch.

"Oh, Lincoln..." I whispered.

"I need to get cleaned up." He shifted his body, but I held him in place by his shoulders. Lincoln's attention moved to my upper arm. Purple-and-black fingertips stained the thin skin of my inner arm. I watched his nostrils flare once.

My hand moved instinctively to cover the bruise. "I swear it's okay."

"No." I didn't recognize the hardness in his voice as it was directed toward me.

"Truly. I'm all right. I took care of myself." I needed him to understand that I was rattled but otherwise unharmed, mostly.

"Took care of yourself?" Lincoln sounded outraged.

Blinking, I struggled to understand the dark tone laced in his voice.

"You think you took care of yourself?" Lincoln took a step back and unwound himself from my embrace. "Joanna, I don't think you realize what you did today."

A hot spark of anger flared in my jaw. "What I did? What is it that you think I did?" Lincoln stood, exhaling into the silence. "Well?" I placed my hands on my hips. "Besides covering for *your* guide service instead of my own? Besides kneeing some prick in the balls because he overstepped his bounds? What is it exactly you think that I did wrong today?"

"Look, I'm not saying you brought this on yourself, but—"

"*Excuse me?!*" An incredulous intake of my breath brought a renewed energy coursing through my body. Anger at the men who touched me I had seen coming, but this?

"No. Joanna. That's not what I—damn it. Ok, look. You're a woman, alone, with strangers."

I hitched an eyebrow. At my silence, Lincoln continued. "You think you can just go out alone and do everything yourself. You're not like other women, and I can't be standing around waiting to come to your rescue."

You're not like other women.

The familiar words gutted me when they spilled from Lincoln's mouth. How many other men had told me that? That I was too independent, too strong, or too different. I would never be the one he chose in the end.

"I never asked you to rescue me." I was scrambling to hold together the scraps of my dignity. "What the hell is going on with you?" I searched his eyes for something, anything, that could clue me in as to why the conversation was spiraling out of control.

"I can't do this." Lincoln's body went rigid, his shoulders straight, and he stared through me.

"Lincoln, what are you saying?" My hands were frigid and shaking.

"I'm saying this is over." His eyes never met mine. Lincoln stood with military precision, as he tore my heart from my chest.

Desperate for him to understand what I was feeling, I pleaded, "I care about you. Talk to me." My voice cracked, and I was seconds from full-on hysterics.

He wants a real woman. One that's soft and sweet and

normal and doesn't put herself in a position like you did today.

Humiliation burned on my cheeks. I felt crushed and emptied. Building a wall was the only way I knew to protect my heart.

Ice filled Lincoln's eyes, but I lifted my chin in defiance. He pinned me with his stare before turning his back to me.

"I thought you were a good man." I flung the words at his back and cursed the tears that tumbled down my cheeks.

Lincoln wrenched open the front door and turned his head over his shoulder. "You were wrong."

I DESERVED the hollow snap of Joanna's cottage door as she closed it behind me. The weight of my shoulders and the burn in my jaw were nothing compared to the scooped-out feeling that resided in my chest.

I was furious. Furious that I had pined for this woman for so long. Furious that she was more than I ever expected, more than I deserved. Furious that she got under my skin and made me imagine the possibility of sharing a life with her.

Fifty feet of space between her cottage and mine wasn't nearly enough. I slammed my front door so hard a crack splintered across the small window.

Fucking great.

I pressed the backs of my battered hands against my eyelids, wincing at the sharp sting of my swollen eyebrow. I tried to forget the pain that had crossed Joanna's face as I shut her out. The pain that I had caused by being dishonorable and a fucking coward.

When I spat my words at her, she had believed them so readily. But someday she would realize that I had done her a favor. I had given her the chance at a life she deserved. Some new asshole would swoop in and worship her. He would be kind and steady. This man would give her a home with sandy-haired babies that grew up on the rivers of Montana. He wouldn't have to battle any demons or justify transgressions done in the name of duty. This man would love her, body and soul, and I would hate him with every fiber of my being.

~

RELIEF FLOODED MY VEINS WHEN, after three days, Joanna hadn't moved out of the neighboring cottage. It was a unique kind of hell—knowing she was so close, wondering if she was okay, but being unable to be certain. Joanna's ability to avoid me was shockingly impressive.

Without any witnesses willing to come forward, Deck told me I had gotten lucky and escaped any charges but to keep my nose clean and lay low for a while. Walking down Main Street toward the office, I was given a few knowing nods, and despite their good intentions, our community accepting my outrage without consequence left me feeling corrupt.

Shame washed over me every time a hand gripped mine and eagerly pumped me for information. Our small town took care of our own, and Joanna had been accepted into the fold. In their eyes, I was protecting her from someone who violated her, but I knew the truth. I had lost control. Facing their kind words was unbearable so I buried myself in work on the farm. I took to fixing the sagging porch steps and battened up broken windows that needed replacement.

Because I was a fucking coward, I let Finn shoulder the business and avoided everyone altogether. On the farm, I punished my back by splitting wood for an hour. I stacked the cords tightly, close enough to the back entrance to the Big House so that old man Bailey would have plenty of firewood and he wouldn't have to carry it too far. I would have brought it right into his house, but he was stubborn as fuck and would have just argued with me about it. I could appreciate his need to be self-sufficient so I left it on the back porch where he could carry it in himself.

"You about done with that?" The back door creaked open, and the old man's craggy face peered through the screen.

"Yes, sir." I clunked another piece on the pile with a thwack.

"Wasn't talking about the wood, son." He leaned into the door as it swung open.

I looked at him. The old man was a legend around here. He was a veteran too, had served his country with honor and gusto. On the shop corners in town, other men recalled his bravery and stories of active combat. Despite his reputation for being a hothead, they all respected him as an elder in our community.

He still walked tall, with only a slight rounding of his shoulders as he edged toward a chair on the porch. The years had been kind to him, and despite knees that ached and losing some of his hearing from working as a tank mechanic in the Marines, he was sharp as a tack. He could also hold his own if he needed to. "Old man strong," Finn had called it once. I figured it was years of staying active, working around the farm, and not letting himself get too soft that worked in his favor.

I continued my assault on the logs, but Mr. Bailey pinned me with a stare. "Jesus, kid. Take a break before you kill yourself." He reached into his pocket and brought a small flask to his lips. His arm stretched out to me, offering it, so I took a hard pull. Bourbon. Bourbon at eleven A.M.

I felt the sharp burn of the liquor, but it soon gave way to emptiness. It was the emptiness of missing Joanna, I realized, and it would eat into my bones and stay with me forever.

I hated myself for what I had done to her. I snuck a look toward her cottage, satisfied with the neatly stacked pile of firewood I had left by the entrance. She might be royally pissed off at me, but at least I knew she wouldn't freeze to death.

"That's what I thought." Mr. Bailey smirked when he caught me looking toward Cottage Two.

"Hmmph."

"I walked that road you're on, son, and it's a hard one." He looked out over the water that lined the property, shook his head once, and took another deep pull from the flask.

"When Lottie died," he continued, "I screwed up. I dug myself an angry little foxhole and refused to come up for air."

Reeling from his words, I placed the head of the splitting maul at my boots. "You were married?"

"Oh, yeah. And she sure was something. She was sitting on a park bench waiting for her friend when I rode past her on my old Honda 125 street bike. Turned that thing right around and asked her if she wanted a ride." His smile, which almost never came out, reached his crinkled eyes. He nodded slightly as he recalled the memory.

"And she said yes, I take it?" I was curious to know more about the man who took me in but never shared much about himself.

"Fuck no." He chuckled. "She was new in town, only fifteen, and I was seventeen and already had a reputation.

Took me five months to convince her father I was worthy of a date. We went for a ride, I bought her an ice cream cone, and took her home. Though I did leave out the part where I tried to get my bike to break down on the way home." He winked at me and laughed again.

I was stunned into silence. Old man Bailey was known for being a hardass and frightened his share of small children when he ventured into town.

"Lottie and I were inseparable after that. She stayed by my side when I enlisted. Hell, I married her at sixteen just so she could go to California with me. Her dad was pissed about that, but they knew she'd run away anyway if they told her no." He laughed at the memory of his late wife.

Mr. Bailey turned back to me and patted a hand on his knee. "Well, it ain't my business, kid, but I've seen you two giggling around here. She's good for you, she brings a lightness to you that you need."

"Yeah, well, we aren't together. Not anymore." The shame that wound through me forced my eyes to my boots.

"I heard what you did for her. Those two got what they deserved."

"It's nothing." My hands twitched. I needed to talk about something—anything—else.

"Well, if you're thinking about her but can't figure out how to talk about her, it's not nothing."

I dragged a hand along the short hairs on the back of my head and blew out a breath. "Yeah, well. It's done."

Mr. Bailey pushed himself up from the chair, his shoulders squared to me. His cool eyes met mine. "Hmph," he grumbled. "I never knew you were such a quitter."

Without waiting for a response, he turned from me and walked back into the house, letting the screen door slam in his wake.

~

"Well, hey there, sweet boy! To what do I owe the pleasure?" I should have figured my mother would have spotted my truck turning up her driveway.

"I'm a grown man, Mom," I grumbled, grabbing the small bouquet of flowers from the front seat before closing the door.

"Oh, hush." She rushed down the steps of her porch and swatted my arm with the dish towel that hung over her shoulder. On her tiptoes, she still only came midway up my chest. I leaned down to hug her small frame, and she kissed my cheek.

Everyone in town might have called her Birdie, but my mother's personality filled any space she entered. Born and raised in a small East Texas town, Birdie lived up to her reputation as a genteel southern woman, even though time had faded her accent and she'd settled into the life of a Western woman.

I unceremoniously presented her with the wilting flowers. "For you."

"And that," she smiled, "is why you'll always be my sweet boy. Now come inside but don't you dare track mud onto my clean floors."

"Yes, ma'am." I couldn't help but shake my head at her back.

Mom still lived in our childhood home where she spent her days gardening, baking, and volunteering at the Chikalu Women's Club. She had a line on every bit of gossip in this town, so I knew I'd have to face her sooner or later over what went down in Colin's bar.

She poured homemade lemonade into two slim glasses,

taking a sip from one and setting the other in front of me. "So...you've been the talk of the town."

I guess we're getting right fucking to it then.

I cleared my throat. "Seems like it."

With a lifted brow—that woman could warm your heart with a hug or freeze hell with a glare—she said, "And what happened with that sweet girl, Jo?"

Sitting in her kitchen made me feel sixteen again. "I don't really want to talk about it."

"Well, I didn't ask if you *wanted* to talk about it, did I?"

I puffed out a breath and finished the lemonade in one long drink. I stared down at my hands, rubbing the web between my thumb and forefinger.

I could see how easily Joanna would fit into my life if I had let her. In my mother's kitchen, I could see her humming along with the radio, Mom teaching her how to make real fried chicken, laughing with Finn over a few beers on the back deck. I had been so close to having it all, but it didn't change the fact that I could never be the man she deserved.

"Lincoln," my mother's voice went quiet, "you carry the weight of the world around on those big shoulders of yours. I think sometimes you forget that you're allowed to put the weight down." Her dark eyes were soft, and her small hand rested on my shoulder.

My throat felt thick, and I could only manage a nod. I had come here because I felt lost. Apparently, being a successful adult male didn't make you need your mom any less. She moved to put the flowers in water, and I couldn't help but think of Joanna and how she'd transformed her dingy, unused cottage into something inviting and charming. Little jars of wildflowers were all over the tables and counters. They'd found their way into my cottage too, and I still didn't have the balls to throw them away.

I was angry at myself for missing her. I had made the decision to let her go. I should have felt better that she was no longer tied to a man who would only drag her down, but all I felt was emptiness.

Mom let the topic rest for now, and for the rest of the afternoon, I helped her in the garden, building three new raised beds and hauling dirt and compost to fill them. Physical labor helped to warm and stretch my muscles, but it did nothing to ease the ache lodged in my chest.

On the drive home, I told myself I wouldn't slow down as I passed the office, just to see if she was there. I definitely didn't take a second lap around the block when I saw her truck parked at the café in town.

THIRTY-TWO

JOANNA

"I CANNOT BELIEVE how little this town has changed!" Honey sat across from me at the café. Her bouncy blond curls were smooth and shiny.

"The whole town reminds me of Gram and Pop. I like when people tell me stories about them." My heart lifted, but ached, at the memory of my grandparents.

Honey flipped through the sticky plastic café menu. I had called her after Lincoln decimated my heart. She listened to my sobs for hours that first night. I wanted nothing more than to pick up and leave—run away—but I had a few more appointments, and with Lincoln not coming into the office, I didn't want to leave Finn in a lurch. So, instead of leaving town for Butte, Honey insisted she come to me.

Mrs. Coulson, our very elderly and very slow server, finally met us at the table. She looked back and forth between us.

"Evening, Mrs. Coulson," I said, breaking her stare from Honey. "You remember my sister, Honey?"

"Oh, I wondered if that was you! My, it's been a long

time." Her sweet face crinkled, and the soft wrinkles of her face deepened with her smile. "I see you've still got a proclivity for flashiness."

I choked out a little laugh as I sipped on my water. Mrs. Coulson also lacked a filter.

"It has been a while." Honey smiled a warm, affectionate smile back, ignoring the backhanded compliment. "I hear you have all been taking care of my Jo." Honey just had a natural way with people. She could talk to anyone like it was just yesterday they last talked. Everyone felt at ease around her.

"Oh, well, our little Jo's been quite the talk of the town, you know!"

Our little Jo. My cheeks flushed at her words. I had never truly felt a sense of belonging anywhere, and somewhere along the road, I had started to think of Chikalu Falls as home.

Mrs. Coulson continued. "She's got our Lincoln in a tizzy, that's for sure. But it's good for him, if you ask me." Her deep brown eyes danced with mischief.

Clearing my throat gently, I shifted uncomfortably in the booth. When Mrs. Coulson winked at me, it took everything I had not to roll my eyes. Anger still simmered beneath my skin, and I held onto it because it was better than feeling the deep bruise of hurt that Lincoln's rejection had left behind.

We ordered our dinners and spent the next hour watching the people of this small town talk and mingle. There was a thumping rhythm about it—the way that people laughed and chatted across tables. No matter where you went in Chikalu, neighbors were family. A deep spot in my stomach ached at knowing I loved this town but would never be a part of it.

After dinner, Honey followed me down the dark roads to Mr. Bailey's farm. She parked her vintage Chevelle next to my old truck.

"You know," she said as she got out and examined the side of her car, "I'll be pissed if this gravel dings my paint job."

I laughed. Honey was a lot of things but used to small-town life—gravel driveways included—was not one of them.

We walked up to the cottage and, despite myself, I peered over at Lincoln's cottage. The curtains were closed tightly and the lights were off. Honey's hand patted my back between my shoulder blades. She rested her cheek against my shoulder in comfort.

As I went to open the cottage door, I frowned at the fresh pile of neatly stacked firewood beside the door. We went inside and unloaded Honey's weekender luggage. She reached inside when I flipped on the lights and let Bud go for a quick run. He yipped and loped straight toward Lincoln's cottage. *Traitor.*

From her bag, Honey held up two bottles of vintage Shiraz, wiggling them side to side. "Got any cups? Let's drown your sorrows tonight."

I pulled two small mugs from the cupboard and we sat knee to knee on the couch, sipping the luxurious wine.

"You spoil me," I said, smiling at her.

"Someone needs to! Plus, I am always down for a good post-breakup wine-fest." At that, we clinked our mugs together. I took a deep sip, letting the spicy liquid warm me. My eyes lost focus as I stared at my mug, lost in thoughts of Lincoln and what could have been.

Honey reached over and gave my shoulder a loving squeeze. "I'm sorry you have to go through this."

"Yeah, you and me both."

"He really beat the shit out of those guys?"

"Yep." I nodded. "It was bad. I hardly got the words out and he was flying out of the office. I didn't see him until later that night, and he looked *awful*. I guess Colin had to pry him off the guys."

"That's kind of hot." A devilish grin spread slowly across my sister's face.

A small smile quirked at the corner of my mouth. Before I could respond, Honey had her hand up. "Shhh! I hear something . . ."

I looked down at Bud who was resting between us, but he hadn't moved. Honey set her mug down and tiptoed to the kitchen, flipping the light off as she entered. She moved her small frame to the side of the door, peeking out from behind the curtain of the window into the darkness outside.

"It's him!" she whisper-shouted.

My stomach flipped.

"I knew he was hot, but you never said he had a body like that! Damn."

I planted myself on the couch, refusing to look at the man who'd shattered my heart.

"Shit!" Honey ducked below the window. "He's coming!"

My eyes grew wide, and my heart hammered in my chest.

Honey kept her hand clamped over her mouth, but tipsy giggles kept escaping around her fingers. I swatted my hand in her direction and put my finger to my lips. We waited a beat, then another. Nothing.

I mouthed to Honey, "Where'd he go?"

She looked at me and shrugged her shoulders. Carefully, I moved off the couch, trying not to rile Bud. I toed to the door, moving slowly next to Honey. When I straightened my body, I let one eye peek out of the window. Through the foggy glass, I could make out Lincoln's large frame entering his cottage and closing the door behind him.

Disappointment flooded my system. I looked at Honey and shook my head, walking back to the couch to down the rest of my wine in one burning gulp.

She straightened. "Did he really turn around? I'm taking a peek."

Honey cracked open the door to get a look for herself. When she moved back inside, she was holding a small bundle of wildflowers wrapped in jute twine.

"This doesn't look over to me," she said. Honey set the yellow and pink flowers on the end table next to me.

I pressed the petals to my nose. "I've been finding little things—flowers, the firewood, treats for Bud. I do *not* understand him."

"He's in love with you, idiot."

A flush bloomed across my cheeks at her words, but I forced it away and sank back into the couch. "Men like Lincoln don't love girls like me, Honey."

Her face twisted at my words as she plunked down beside me. "What kind of bullshit is that?"

"I'm serious," I continued. "Men like Lincoln end up with girls like you—beautiful and funny and feminine." I gestured at all of her as I spoke.

She rested her hand on top of mine. "Jo, you're all of those things. Just because we're different doesn't mean you're less." My eyes filled at her words. "Joanna James, you are hot as fuck, strong, smart as a whip, and can run circles around any man with a fishing line. You're going to be running this county when you decide to get off your ass and open your own guide service. And that," she gave me her best stern look, "is a fact."

"I need to do it, you know." I found my voice and looked at her. "People keep asking me and I think it's time. I'm going to open up my own service and see where it takes me."

"That's my girl!" Honey emptied the last drops of the bottle into my mug and went searching for the second bottle. I couldn't help but replay her words.

He's in love with you.

Why did he have to be so stubborn? Why was he leaving me things? Didn't he know that made it so much harder? If he loved me, how could he push me away? Flashes of anger rose inside of me.

I did nothing wrong. If he can't see how great we could have been together, then that's on him.

I swiped a traitorous tear that tumbled down my cheek.

A WEEK after Honey's visit, I still hadn't seen Lincoln. Since he was a man of routine and order, avoiding him had become easy—out the door during his morning run, avoid the coffee shop around three, no more dinners at The Pidge.

Once I'd fulfilled my commitment to Finn, I would pack up my meager belongings and head back to Butte. There, I could focus on how I would finally start marketing Montana's first female-owned guide business.

In reality, the thought of leaving Chikalu Falls and the warm, friendly faces that nodded and waved when I walked down the street spread a dull, aching sadness across my back. In the short time here, happy childhood memories had flooded back. I would miss Mr. Richardson insisting my groceries were far too heavy, Miss Trina giving me a smile and a knowing wink when we passed.

I would even miss grumpy old man Bailey. I knew by the way he'd try to hide a smile and slap his knee when I reeled in a fish off his riverbank that, beneath his gruff exterior, there was a teddy bear. I had fallen in love with Chikalu—it was a small town with big love.

But I couldn't bear the thought of Lincoln moving on. My stomach soured at the thought of seeing him with his arm draped across the shoulders of another woman, his blue eyes looking at her with the love I wished he could feel for me. I couldn't pretend what we had wasn't real.

The mountain air brought a crispness, reminding me that summer was slowly tilting toward fall. Consumed by my thoughts, I rounded the corner out of the coffee shop— I'd started ordering tea, even though I hated it, because coffee reminded me too much of mornings with Lincoln— when I crashed into a brick wall of a man with a very unladylike *ooof.*

Before my head could snap up, I was accosted by his deliciously clean, pine smell. His arms instinctively steadied me, wrapping a little too intimately around my back.

"I'm sorry," tumbled out of me before I could completely register who was holding me. When I looked up and saw Lincoln's sea-blue eyes, I jumped back, sloshing my tea through the lid.

"Joanna." Lincoln's eyes fixed on me. He looked exhausted, like he hadn't slept in days. Shadows darkened beneath his eyes, and his beard was shaggier than I remembered.

I blew out a breath to steady my war-drum heartbeat.

THIRTY-THREE

LINCOLN

I REALIZED she had been avoiding me, so for three days, I intentionally changed my routine—got a haircut, ate dinner out every night, went grocery shopping in the middle of the week—anything I could think of that would reward me with a glimpse of Joanna. When I saw the sweep of her hair and her long legs step into the coffee shop, I immediately crossed the street, slowed my pace, and tried to time her exit.

"Joanna," I growled when she crashed into me. I tried to hide the hitch in my throat, and my words came out more aggressively than I intended.

Her eyes went wide, and her cute, pouty mouth dropped open in a little O. I stared at it and licked my lips.

You feel so good in my arms. I'm sorry. I made the biggest mistake of my life.

I was starved for her, but I pushed down the thoughts that came erupting to the surface. Freeing Joanna was the only way she could lead a happy life.

When she recovered, Joanna blinked and moved her

shoulder, unwinding herself from my embrace. "Hello," she said. Her voice was aloof.

When she moved to walk past me, I stepped left, blocking her path. Her eyes met mine again, but this time, surprise was replaced with fire.

There's my warrior. My heart galloped in my chest.

"What are you doing, Lincoln?"

My brow furrowed. *I have no fucking clue what I'm doing.*

On a frustrated sigh, she shifted to move past me again. "If you have nothing to say to me, I need to go."

This time I let her pass, my legs rooted to the ground. I wanted to tell her everything—that I fucked up, that I loved her, that I wanted to marry her, have babies with her, and do anything in my power to make her happy—but I froze. She deserved so much more than I could ever be for her.

She took several quick steps away from me before turning over her shoulder, her eyes glittering with unshed tears that ripped my heart out. "Please stop leaving things at the cottage."

As she turned away, the distance between us expanded as I watched my soul walk away from me.

And then, only two days after seeing her, she was gone from my life.

"You ARE A FUCKING TRIP, MAN." Finn shook his head and plopped his frame down on the barstool as I scowled at the beer I'd been nursing.

He slapped a hand on my shoulder, but I shrugged him off with a grunt.

Taking a deep pull of his beer, he eyed me carefully. "I'm serious, man. You did this to yourself, you know."

"You don't think I know that?" I spat the words in his direction.

"Oh, I know you know. But it's my job as your brother, and her friend, to make sure you know what a dumbass you are."

I grimaced and drank another long gulp.

After accidentally-on-purpose running into Joanna outside of the coffee shop, I spiraled deeper into chaos. My nightmares were unrelenting—every night I woke up sweating and shaking. Being at home was no longer a comfort. Everything reminded me of her, and I was always on the razor's edge of a panic attack.

Distracting myself was the only way I knew how to deal with feeling like total dog shit. So tonight, it was listening to Colin and the house band, having a few beers. Trying to forget about letters and what-ifs and complicated feelings.

"All right, well, if you're going to pull the whole 'mopey zoo lion' thing, I'm going to need another drink." Finn signaled to our server for another round.

"I'm not moping," I lied.

"The fuck you aren't," he scoffed. "Look at yourself." Finn gestured toward me with disgust.

I really didn't want to be talking to Finn about this. I knew he cared about her, and him knowing the depths of my love for Joanna would only create a bigger mess of the steaming pile of shit that was my life.

"Look, she's—"

I cut him off. "I don't want to know a damn thing about her. Do you understand?" I pinned him with a stare, ice running through my veins. But after a beat, I couldn't help myself. "Just tell me...is she okay?"

The throbbing in my temples was unbearable as Finn looked at me with a mixture of disgust and pity. "You know what I think you see when you look in the mirror, Linc?"

Jesus, here we go. I stared ahead.

"I think all you see is a dark, resounding loneliness stretched out ahead of you," Finn said.

The hammer of truth in his words caused a buzzing in my ears. "What's your point?" The band switched to an upbeat song, and my legs twitched to escape.

"My point is, brother, you're fucking wrong."

I shook my head at Finn and the words tumbled out of me. "You couldn't understand. I stole her from under you. Do you realize that? What kind of man does that to his little brother? What kind of man almost kills someone with his bare hands because he can't control himself? Is that the kind of man Joanna deserves?" My voice amplified with every question, earning wary glances from the tables next to us.

"Is that what this is?!" Disbelief laced through Finn's voice. A short laugh burst from his chest. "Lincoln, you did not steal her from me."

"I knew that you had feelings for her before I made a move. It's inexcusable and I—"

"What the *fuck,* dude? I'm gay." Finn flipped his arm up in my direction, and the table next to us turned, slack-jawed and all too eager to listen in. "You've got your head so far up your own ass that you don't even see what's right in front of you!"

I was stunned into silence by Finn's admission.

Finn is gay? What? Oh, shit, Finn is gay.

Without missing a beat, he barreled on. "You thinking that I had some claim on her is just an excuse. An excuse to punish yourself for feeling anything real. For believing that you're unworthy of love."

I steadied myself and stared at my beer bottle. "I couldn't stand to see her throw her life away. She deserves so much more than I could ever give her."

"Also bullshit."

"Finn, this is...a lot." I exhaled, but it did nothing to ease the tension in my back.

"Yeah, well, this isn't exactly how I planned to tell you, but you gave me no choice. I had to say something before you went nuclear."

"I mean . . ." I fumbled for the right words. I couldn't care less that Finn was gay, but I was also completely surprised. My mind flipped back to all of the unrequited flirting from the girls in town and him dodging conversations about girlfriends. How long had my brother been keeping this part of himself hidden because of me?

Fresh shame washed over me.

"Finn." I looked at my baby brother. He was good and strong and kind. His love was more than I deserved. "I'm sorry you couldn't tell me sooner."

"Ah, man. Take it easy on yourself. If it makes you feel any better, I think most people kinda know. I just don't make a big deal about it, ya know?" He shrugged his broad shoulders and smiled into the sip of his beer. "Mom knows. Dad did too. I asked Jo not to tell you before you two hooked up."

"She kept your secret," I said. A warm glow formed around the thought. Joanna knew how important it was for Finn to talk to me himself, and despite the long talks and late nights whispering secrets to each other in the dark, she had kept Finn's secret safe.

I will never love another woman.

In that moment, I looked down at the torn Valkyrie

wings tattooed on my forearm, and I knew I would spend the rest of my life missing that girl.

"So you actually did it." Old man Bailey had a knack for sneaking up behind you if you weren't careful, reminding me that even though I was a highly trained Marine, so was he.

"Did what, exactly?" I asked as I nailed a sagging shutter against the Big House.

"You chose to be an asshole rather than face reality," he said simply.

"Reality?" I spoke around the nail I was holding between my lips.

"You're in love with that girl and she loves you. But you're too chickenshit to admit that you can have more than what you've allowed yourself. More than living in some rundown cottage, taking care of a crabby bastard like me."

"You don't need taking care of." His words burned in my gut, and I couldn't meet his stare.

"Hah. We both know that's bullshit. If it weren't for you, I would have died in a pile of rubble when this house finally came down around me." He had a firm grip on a porch post and gave it a firm shake. When he paused, I glanced at him and saw his eyes soften. "Also kept me from dying of loneliness too, son."

My hammer paused, and I sagged against the building at his words. This man had taken me in when I was too scared and confused and hotheaded to function in my mother's home. In those days, I'd tried to drown out the nightmares and memories with booze and women. He gave me a safe place to go crazy and helped me come out on the other side of it. Taking care of him gave me a sense of purpose and direction. I hadn't realized what he was getting out of the deal too.

"Looks like you've got some thinking to do." He nodded toward Cottage Two. "But if you're so over her, go clean it out then." He nodded again toward Joanna's cottage and walked back into the Big House.

IT TOOK another four days for me to grow the balls to walk into her cottage. Gooseflesh rippled down my arms as I pushed the door open and her citrus scent assaulted my senses. It knocked me back. I gritted my teeth through a swift intake of breath and pushed my way into the empty space.

Every trace that Joanna had occupied the cottage was gone.

My heartbeat stuttered at the thought. All of the little jars that held wildflowers or cattails were scrubbed and tucked away in the cabinets. The bed was stripped, and the sheets were washed and neatly folded at the foot of the mattress. My eyelids burned, and I pressed my fingers into them.

I felt her absence in this space, and it made me want to burn it all down around me. Nothing in my life felt right without her in it.

I moved toward the door; I couldn't deal with the echoing drumming in my head. As I passed an end table by the couch, a small frame caught my eye.

It was a printed-out photograph of the selfie I had taken and sent to her sister. In the photo, my girl was sweetly tucked under my arm. I was grinning like an idiot—I think I loved her even then—and she was looking up at me. I barely recognized the carefree, happy man in the picture. For the first time, I looked at Joanna in the picture, looking up at me with her bright eyes.

She loved you too.

A tightness curled under my ribs. I had fallen in love with Joanna, and she loved me back. She loved me. Joanna never cared that I was broken or that sometimes I needed my space. She loved all of me and I had pushed her away—not because I was protecting her, but because I was protecting myself.

A frenetic energy buzzed underneath my skin.

Do the right thing for the right reasons.

I wanted it all back—I had to find a way to fix this.

THIRTY-FOUR
JOANNA

"It's a damn shame he never got to see you in these." Honey was upside down on the bed, her head hanging off the side and holding the strappy black thong like a slingshot.

Pressing my lips in a thin line, I snatched the lingerie I'd purchased from the Blush Boutique out of her hand and stuffed it into a drawer. "Knock it off."

Her hearty laughter did little to wash away my sour mood. It had been nearly a month since I left Chikalu Falls. Autumn had settled into the West, bringing cool breezes and crisp nights, but no sign of Lincoln. A small ember of hope that he'd come to his senses and see how good we were together still burned inside of me. But I couldn't wait for him. Sitting around the cottage was too painful so I had packed my belongings and returned to Honey's apartment in Butte.

Invigorated by newly found determination, I scoured the local public lands, finding new and interesting places to bring clients. Before leaving town, I had reached out to the Chikalu Women's Club about setting up a fishing program for veterans. Nature had healing qualities, I knew it from experience, and I wanted to help in any way I could. I met with similar small-town groups, brainstorming how to form an outreach program. The buzz about the program reached clear across the county, and I had four meetings set up to discuss how to get supplies, pair the veterans with a guide, and create groups for the men and women to socialize over the water.

It was different than what I had imagined but was quickly becoming so much more than I could have dreamed. Honey made a few phone calls, and before I knew it, a launch event was being planned. My phone was blowing up with several calls a day from people who had heard about the newly formed program and either wanted to sign up or volunteer to guide.

I called it Project Eir to honor the Valkyrie goddess of healing. Eir was a badass warrior and so was I, but I would be lying if I didn't say it also made me think of Lincoln and the time we shared. The sharpness in my chest was still there every time I thought about him.

THIRTY-FIVE
LINCOLN

I felt like a fucking idiot.

For the past several weeks, I did everything I could to salvage my relationships. I spent more time with Finn and my mom, Deck and Colin, and Mr. Bailey. I stopped shuttering myself away despite the uncomfortable feeling that bloomed in my chest sometimes.

I knew I had to be a better man for myself, for them, and for Joanna. She might not ever forgive me for pushing her away—punishing her for my own fears—but until I was worthy, I was determined to work on myself.

I was so fucking proud of her. Word spread quickly in the county about Project Eir, and the buzz in our community swelled with pride for our girl. Once I had heard that she was planning a big event, I knew it was time.

Blowing out a stream of breath, I dialed the number.

"Hello?"

"Hi, is this Honey?"

"Well, holy shit."

So much for subtlety. I cleared my throat. "Hi, Honey, it's Lincoln."

"Oh, I know who you are." Well, she wasn't giving me an inch.

Fuck. Fuck. Fuck.

She hadn't hung up on me yet so I took the opening. "I need your help."

"What in the world makes you think that I would help you with shit?" I had to smile at Honey's loyalty to her sister. I liked knowing Joanna had someone to watch her back.

"I need to see her," I started. "More than that, I need to make up for everything I put her through, the things I said to her."

"You pushed her away, Lincoln. It's not easy for her to be vulnerable, and the second she was, you destroyed her."

My voice was thick with emotion. "I know. I thought I was protecting her."

"Protecting her from what?!" Her voice pitched upward.

"I don't even know anymore. Myself, maybe? I'm aware that she deserves so much more than me, but I'll be damned if another asshole takes my place. I need to show her it's always been her." I hissed out a breath. Saying all that out loud wasn't easy, and my insides felt raw.

Honey's voice softened at my confession, but her words were daggers. "Well, you better not fuck this up again or I'll have your head on a platter."

THIRTY-SIX
JOANNA

"I've done all I can, Jo. The space is booked." Honey's stern PR voice rattled my jaw over the phone.

Three days before Project Eir's main launch event was supposed to happen, she called to tell me the lodge we had booked was suddenly unavailable.

"How is that even possible?" I tried to hide my annoyance at my sister—she was working for free, after all.

"They said that there was a double-booking. It happens." A curious trill in her voice had me squinting my eyes.

"Honey, I have sixty people counting on us for a day of fishing, food—what the hell am I going to do?!"

"Look. I will take care of this. I made a few calls and there's another location that will be perfect, but you have to trust me." With that, she hung up.

Panic skittered through me. I knew the county too well. I had a feeling that Mr. Bailey's farm was *the perfect location* that Honey was talking about. Even the *possibility* of running into Lincoln after a month of hiding my broken heart was unbearable. Had he moved on? Would I see him? Was he as miserable as I was?

I still felt a sharp wrench under my ribs every time I thought of his muscled arms wrapping around me, tucking me into his side. I missed the way he smelled. I missed the uptick of his mouth when I teased him and he tried not to laugh. Allowing myself a rare moment of weakness, I tilted my head back against my pillow. I closed my eyes and traced my fingertips over my lips, imagining Lincoln's kiss lingering over me.

"This sure is something, girly." Mr. Bailey stood at the edge of the porch, shaking his head at the cars and trucks that lined his gravel driveway.

"I truly can't thank you enough."

His eyes slanted at me, but I caught the sparkle in them just as he winked and turned away to walk inside the Big House. I knew that hard ass was a marshmallow inside.

I looked up at the Big House. It had new black shutters, and someone had sanded down the peeling paint, prepping it for a new coat. Care and love were going into restoring the once beautiful house. I let the wave of sadness pass over me and then tried to replace it with the joy of knowing Mr. Bailey's home was being cared for.

I tapped my thumb against my thigh, trying everything I could think of to expend the nervous energy radiating through me as I waited for our event to start. My cheeks hurt from the plastic smile I'd set in place.

"Stop making that face." Honey walked up the stairs to stand by my side.

"I'm not making a face." I scowled at her. "I'm smiling."

"Well, you look like you shit your pants. Just relax."

A little shotgun burst of laughter escaped me, and my first genuine smile of the day spread across my face.

"There you go." Honey bumped her hip against mine. "Look around, sis. You did this." She tipped her chin in the direction of a large white tent down by the riverfront. People were milling around, shaking hands, checking out equipment. There was a buzz of excitement in the air. I caught Finn's eye by the water, and he shot me two enthusiastic thumbs-up.

"Crazy, right? I can't believe the turnout." My eyes darted nervously around the crowd, and I sank my teeth into the inside of my lip.

"JoJo, I always knew you would do amazing things. Enjoy it." She glanced over and caught me staring at Lincoln's front door. My traitorous thoughts tried to will him into existence.

Her gaze followed mine when she spotted Colin hauling trays of food out of the back of his truck. He insisted that The Dirty Pigeon cater our event, free of charge. My heart tugged, and I was so thankful for him.

Honey tipped her head, peering over her sunglasses. "Who is *that*?"

I smiled. I had wondered how long it would be until she noticed Colin. "That's Lincoln's friend Colin. He owns the bar in town."

"Mmmm." She licked her lips and shimmied her shoulders. Well, Colin was in trouble. Before leaving me, she hugged my shoulders and squeezed. "Incoming," she whispered.

I looked away from Honey to see my mom and dad walking up the gravel driveway. I was stunned they had made the trip back to the town they tried so hard to forget.

"I told them how important this was to you, and I wouldn't let them make any more excuses. Now they can see you shine." Honey winked at me and my wide-eyed expression. She walked down the porch steps, gave our parents a quick hug, and made her way toward an unsuspecting Colin. I slowly raised my hand in a wave, catching my dad's eye.

"Hi, sweetheart!" my dad called as they walked toward me.

"Hey, Dad. Mom. Thank you so much for coming."

"Joanna, this is..." My mother looked around.

I whooshed out a breath. "It's a lot, I know. I can't believe so many people came."

"This is really impressive, darling." My dad nodded in greeting as people walked by.

Suddenly, my mom wrapped me in a tight hug. "We're very proud of you. I'm sorry we didn't understand it earlier...how much this means to you." My dad reached out to rub a circle on my back.

As we separated, Finn walked up, his goofy grin wide across his face. "Okay, boss. You're up." He tipped his head toward the tent.

I set my shoulders and lifted my head. My mother squeezed my hand, and I took one deep breath before walking down to the tent to welcome everyone.

I HIKED UP THE RIVERFRONT, admiring the small groups of men and women packing up and leaving the water. Most were experienced on the river and spent the time chatting with each other. The air danced with laughter, and I felt a lightness in my heart that I hadn't felt in a long time.

The event—the first of many, I hoped—was a hit. We had volunteers signed up and veterans looking forward to having someone to fish with on a regular basis. A few landowners offered access to the river on a rotating schedule. It was a resounding success. I breathed deeply and raised my face to the fading sun. I closed my eyes and let the warmth wash over me.

"Joanna Banana!" Finn's deep voice rumbled behind me, and before I could react, I was scooped up. I laughed as we twirled, and Finn gave me a big squeeze before letting my boots touch the ground.

"Shouldn't you be packing up?" I poked at his shoulder.

"Nah. I saw your pretty face, and I had to come over to tell you how amazing you are. I really miss having you around."

My smile faltered—ever so slightly—at his words, but I recovered just as quickly. "Things have been really busy. I'm so grateful people were interested in signing up and volunteering. My parents even came. Can you believe that? They went back to the motel, but I hope you get a chance to meet them." I peeked up at Finn. The conversation felt strained and awkward.

I walked side by side with Finn, looking down and trying to avoid asking about Lincoln. He avoided the topic too, and our rhythm felt off.

"Look." Finn stopped and faced me, placing his broad hands on top of my shoulders. "I know I'm a shitty friend for bringing him up, but I have to tell you—I told him."

I closed my eyes. "You're not a shitty friend. I'm fine," I lied. "How did that go?" I searched his kind face and found his eyes were clear and happy.

"He was surprised. I kind of threw it at him in the middle of his sulking over you." He shrugged his shoulders.

"Actually, I yelled it at him in the middle of the Johnson family dinner so I'm sure they'll be talking about that for a while." Finn's straight smile spread widely across his face.

I couldn't help but laugh. Finn was nothing if he wasn't joyful. He draped an arm over my shoulders and pulled me in for a quick hug. He continued. "Linc told me that you kept my secret. I knew you would, but it means more to me than you know." The seriousness in his face had me stopping my gait.

I smiled up at my friend, pushing away the sharp pain that tucked itself under my ribs at the mention of Lincoln's name. Finn noticed my shift in demeanor so he quickly changed the subject and started rambling on about how we could expand Project Eir.

I listened half-heartedly while we walked, and I tossed a stick to Bud. When I flung it left, Bud started after it, then stopped and veered right, running straight up the small hill toward the cottages.

I whistled, but he ignored me. I tracked his movements and stopped when I saw Lincoln standing on top of the hill, hands in his pockets, looking down at Finn and me.

Bud tore off in his direction, running happy little circles at his feet. Lincoln reached down to scratch Bud behind the ears, and my heart sputtered in my chest. My feet were rooted to the ground.

As I gaped at Lincoln, my chest felt tight. I could appreciate the long lines of his muscular thighs, and my core ached in response. My eyes moved upward to his trim waist that gave way to a broad chest. Lincoln had his hands in his pockets, and a small smile played at his lips.

He looked *good*. Rested and self-assured. I stepped out from under Finn's arm and absently ran a hand over my flyaway hair. Panic rose in my throat.

What is he doing here? My eyes searched Finn's.

Finn just looked at me and smiled. He leaned down and kissed my cheek before whispering, "You've got this. You can do this next part on your own."

Finn stepped away, raising a hand in greeting to Lincoln before walking toward a group of fishermen.

Lincoln ambled toward me. My heart raced faster with every step he took closer to me. I thought of Finn's words and sucked in a deep breath, willing my nerves to settle.

When he finally reached me, he stood tall, looking down at me. His face was strained, but his eyes were soft. "Hello, Joanna."

I swallowed the hard lump in my throat and willed my voice to be steady. I looked up to meet his steely blue eyes.

A thousand emotions swirled inside of me. Excitement. Hurt. Longing. Anger. Love.

Love.

No matter how long we had been apart, my love for Lincoln swelled in my chest. I cleared my throat, hoping my voice would not betray me.

Lincoln reached up, brushing a stray hair from my eyes. His fingertip traced down the side of my face, and he let his palm linger, just a moment. I wanted to lean into his hand. Close my eyes and feel the warmth of him pass to me. Instead, I gaped at him, unsure of what to say.

"I am so proud of you. Everyone in town is talking about this."

"I'm surprised you came." The steadiness in my voice shocked me, and my insides did a little fist pump.

"I didn't want to upset you, but I needed to see you." Lincoln dropped his hand, reaching around to his back pocket. He pulled out a thick envelope and paused. "I have something for you."

A pressing rhythm drummed inside of me.

Lincoln placed the envelope into my hands. "I hope this helps to explain everything."

As I stared at the crisp, white paper, a thousand questions burned in my mind. Lincoln placed a hand around the back of my neck as he leaned forward. He smelled like pine and campfire smoke, and I closed my eyes, inhaling the warm, masculine scent. I was not strong enough to resist his lips against mine. He bent lower, and I felt his full lips press against my cheek.

Lincoln pulled back and walked away. I held the letter to my chest, tears burning at the corners of my eyes. I looked around to see if anyone else had noticed me melting into the ground. The crowd was dispersing, people were shaking hands and driving away in their cars. The big white tent was being disassembled. I watched Lincoln join Finn and Colin as they loaded up the last of the serving dishes.

On the back porch, Honey was charming Mr. Bailey. I couldn't wait. I had to know what was inside the envelope. I pumped my legs in swift strides up the side of the hill. When I was sure I was out of view, I jogged behind one of the nearby cottages. I tore open the envelope to find a letter in Lincoln's masculine handwriting.

THIRTY-SEVEN

LINCOLN'S LETTER

Dear Joanna,

I don't know how to begin to tell you all of the ways that you have changed me, so I might as well try to write it all down. I was twenty-two the day you changed my life. I tried to ignore it, but I opened your first letter after three days of it calling to me.

Out in the desert, the days were unrelenting. Corrosive. But I am a Marine. I did my job and I did it well. Whenever I felt like there could be (and probably should be) something more than that, I felt like an imposter. I punished myself for those feelings by working harder, being even more focused.

You don't even know it, but you helped me see that there was still beauty and good in the world—especially in moments it was hard to remember that. You helped me laugh. You told me stories from home and kept me connected when it felt too easy to drift away.

I know that I should have written you back. I wanted to. Every time I got a letter, I wanted to write to you. But how do you put into words feelings that you don't even understand yourself? So I carried you with me. Your letters, the wings, they were all reminders to be a good man.

I spent two thousand eight hundred sixteen days in the Corps training to follow orders and make the right decisions at the right times. But what I failed to learn was how difficult it would be to find myself again—let someone else in—when I returned.

When I came back, I was angry and scared. I became obsessed with secretly finding the woman from the letters, but I had no idea that I would find you. You have changed everything. The day I saw you, everything inside of me said "you finally found her." I knew in my bones that you were who I had been looking for.

But while I was searching for you, I never had to worry about losing you. I know I messed up—losing control when someone hurt you. I don't regret what I did to them but I do regret everything that happened next. I should have trusted you enough to open myself up.

I'm trying to do better. I found a therapist who works with combat veterans to sort through the mess in my head. I'm learning that I don't have it all figured out and maybe it's not my job anymore to control every situation. I realize that what I have been doing to myself has gone way beyond what I can handle alone.

I won't ask for you to wait for me, but I need you to know that I will carry you with me for the rest of my life. I won't see another wildflower or hear another sad country song and not think of dancing with you in the kitchen.

Behind this letter you'll see a deed to the Big House and all of the property around it. Before you freak out, you need to know this—Chikalu is your home. Please don't go. This town needs you.

Joanna, my heart beats to the rhythm of yours and the best thing to ever happen to me was finding you.

All my love,

Lincoln

THIRTY-EIGHT
LINCOLN

FROM THE WINDOW of the Big House, I watched Joanna stare at the envelope. She moved it in her hands, looking at the front and back. I was a fucking wreck. My gut clenched. My veins burned.

I didn't know if she would open it there or—fuck— maybe even throw it away without a second thought. I knew I didn't truly deserve any more than that for what I had put her through.

I watched as she moved gracefully up the side of the hill, picking up her pace as soon as she thought she was out of view. Joanna tore open the letter, sinking back against the side of the cottage.

My pulse hammered as I watched her read the letter. Her hand moved to her mouth. I'd never been good with words, and I hoped it would be enough to show her how much she meant to me.

The old man's hand clamped down on my shoulder and gave it a squeeze. "If she didn't love you back, she wouldn't still be reading," he reassured.

Jesus, I hoped he was right.

Joanna wiped at her eyes and pressed the letter to her chest. I had to calm my breathing to not throw myself into a panic attack.

In, two-three-four. Hold, two-three-four. Out, two-three-four.

My spine stiffened when I saw Joanna look up from the letter, wipe her eyes again and look around.

She moved quickly, out from the shadows at the side of the cottage. All of the crowd had gone. Her long legs moved swiftly under her, and she walked into the open area between the cottages and the Big House.

Was she leaving? *Please don't leave.*

When her head snapped up, our eyes met through the window glass. Tears shone in her green-gray eyes, and I knew.

My girl had come home.

I moved away from the window, pushing open the back door. "Joanna!" I called out to her.

She took off like a shot, barreling toward me. My strides ate up the distance between us, and I leaped off the deck. I couldn't get to her fast enough. As I raced across the lawn, Joanna's strong body slammed into me, her legs wrapping around my waist as I lifted her, holding her hips tightly against me.

I held her close, pressing one hand on her upper back. I slanted my mouth across her neck, trailing frantic, wet kisses along her soft skin. I could feel her heartbeat hammer against my lips, and it drove me further out of my mind.

I was starved for her.

"Baby, I am so sorry." I pulled back to look at her beautiful face. She held my face between her hands, and those gorgeous green-gray eyes were swimming with tears but looking right at me. I rested my forehead against hers. "I am so sorry for everything I put you through."

"Shh," she whispered and stroked the back of my head.

"No, I need to say this." I swallowed hard, and my breath came out in ragged drags. "I never meant to disappoint you, and there's a chance I'm going to again. But I need you to know." I looked at Joanna and my heart tripped in my chest. "I love you. I have always loved you."

Joanna tightened her arms around my shoulders, pulling me into her. "I love you too, Lincoln."

We stood there, clinging to each other, afraid to let go. I pulled a deep breath into my lungs, smelling her citrus shampoo, and I never wanted to let her go again.

"Lincoln, the letter. The house. It's too much."

"It's not. You deserve this. I want you to have it."

"But I don't understand." Joanna shook her head.

I reluctantly lowered her to her feet and ran my hands down her arms. I twined my fingers with hers. "Five years ago, the old man was selling his house and property because it had become too much for him to take care of. I bought it, figuring it was the least I could do for him after he took me in. But the moment I saw your face light up when you hiked onto it, I knew it was meant to be yours."

She squeezed my hands and rested her head against my chest. I lowered my lips to her hair. I couldn't get enough of this woman.

"So, does that mean I can move back into Cottage Two?" she asked. The laughter in her voice filled my soul.

"Fuck no." I laughed. "We're moving into the Big House." I smiled at her confused face. "I've been arguing with Mr. Bailey ever since I bought the place about moving into the house. He wants the cottage, but that just never felt right to me. But now, if you want it—want me—we'll make it our home."

"I have never wanted anything more than you, this place, and a grumpy old man to go with it."

Joanna kissed me again, deeper, and I felt my cock thicken between us. She felt it, too, because she pitched her hips forward, pressing into me.

"Lincoln," she breathed between kisses, "take me home."

On a growl, I bent down and threw her over my shoulder like a fucking caveman. Joanna yelped, and I slapped her ass as I stalked toward my cottage.

I was barely in the door before I kicked it closed and hauled her against it. Her legs were trembling, and my mouth covered hers, my tongue tasting her. My hand grabbed roughly at her hip, and I groaned at the feel of her beneath me.

Joanna pulled at my shirt, lifting it off my chest as she dragged her tongue and teeth over my sensitive skin. Little shocks of electricity buzzed beneath her mouth. I needed to feel her skin on mine.

I tore off my shirt and ran my hands up her sides, pulling her shirt off with one motion. She reached back, unclasping her bra and letting it tumble to the floor. I palmed one perky breast and lowered my mouth to the other. I sucked and teased the hard pebble of her nipple.

"Yes," she whimpered. Her hands were clawing at my belt buckle, and my cock was throbbing to be inside of her. "God, I've missed this, Lincoln."

Needing more of her, I dropped to my knees in front of her. I pulled the tab of her jeans, releasing the button. I slowly dragged the zipper down, revealing a smooth, silky scrap of fabric.

I licked a line along the top of her panties as I pulled her jeans down her hips. I sat back on my heels and watched as she slipped her legs out of her pants. I could see a line of wetness from her arousal, and I about lost my damn mind.

I dragged a thumb up the wet crease in her underwear, circling the tight bundle of nerves as I licked the sensitive skin where her leg met her center. Her deep moan made my cock throb in response. I reached down and palmed it once.

Joanna pressed herself back against the door as I hitched one leg up and rested it on my shoulder. Teasing her slit, I moved my fingers over her. She tipped her hips forward, begging for more.

"You are everything." I dragged the flat of my tongue up, stopping at her clit and circling it with my tongue. I sucked it in deeply, and her hand tangled into my hair. I groaned into her as I devoured her sweet pussy and she climbed higher. Her thigh beside my face quivered with need.

"Lincoln, please," she begged. Giving my girl the release she needed had me increasing the pressure. I slipped a finger inside of her and felt her heat clamp down on me. My cock was aching to be inside her—the heaviness between my thighs was shockingly intense—but I was determined to drag this out for her, make her feel incredible.

Using my hand and my tongue, I brought Joanna to the edge and then slipped another finger into her soaked pussy. She was soft and wet and warm, and I lapped up every drop of her. Gently, I teased her clit with my teeth as I pumped my fingers into her.

On a cry, she called out my name and I felt her legs go liquid. I peered up and saw her face flushed, eyes heavy-lidded, and a smile danced across her beautiful face. As I stood, I pulled my fingers from inside of her and brought them to my lips, tasting her again, and I looked into her eyes.

Fire and desire rose in her eyes as she watched me lick her arousal from my fingers. Unbuttoning my jeans, I let them drop to the floor. I pulled out my dick, hard as steel, and stroked it from root to tip.

"Get over there," I said, motioning with my head toward the kitchen counter. Joanna bit her lower lip, and a surge of pressure throbbed in my cock.

Joanna moved quickly toward the counter, and I grabbed her hips, helping her up. She tried to reach down and feel me, but if she touched me, I knew I'd come right then and I had to be inside her. I moved her hips forward and lined my cock up to her entrance. I rubbed the head of my dick up her pussy, coating the head with her juices. We both moaned.

Sliding it back down, I moved my hips forward, easing into her tight pussy. I felt it pulse around me, and my body needed to move. I drove a steady rhythm, worshipping her body as I chased my own release.

A bead of sweat trickled between Joanna's perfect tits. I saw her nipples tighten and felt her press her legs into my ass. I leaned forward to lick a path from her pink, peaked nippes to her neck. I traced my tongue into the dip of her collarbone and felt her heartbeat drumming wildly.

"Oh, baby, I need you. I need this." I hammered long strokes into her.

"Yes, yes, yes," she panted over and over.

I reached a hand forward, playing with her clit, begging her to come again, come with me. Her clit throbbed, and I lost any semblance of control. Her pussy clamped down around me, and I felt the gush of her orgasm as my own tore through me. I kept pumping into her as I filled her with deep, hot spurts.

Coming down from my own orgasm, my legs felt weak. I had handed every part of me to Joanna. She had my body, my heart, my soul.

Our heavy breathing filled the silence in the cottage. Still deep inside of her, I moved my hips.

"Mmmmm," she groaned.

I lifted my hand to her face, brushing the small pieces of hair that stuck to her forehead. "You are so beautiful."

Her eyes sparkled, and I fell even harder for this amazing, stunning woman. I would spend the rest of my life trying to be the man she deserved.

My voice felt thick with emotion. "Finding you was the best thing to ever happen to me."

She looked at me and smiled. "My sweet man." She ran her hand along the scruff of my jaw. "I think we found each other."

THIRTY-NINE

EPILOGUE

JOANNA

The smell of cinnamon coffee pulled me from sleep. I inhaled deeply, stretching my arms above my head. I knew he wouldn't be there, but I reached over absently, feeling Lincoln's side of the bed still warm.

On a little moan, I leaned over and grabbed his pillow, inhaling the scent left behind. My heart made a happy little tumble at the intoxicating mix of pine, smoke, and *good-smelling man.*

Pulling myself out of bed, I wrapped myself in a fluffy robe. Winter was clinging desperately to the Montana mountains, and the morning chill lingered.

I padded down the large wooden stairs of the Big House, feeling the smooth, dark wood of the railing under my hands. I still couldn't believe I lived here. The house needed work, but over the winter, Lincoln had taken advantage of the slow season and worked doubly hard to fix it up.

Windows had been replaced, loose porch boards repaired. Once spring finally broke, we planned to give the house and the expansive wraparound porch a fresh coat of white paint. I loved seeing the old house come to life and transform into a beautiful home. Our home.

I turned the corner into the wide, open kitchen. On the island, I found a fresh pot of coffee and a note from Lincoln.

Morning run, then helping the old man in the barn. Come find me so I can kiss you.

-L

Happy little butterflies danced in my stomach. With one look, that man could still make me feel like the prettiest girl in the room. I couldn't wait to find him and cash in on that kiss.

I often found little notes around the house or in my truck or backpack from Lincoln. He said once that it was to make up for all of the times he didn't respond to my letters. He didn't know it, but I kept every single one—even if they were unimportant or silly—tucked away in a shoebox. His notes made me feel special, just like the bracelet he made me our first night camping. It didn't really match anything I owned, but taking it off didn't feel right, so it had become a part of me, a lot like Lincoln.

I tucked the note into the pocket of my robe, poured myself a hot cup of coffee, and walked out onto the back porch. Quiet mornings in that exact spot were my favorites.

I tucked my legs under me and let the coffee warm my hands as I watched the fog lift off the water. The river wound around the small hills and fields of our property.

Home.

Lincoln and I were making a home here, and it was shaping up to be pretty incredible. Mr. Bailey begrudgingly ate dinner with us most nights, and he was teaching me how to play poker. On chilly nights, Lincoln and I would light a fire and watch the flames dance in the fireplace while we talked about the fishing business, Project Eir, and our dreams of building something that truly connected people in our community to nature.

I still couldn't believe how I ended up finding my home in Chikalu Falls after all these years.

One morning on the back porch, Lincoln had come up behind me, wrapped me in his strong arms, and whispered, "Baby, look around. This... all this? It's yours."

I leaned my head back and nuzzled the scruff on his jaw. "No," I said. "It's ours."

Sipping my coffee, I remembered Lincoln's letter and how electric it felt when he ran off the porch toward me. He couldn't get to me fast enough. *Me.*

There were still some days I couldn't believe that Lincoln Scott was mine. He still tended to be growly and overprotective, but I understood him, and he accepted me for exactly who I was.

I was so proud of Lincoln, too. He continued to go to therapy to deal with the weight of his experiences in the military. His nightmares still scared me, but with the help of his therapist, they were becoming fewer and further between. Lincoln swore up and down that the best thing to do when he had them was to be there and hold him.

Finn's dream of us guiding together finally came true. It didn't make a whole lot of sense running competing businesses, and with Project Eir taking up a lot of my time, serving fishing groups with Finn didn't even feel like work. Although, I still vetoed the new names he tried to come up with. (FiLiJo? Ew. No.)

By working so closely with Finn, Lincoln was able to work behind the scenes for the business, and that made him much happier. Occasionally he would join us, but he was most content when it was quiet around the office. That also allowed Lincoln and Finn to start to focus less on their business and more on being brothers.

We met the man Finn had started dating about a month ago. He owned a coffee shop in Bozeman and met Finn while he was in town. Finn said that sparks flew over lattes, and that was it for him. He and Lincoln bonded over the merits of The Punisher versus Daredevil, but I was still not really sure if they were talking about movies or what. Regardless, seeing Lincoln and Finn's relationship grow over the past several months had been amazing.

Before moving to Chikalu Falls, I thought I had everything I needed, but someone to love. Turns out that I also needed a home, friendships, and to truly belong. I think Pop would be happy to know I'd set down roots in his hometown, and now I could bring flowers by the cemetery. I went there sometimes to tell him and Gram all about how much my life has changed.

～

LINCOLN

I HAD WORKED like a dog all week trying to get the barn ready. Joanna had gotten it in her head that horses would be the next logical addition to Project Eir. She claimed that not only were horses therapeutic, but they would make a more memorable experience for the veterans and clients who camped on our land. That girl sure could dream big.

I knew it would take a while, but I was going to be damn sure that Joanna's dreams came true. Funny thing is, somewhere along the line, her dreams and mine got all tangled up and I really couldn't separate the two.

Tonight, the trout were running so I encouraged her to fish along the bank. Watching my girl fish was one of the most peaceful parts of my week. Her legs were strong as she waded out into the river. The water rippled and danced, reflecting pinks and oranges from the fading sunset. She was silhouetted, but I could tell she had found her rhythm. Back and forth she moved, casting and moving with the water.

I touched a hand to my pocket. I didn't carry Joanna's letter with me anymore—I didn't need to when I had the real thing to come home to every night. I had put the letters away in a lockbox to keep them safe, and every so often, we'd take them out and I would read them with her. I loved to tell her why something made me laugh or what my favorite part of a particular letter had been.

Tonight, I didn't carry a letter with me. Instead, my hand felt the outline of the ring I had picked out. I knew Joanna didn't *need* anything fancy, but screw that. With some help from her sister, Honey, I had designed a ring that was feminine and bold and a little bit vintage. When I saw the mock-up, I knew it had to be hers.

The diamond was probably a little big, but I was going to marry the fuck out of that girl and everyone was going to know it. I smiled and shook my head at that thought. I might pretend to wear the pants in this relationship, but everyone in three counties knew Joanna had me wrapped around her finger.

It felt like it took forever for the ring to be ready. I would have married her months ago, but she deserved for everything to be perfect. Knowing Joanna, perfect for us was here—outside on a gorgeous night with the sun setting and our home waiting for us at the top of the hill. Honey insisted on an engagement party tomorrow, but tonight would be the two of us, wrapped up in each other.

Standing, I looked at her, and my heart beat faster. *That's one hell of a view.*

WANT a peek into Joanna and Lincoln's happily ever after? Click here to subscribe to my mailing list to read an exclusive FINDING YOU bonus scene!

Next in the Chikalu Falls series is Honey and Colin's story KEEPING YOU. Keep reading for a sneak peek!

SNEAK PEEK AT KEEPING YOU

Honey

OKAY, so maybe flipping the entire Sunday morning church crowd the bird was not one of my finest moments.

Or snatching the mimosa off that old lady's table and downing it in one gulp.

But hear me out...

Sunday work brunches were my least favorite part of the week. Sylvia, my boss and an actual demon from hell, thought the meetings would build team morale and while they were "optional" it never felt that way. I sucked it up, and woke up extra early on Sundays just to get ready.

Everyone that worked at Sylvia Jay PR had several expectations to live up to—impeccable fashion, full-face makeup, ruthless attitude. When I started with the company, the allure of a high profile job and getting out of bum-fuck nowhere was intoxicating. I could leave behind the cowboys and miners of Montana and use this job as a stepping stone to somewhere more exciting, like New York or L.A.

After three years of it, I was starting to realize that in order to get ahead in this company, you were forced to step on the backs of anyone in your way—including your colleagues and friends.

Sitting at brunch, I watched Sylvia drone on, again, about branding, scouting, and *using our assets*. She emphasized this by slapping her own ass.

Jesus.

"This," Sylvia drilled a hot pink lacquered nail onto the white table cloth, "is a business. You need to do what it takes to get the job done!"

"Take Megan, for example," she continued as we all shot poor Megan tentative glances. Getting called out by Sylvia was never a good thing. "Megan? Did you meet your deadline this week?" Sylvia's eyebrow hitched up as she coolly looked down her sharp nose at Megan.

Megan cleared her throat, "I did not." She looked calm, but under the table I could see her high heel bounce up and down.

"Exactly," Sylvia rested her hands on her hips. "You failed, Megan. Again."

Megan's head drooped slightly. I wanted to reach out and rest my hand on hers but we weren't really close, so I tried to give her a look that showed her I was sorry she was put on the spot like that. God, Sylvia was such a bitch.

"So the lesson here, ladies, is that when you're a failure, you're off the team. Megan, pack up. You're fired." No one dared to gasp at the abrupt dismissal of Megan, but it was shocking. Megan led in client recruitment most weeks and her father had recently died, which was probably why she got behind in her work. My jaw hung open.

Sylvia looked around the brunch table, daring anyone to

speak. The women around the table glanced at their manicures or picked absently at their skirts and napkins.

This was team building?

Sylvia took a sick joy in pitting us against each other, making everything from our numbers to our clothing a competition.

"And Honey?"

Fuck.

I lifted my chin to meet her gaze.

"Where are we with the social media reviews for our new client?"

Clearing my throat, I stood. "Actually I am looking to get more product into the hands of their target audience." I smoothed my pencil skirt down my thighs. "The initial reviews are less than favorable. I need to get something that we can use."

"The client expects a full social media takeover, including product reviews, next week."

"Yes, I know the deadline, and I'll meet it, but right now there's nothing coming in that I can use. People actually *hate* the product."

"I don't see the problem here."

Is she fucking serious?

"Um, well . . ."

"Make. Them. Up." Sylvia rolled her eyes so hard I was surprised they didn't get sucked into her skull.

I blinked once, but recovered quickly. "I'm sorry, Syl. I can't do that." Not only was blatantly making up product reviews unethical, it was actually illegal.

"Do we have a problem here?" Her arms crossed over her large, fake breasts.

I ticked my jaw and the words came tumbling out of me.

"Yes, apparently." I leveled my eyes with hers. "I won't make up reviews. We can leave the reviews out, or wait to get in some that aren't so awful, but I can't just fabricate them."

Anger flared on Sylvia's face. "Huh. I'm surprised by you, Honey. You're driven, talented. I didn't realize you were also a bleeding heart." A small chuckle rippled through the table. I looked around and saw plumped up lips pressed together, eyebrows raised. The women I had called my friends were all enjoying the show.

"I may be driven, but I'm also honest. Their product sucks, and everyone knows it. I can spin it to make it look a little better, but if I don't have any actual customer reviews to use, then so be it." I tossed a blond curl over my shoulder and glared at her.

I'd always been like that—backed into a corner and I stand my ground when any normal person would know it would be a great time to shut the fuck up. But I was just not wired that way.

Sylvia's eyes slitted and she looked around the table. "Anyone else have a problem with how we do things here?"

Slow, quiet murmurs and head shakes passed around the table. Sylvia raised both her palms up, as if to say "see, you're the one not falling in line here."

I was stuck, rooted on my feet. I needed this job, and the promotion I'd been working toward for over a year. Over the drone of her voice, my mind flicked back to my string of colossal fuck-ups.

Leave your dreams behind to chase a man. Check.

Follow him around like a love-sick puppy. Check.

Lose your ability to make a single decision for yourself. Check.

Gather the scraps of your dignity when you discover he's fucking your roommate. Check.

Live with the reputation of being a flake. Check.

Shame burned hot in my cheeks. This job and its fancy office had been my fresh start. A new, serious, and independent me.

"If you think for one minute," Sylvia continued, "that you hold any value outside of my company, you're kidding yourself."

If I just sat down and shut up, I could figure out a way to make both Sylvia and the client happy.

Did I do that? Of course I fucking didn't.

Instead I wheezed out a breath. "You know, Syl," I sipped the last of my mimosa from the champagne glass. "Working for you has been the most soul-sucking three years of my life. Go fuck yourself."

At the audible, pearl-clutching gasps from the table, I put the champagne glass down with a *snap*, grabbed my purse, and walked toward the door. On the way out, I saw a full mimosa at the end of the table of sweet old ladies enjoying brunch after church. I snatched up the glass, downed it all in one gulp while flipping my former employer and the rest of her Barbie cut-out minions the middle finger.

"You. Dɪᴅ. Nᴏᴛ!" My sister Jo squealed on the other end of the telephone.

"Yeah, pretty much did."

"I can't believe it! What did they say? What are you going to do?"

Rolling the dough into a fresh batch of cinnamon buns,

I held the phone between my ear and shoulder. "Hell if I know, sis. I didn't wake up today planning to be jobless."

"This is crazy. I can't believe you just . . . did that!" Joanna was always the level-headed older sister. She marched to the beat of her own drummer—she was actually a female fishing guide several counties over—but she was reliable, steady. Unlike me, she was more cautious and actually thought things out—things like having a backup plan before randomly quitting your only source of income.

For the first time, I started to get a little nervous about what I had done at brunch. I had plenty in my savings account since my only expenses were my apartment and the clothes that I needed for work, but Butte, Montana was a small city. I'm sure word was getting around quickly that I'd stormed out, made a scene, and if Sylvia had any say, she'd be calling around to blacklist my name by dinner.

Me and my damn mouth.

"I'm sure I'll figure something out." The oven creaked open as I placed the pan of cinnamon buns inside.

"Are you stress baking again?"

"Maybe," I admitted. "I thought it would make me feel better but so far it isn't working."

"Hon, you know you can always come see Lincoln and me. We'll happily take some of whatever you're baking!"

I laughed. "I'm good. Really." I was working hard to convince myself just as much as her, that I was really okay with my life right now.

I changed the subject, hoping to move the focus away from me and onto her upcoming wedding plans. "Have you set up any appointments for dress shopping?"

"I don't know," she hesitated. "There's a little shop here that I wanted to look at but I don't think I need anything too over the top."

"Joanna," I scolded. "You are marrying a broody, handsome, brick wall of a man next year that you waited a *long* time for. Don't you want him to fall to his knees?" Only part of me was teasing her--I knew she'd look amazing in whatever she chose--but sometimes Jo needed a hype woman and I took that job very seriously.

"If I promise to let you pick it out with me, can we please stop obsessing over the dress?" Joanna's voice was laced with laughter.

"We're going to find you a dress so hot that the way he looks at you will be wildly inappropriate. The whole town will be scandalized."

Jo bubbled with laughter and I peeked at the cinnamon buns slowly rising in the oven. I'd successfully averted more talk about me and the life that was crumbling around me and the stark contrast of her life and mine.

I was thrilled for her. Lincoln was her best friend's older brother and while he was deployed overseas, Jo had written him letters. He didn't know her at the time, but had kept every single one.

Joanna deserved how the pieces of her life were clicking together. She was meant to find her special someone.

I, on the other hand, tended to avoid deeply romantic relationships. Young and dumb, I'd completely abandoned my dreams of culinary school in New York to follow my high school boyfriend to state college. From that I learned the hard way that relationships have the power to change you, make you vulnerable, without you even realizing it.

Plus, serious boyfriends took up way too much time and there were always unrealistic expectations, and meeting families, and "fixing" each other.

No thanks.

I preferred my relationships to be mutually satisfying, brief, and hot between the sheets—that was a must.

We chatted a few more minutes and I mulled over her offer to visit her in Chikalu Falls. It was a small mountain town at the base of the Kootenai National Forest, and I was convinced there was something in the water. That place was crawling with burly, handsome men. The strong jawline of one particularly hot bar owner clicked through my mind.

Maybe a quick trip out there wouldn't be so bad after all . . .

After hanging up with Jo, I flipped through my closet and contemplated what could be next for me. Everything I owned was designer. It had to be in order to fit in at Sylvia Jay PR. Skirts, heels, blouses, and jewelry were all luxury items. Anything less was unacceptable there. I had built my life on a superficial facade but, secretly, one of my favorite parts of the day was coming home, whipping off my bra, and snuggling into oversized pajamas. No one ever saw me so undone, but it kept the tension in my jaw from compounding, and helped the little annoyances melt away.

Baking was the same way. I had inherited my Grandma Nana's love of baking. It calmed me, excited me, and I loved the thrill of taking an old recipe and enhancing it. My neighbors loved it because by the time I got done mixing and prepping and baking, I wasn't really in the mood to eat any of it.

As I waited for the cinnamon buns to finish, my phone buzzed with an incoming text.

Chad: I'm in town tonight. Busy?

Chad was a real estate attorney that made his money traveling through Butte and surrounding small towns. We'd been sleeping together on and off for about a year, but it wasn't anything serious. He had a big dick and he knew how to use it. Tonight, I found myself more annoyed than excited.

Me: What did you have in mind?

Chad: Drinks at the Monolith hotel bar? I'll be done with dinner about 10:30.

After dinner drinks at the hotel bar definitely meant he was looking for a hookup and it had been months since I'd had sex. For some reason the casual flings I'd always enjoyed just weren't doing it for me. I mulled the possibility of Chad showing me a good time. I wasn't really feeling it, but didn't have a good reason not to go, either.

Me: Sure. See you then.

A little zip of unease ran through me. Maybe I could forget all about quitting my job with zero future prospects and focus on feeling something *good* tonight. I blew out a quick breath. Chad and I were going to have a great time.

⁓

Chad was not a great time.

I showed up at the hotel bar just after ten thirty, as we'd agreed. Forty minutes and two dirty martinis later, he finally showed up.

Tall and broad shouldered, Chad caught the eye of every woman—and a few men—in the bar. He had a megawatt smile with straight, white teeth. It was no wonder he was so successful—he could wheel and deal and charm anyone within a fifty mile radius. His hair was puffed and styled back away from his face and every time he smiled, I imagined a little wink and cartoon sparkle to pop around his face. The unease I felt earlier hadn't gone away and I shifted uncomfortably in my seat.

When Chad reached my stool at the bar, he didn't bother apologizing for being late, but rather leaned over and placed a kiss on my cheek.

"Hey gorgeous. It's been a while."

I swiveled in my seat, swapping my legs, one over the other as I turned, "Hey yourself."

Chad signaled to the bartender and ordered a top shelf Old Fashioned. As he swirled the dark liquid in his glass, he eyed the hem of my skirt riding high on my legs. I knew exactly what he wanted.

We made unimportant small talk. He told me about his work, I avoided telling him about quitting my job. It was all surface chatter, and I struggled to stay focused on Chad. There was a nagging desire to leave the bar, go home, and cuddle under the covers with a true crime documentary on Netflix.

Determined to salvage this day and try to have a decent time, I focused my energy on appreciating Chad's lean waist, long fingers, tight abs. After several minutes of openly gawking at him, I didn't feel a single surge of desire.

He finished his drink quickly and turned to me, licking a drop of whiskey off his lip, "You ready to go upstairs?"

Chad's directness was one of the things I typically liked about him. He wasn't interested in a relationship and neither was I. We knew exactly what the other person wanted and we were willing to give it. Tonight, however, I was not feeling it. At all.

I suddenly felt hot. I flipped my hair off one shoulder and blew out a breath.

Why the hell am I having second thoughts about this? Go let this gorgeous man do dirty things with you.

Unfortunately, my lady bits weren't getting the message. No matter how well-fitted his dark navy suit was, it wasn't doing a thing for me tonight.

No one's done it for you for months...not since him.

My mind briefly jumped back to a hot-and-heavy night I spent tangled in the sheets when I visited Jo in Chikalu Falls. I buried the worrisome thought that Colin McCoy may very well have ruined me for all men forever. I hadn't slept with anyone since, and my apparent hang up was becoming a real problem.

"You know," I started, "I'm sorry Chad. These martinis really got to me tonight. It's late and I think I'm going to call it a night."

He stared at me. "Are you sure? I'm only in town tonight."

Damn it, woman. Get your shit together.

"Yeah, I'm sure. I'm sorry, Chad. Next time you're in town, give me a call." I unfolded myself from the stool and grabbed my purse.

"Of course, I understand. Can I call you an Uber?" Chad was only interested in sex, but he also wasn't a total prick.

I rested my hand against the side of his clean shaven face. "I can take care of myself, but thank you. Next time." I smiled at him and walked away from the bar and into the crisp night air.

The blast of cool air felt good on my tacky skin. What the hell was that all about? A hot night with Chad should have been a fun distraction. I even wore my new lingerie with the black lace bodice, but I couldn't get the nagging feeling that it was *so wrong* out of my head.

I essentially cockblocked myself.

Fantastic.

Hailing an Uber from the app on my phone, I stood under the lights at the hotel entrance. Twenty four hours ago I knew exactly where my life was headed—a well-paying job, new promotion on the horizon, a gorgeous apartment overlooking Downton Butte, a sexy man just a phone call away.

Now none of that felt right. None of it felt like *me*.

If I was going to turn my life around, it needed to start right now. I was a total drama queen at brunch, so why stop now?

A new life. One with rules—rules designed to protect me from myself.

No Shitty, Meaningless Job.

No Fake-Ass Friends.

No Men.

The thought of a different life rooted and bloomed deeply inside of me. My entire existence, people saw Honey James as a pretty face without much substance to go with it . . . but not anymore.

Freshly determined to make something more of myself, I pulled out my phone and texted Jo.

Me: I think you may be right about a fresh start. You still have an open cottage?

Jo: Eek! I am so excited. Chikalu won't know what hit 'em!

With a sharp exhale of breath, I slid into the seat of the Uber and wondered how the hell I was going to start over again.

◦≈◦

CLICK HERE to order Keeping You

～

THANK YOU, again, for reading FINDING YOU. I can't thank you enough for giving me a chance on my debut novel. A review on Amazon and/or Goodreads would mean the world to me and makes a huge difference for new indie authors like me!

ALSO BY LENA HENDRIX

The Chikalu Falls Series

Finding You

Keeping You

Protecting You

Choosing You (novella)

The Redemption Ranch Series

The Badge

The Alias

The Rebel

The Target

The Sullivans

One Taste (charity novella - early 2023

One Look (coming March 2023!)

ACKNOWLEDGMENTS

Dude . . . I wrote a novel! Even I can't believe it. I would not have even attempted this without the love and encouragement of so many people.

First, my husband who kept my dirty romance novel writing a secret with me. He listened to every crazy scenario, nodded his head, and even offered advice knowing full well that I was never going to take it. My kids who often asked, "What are you writing?" and believed my lies. Bless your naïve little hearts. One day you can read it—nope. Scratch that. Don't read Mama's smutty novels. I love you "too high!"

My beta-turned-alpha readers: Ariel and Jenn. This book would never have seen the light of day without your love and support. I appreciate both of you for giving me your honest feedback and unending support. We're thousands of miles apart but our love of good writing, great wine, and romance kept us connected. Thank you for keeping me sane.

Nancy, you gave this book the polish it needed. I appreciate every bit of feedback, even when I was so nervous to hear it. You helped boost my confidence and encouraged me to give this a real shot.

Sara, my darling proofreader. Thank you for helping me find all those little details. Clearly, I have zero mastery of a comma, and use *that* way too often. Thank you for your attention to detail!

Kim, thank you for your patience and creativity. I so appreciate all of your insight and input. Thank you for helping me realize that I have a very specific "type" and that it's okay to put someone on a cover who doesn't fit that type (Hint: That's not this cover. He *is* my type. Oh, baby.).

To the goddess herself, Melanie Harlow. I cannot begin to express my gratitude for the mentorship you have provided. It was your generosity and wealth of knowledge that pushed me to think, "Hey, I might be able to do this." I would be *nowhere* without your kindness and willingness to share your knowledge with other newbies like me.

Finally, thank you to each and every person who read this book and gave a new author a chance. Now, let's go on an adventure!

ABOUT THE AUTHOR

Lena Hendrix is an Amazon Top 20 bestselling contemporary romance author living in the Midwest. Her love for romance started with sneaking racy Harlequin paperbacks as a teenager and now she writes her own hot-as-sin small town romance novels. Lena has a soft spot for strong alphas with marshmallow insides, heroines who clap back, and sizzling tension. Her novels pack in small town heart with a whole lotta heat.

When she's not writing or devouring new novels, you can find her hiking, camping, fishing, and sipping a spicy margarita!

Want to hang out? Find Lena on Tiktok or IG or join her Facebook reader group!

Printed in Great Britain
by Amazon